# STALKING KILGORE TROUT

R. C. Thom

# CONTENTS

# INTRODUCTION

First a warning, my stories deal with ideas and some are dangerous to some people. My hope is that there is something offensive for everyone here. If you are religiously sensitive, offended by base language, that is to say locker room words—or ideas outside of your choir, this is not for you. If you enjoy poking a finger in the eye of religion, history, science, society and politics, you are in the right place. My intent is entertainment that tickles one's intellect; I will count it a success if you walk away laughing and thinking and a little angry.

I admit it; I'm a fan of Kurt Vonnegut. This anthology is a tribute to him. The late Mr. Vonnegut is why I've read, why I write, and why I explore the universe and the human condition. I discovered him in the 1960's at a young age and he rocked my inner world. So the following is a collection of stories after his influence. I hope to honor his memory here.

To me, Vonnegut was an idea man. Sure, he wrote good characters but for me they were there to illustrate his ideas and observations. Perhaps that is why, when I write, I start with ideas and create characters that flesh-out concepts. Like Vonnegut, I enjoy taking an idea to the extreme with humor. Vonnegut's are hard shoes to fill. Also, my aim is to tell a good story.

For you non-Vonnegut people, I'll explain my title, *Stalking Kilgore Trout.* Kilgore Trout was a fictional person of Vonnegut's. It's been said that Kilgore was Kurt's alter ego, but there is evidence to the contrary. The character appears in many Vonnegut stories and in each, Trout serves a different purpose. That is fitting, if Trout is Vonnegut, Vonnegut wasn't a one dimensional man. One of Trout's characteristics may be biographical of Vonnegut; Trout was constantly writing and immediately rejecting what he just wrote. I've read that in Kurt's early writing life he did much the same. It's a writer's thing, I think. All writers write trash before we find our voices. Maybe Trout is a nod to struggling writers; Trout was that for me. But as you'll see in the title story that's not true for everyone.

Vonnegut had his favorite ideas and I have mine. I'm fascinated by concepts surrounding history, aliens, politics, God, GLBT issues and the core realities of our human condition. It's fun to mix them all up. I've asked myself many bizarre 'what if' questions and wrote ridiculous answers. Also here you will read serious stories with serious questions or observations and ideas concerning human nature. Looking at life, I've got to laugh. Vonnegut did a lot of that sort of thing too, "and so it goes."

# FAIRY DUST

In the hundred years since the Roman Empire had withdrawn, everything had changed. Craft goods were seldom traded or even found. The roads were not safe. Fine textiles had become especially rare in southern Gaul. Roman commerce had made an exodus, but not Roman ideals. Thus, Markus felt proud as he walked the old Roman road in his clean linen tunic, tightly woven cotton britches and a leather belt with a brass buckle featuring the image of Romulus and Remus. Even his new-made leather sandals fit.

His parents spent all their assets to make a good impression in hopes that the wizard, Merthel, would keep Markus for an apprenticeship. Merthel had the king's favor. Perhaps it would rub off. In these dark days, his parents had invested in bright hopes for their son, and, with Markus away, there would be one less mouth to feed.

'These are perilous times for a boy, nay, a man of twelve years to walk unprotected roads so finely arrayed and alone,' Markus' father had warned, 'be aware and be careful, my son.'

An excited Markus did not scrutinize his whereabouts. His distractions of mind, of magic and wonders untold, paid no heed of the road. He demonstrated no caution.

Thus, he was caught. Two highwaymen slipped from the ruins of a Roman toll station. Markus did not see them blocking his path until he nearly stumbled into them. It was too late to run.

"What have we here?" said a tall, fat and bearded man.

Boils and cysts covered his face transforming this man into an ogre. The almost-apprentice stammered, but did not answer. The robber's face oozed. He wore dirty, smoke-tanned skins. His long hair was matted like sheep's wool past shearing. He smelled of earth, fire and filth. Markus fell to his knees, quaking and overwrought. The robber held a staff in his left hand, carved of an oak sapling with its root ball carved into a mallet.

A smaller, younger robber, similarly dressed and outfitted, said, "Father, he's got money. Look at them clothes. Let's kill him."

The ogre-man's thick arm came swiftly, backhanding the littler highwaymen and knocking him off his feet.

"Fool! No need to kill so fast! Blood on that linen," he grumbled. "There are things of value in this world not gold or silver. Think, use your head! He's a boy, on an errand. These fancy rags ain't his own."

The man gracefully swung his staff and pressed the club up against the Marcus' chin, leaving a grease smudge that smelled of rotting blood and mayhem.

"What of you, boy? Whence you go? Tell me quick or die."

Markus shook uncontrollably. Highwaymen of these parts were not known for giving quarters. Had Markus known who this was, he surely would have fallen dead with fright. For this was Goblin the head-knocker of Gordon, a criminal of some renown. His fame came by his knack for knocking one's head clean off with a stroke of his staff. Markus answered.

"Sir, I am apprenticed to Merthel," he said. "I have no money. My sire spent all he had to make my presentation. Your wisdom is great, save my soul."

"Your soul," the robber bellowed with spittle spewing into his beard. "Only Christ can save your soul, fool! And you go and apprentice with the pagan magician?"

Goblin wound his weapon, ready to decapitate Markus, when his son grabbed the staff.

"Hold, Father," the boy said. "Merthel is said to be rich, but no one can approach him. Can't we trick him? Can't I wear these clothes and enter his cave?"

The young robber had only worn rough hemp and skins in his fourteen years. These fresh clothes enticed the boy. Goblin released a loud laugh and stamped his staff on the paving stones.

"Now you're using your head, Thomas my boy."

Goblin demanded that Markus strip. Well pleased, the robber then let the boy run away naked. Thomas washed in the cold spillover of a nearby, ill-repaired aquifer; which came from the mountains beyond Merthel's cave. Washing was the Roman devil's way, but looting a famous pagan would pay for God's forgiveness.

The clothes didn't fit well, as Thomas was taller. The feel of the soft clothes made his penis erect. Luckily, Goblin didn't notice and beat him for it.

"Now listen to me, Thomas my boy. Gain his confidence. Take time. Learn of his treasures. I'd wager his secrets are well-hidden. Take my dagger. Conceal it. Don't make a move until you've learned all."

Goblin's words bounced away from Thomas like arrows from a bronzed Roman shield, not unlike other lacks of comprehension Markus had for his father's lectures.

"Yes Father," Thomas said taking the dagger. But, his attention was focused more on the erection his attire prompted.

"We better go quickly, Father," Thomas said. "Merthel must be waiting."

Fearing the wizard could hear their approach, Thomas and Goblin walked in silence to where Merthel's path intersected the old stone tiled road. Goblin hissed a harsh final warning as they parted.

"Remember my instructions and don't stray! Go quick and don't stop."

Once out of his father's sight, Thomas relaxed as he made for Merthel's cave. Alone, Thomas stopped to relieve his dammed humors. Thomas lowered his britches and took his true master in hand.

With that distraction released, Thomas found his way without mishap. Merthel's unworn path was mysteriously discernible through the steep and thickly forested climb. The people called this route the Path of No Return and only took it if invited. The fear of Merthel's magic afforded his sanctuary more protection than any army of the king would give. This land's enchantments were well known yet few hostile eyes lived to report them. Merthel's path gave way as Thomas proceeded.

*It's as if he expected me*

When Thomas looked behind, there were no signs of his passing. The entry of Merthel's cave was four horses wide and two horses tall and hemmed with a lattice of thick squared interlocking timbers, well-jointed and in-filled with cut stone and mortar. At the center was an ornate oak plank door carved with dragons, mermaids and a Minotaur. Thomas approached the door, cautiously, as his limbs threatened to betray him with trembling. He raised a hand to knock, but the door swung open on its own. A voice called from deep within.

"Markus don't be afraid. Come in; come in, my good lad."

*Markus must be the boy's name, I must answer to that.*

Thomas passed into a shallow, empty cave lit by one torch. The cave had been cleaned and was filled with strange odors; otherwise, it was like many Thomas had seen before. The door shut behind him. He stood in a foyer. Another man-made stone wall, with a plainer door, was at the deep end of the room. Thomas opened the inner door and entered a well lit cavernous room. Blinking with amazement, his eyes wandered widely.

Oaken shelves overflowed with books and scrolls. They filled racks taller than Thomas' father, some finely made while others were roughhewn timbers. Candles, oil lamps, papers, papyrus scrolls, leather bound books, velum parchments, quill pens and inks covered the tables: Never had he seen so many books all together. Remembering and heeding Father's order, Thomas observed everything and tried to memorize the details.

Abounding tools of alchemy such as stone-made mortar and pestles of many sizes, small copper kettles and clay or glass jars were amid unrecognizable tools of brass. Thomas imagined such were things made for sailors, or astrologers, or doctors, of their purpose he could not be sure. Small olive oil lamps burned. Iron braziers glowed under iron pots which percolated and smoked bitter odors.

On the gray rock walls, which had been dressed smooth, there were hung Persian carpets, maps, unrecognizable furs, and tapestries. The furthest wall was left natural and on it was painted renditions of animals that Thomas had never seen before. A wedged boulder firmly blocked a cave branch in that wall.

Thomas spun. All about there were lamps on expensive brass stands twice his height. Amid chairs and dressers that might have been made for kings there also stood haphazardly other items of furniture more fit for slaves. There were more accoutrements than found in a church, they were more liken to those items of a castle he guessed.

A fire pit with a low stone wall occupied the center of the room. A spit made of gears and wheels turned unaided roasting a fawn over hot coals. Iron pots were suspended above the pit, too. Soot blackened the ceiling. The entire room vaulted to a point high above the cook-pit where a hole allowed light to stream in and smoke to escape. Thomas saw no weapons. This emboldened him, but neither did he see gold or silver or anything else of *real* value. He noted nothing he could steal to show his father. He stepped farther into the room.

"Hold there, apprentice," the wizard said from an unseen nook, "Step lightly, for this place is hallowed ground. Pray the gods grant you wisdom in this place."

Merthel appeared from a shadow. His plump face was deeply wrinkled. His thin hair and groomed beard were long and gray. He wore the same long brown robes and had the same overfed stature as the Christian friars. Father would not rob these fat churchmen for fear of their God. Yet, Merthel was not like the friars. His dress and face were clean. His bulbous noise showed no sign of excessive drink. Rather unlike the churchmen, Merthel's eyes burned clear and bright. In spite of his girth, Merthel seemed frail.

*He is no match for me.*

Merthel lifted both hands above his head and spoke in a thunderous voice. Thomas did not understand the tongue. The sound unnerved him so much that his heart stopped and his feet stalled.

"Ah yes, that's better, my lad. Now, you shall not be struck dead. Only the invited can walk here, until my death or the influence of greater magic."

Merthel slapped his open palm on an oak plank table.

"Ha! Greater magic, indeed," Merthel said with a laugh.

He waved his hand.

"Come, my lad, come now and let me see you," the wizard said.

The beckoning of Merthel had somehow unbound Thomas' feet. His heart resumed. He walked slowly toward the wizard as if barefoot on sharp rocks, but the floor was polished flat. His eyes darted to and fro looking for the shine of treasure. *Nothing, nothing to steal!*

"You have respect for this place. That's a good boy!" Merthel said. "This is a good start for us in this holy place. This is a dangerous place."

Merthel looked quite pleased with himself.

*Dangerous for you old man. I am not a boy, but a man.* Thomas noticed a resemblance between Merthel and his father. Thomas gritted his teeth and bit back anger.

*I will be no one one's boy after this day.*

"Master," Thomas said, "your enchantments are famous and so too the danger of this place. The magic you wield can only come from the gods, but I see nothing here of your wealth. Your legend is greater than you."

The old man bellowed with laughter.

"Ah the ignorance of youth," Merthel said. His countenance soon changed.

He drew himself tall and straight and waved his hand. "Do you see all this? This is worth more than all the gold of the fallen Empire. This is food you cannot eat but will feed your mind. This is a place of knowledge. That is the commodity of kings."

"How so, Master?" Thomas asked meekly.

"Do you see theses scrolls?" Merthel said pointing to a rack with hundreds of rolled manuscripts. "They come from Alexandria, the Alexandra that burnt! Kings would pay great sums for what is held in that collection alone, if they knew how to read the secret languages. The keeper and interpreter of these books may name his price."

*I would need a caravan to transport them to where they would do me good.*

"For it is not the books themselves that have value, no. It is what they teach. I have books from every land, books of great forgotten wisdom."

The old man shuffled over to a nearby table. On it was a rust brown rock that looked like an Aegean sponge, the kind commonly found within the ruined public baths the Romans had built. The rock sat in an ornate bronze cradle. The texture reminded Thomas of his father's face, pocked and rough.

"This philosopher's stone was once worshiped in Egypt," Merthel explained. "It was once the center piece of the great temple of Karnack. Hidden within this stone are elements that Aphrodite herself fused into it when the cosmos were founded. Its dust will allow any man to procreate like a god and produce exceptional heirs. Its dust drove Nero and Caligula mad with lust! Alexander himself used it to impregnate his concubines. His father, Philip, would be without his heir if this stone were not captured from Egypt. With the dust of this stone, no man can resist its urgings. Even those men who have no proclivity toward women will fornicate against one's own nature under its spell."

*Who would trade a rock for grain?*

Thomas looked past Merthel. He spied strange glass jars unlike anything he had seen before on the self behind the wizard. Each shiny yet clear jar, in blue or green, had a fitted corkwood stopper. Earthen jars were all he or anyone of Gaul had known since Rome withdrew. Only priests had glass, and only as candle holders. The jars contained dirt, herbs or leaves. One held dried bat wings.

*Useless! At least jarred beans can yield crops. Yet these magic vestals hold no beans or seeds.*

"Now that's a good eye, my boy," Merthel said with enthusiasm. "What you see behind me is rare, rare indeed. Roman glass like this has not been made in a hundred years: Worth its weight in gold. The art of its industry was lost."

Merthel lifted a green vessel from its perch and extended it.

"But this glass, valuable though it may be, is greater for what it contains: the dust, extracted from God-Stone at great peril. All this glass is worth its weight in gold."

*Worth more than gold! And a size I can carry!*

"So, my good lad, what say you: Ready to apprentice with me? Learn what I teach you well, and your rewards will be great, slow to come, but great."

"If it's all the same to you, Master," Thomas said, drawing out his father's hidden dagger, "I will take my rewards now."

Thomas charged and thrust the dagger deep into Merthel's torso. Merthel collapsed. Thomas immediately ransacked the room searching for booty. Merthel lay helpless and bleeding, desperately clutching his wound. Finding nothing he could carry away, Thomas turned to the jars and dumped their contents to make ready his escape. Merthel looked up at Thomas as the thief poured out the God-Stone dust. Merthel laughed.

"What gives you such pleasure old man that you laugh at your own death?"

"No," said Merthel, "I laugh at yours, you will die in torture. My magic holds the mountain back as long as I live. You could dig yourself out, but you will be too preoccupied. You released the Goddess' bane you…fool…"

With that, Merthel expired.

The roof caved into the foyer room, filling it with ruble. It left Thomas trapped in the great room, alone, with a sudden, irresistible, raging erection as company, a feeling of a kind he never felt before.

*I will find my way out once I satisfy my need.*


## Sixteen Hundred Years Later

It was going to be one of those days. I knew it as soon as I read the memo. It didn't take a magician to recognize this bad omen, but even a crystal ball couldn't have predicted this day's outcome.

I worked here at the Houston Astrophysics Laboratory's Planetary Studies Group with Peter Christopher for the last five years. I have to say, it's been no picnic. This ought to be a planetary scientist's dream job, since I'm privileged to work with meteorites, my favorite subject of study, but I was stuck working alongside an oxymoron. Transferring to Texas seemed like a good idea. Once I started working with redneck-scientist Peter Christopher, the job became much less a scientific pleasure and more an exercise of political eggshell dancing.

Peter is good at analysis. Don't misunderstand. He's careful and thorough, to be sure, but his distracting attitude and volcanic mouth took all the magic out of doing science for me. But then "Merlyn's Meteorite" arrived and things changed radically.

When I received the memo requiring that Peter and I attend a meeting with renowned archaeologist and gay rights activist Edmund Thomson, I knew Peter would go off like a rocket. I cringed as I handed him the memo and braced for blast off.

"Another useless meeting, balls!" Peter said, tossing the memo on my desk, "I can't believe I got to go listen to that goddamn archeology fag tell me how to do my frigging job."

Peter's fat face turned the color of iron oxide as he thundered and pounded on his desk. He spewed every anti-gay sound-bite I ever heard, finishing with the classic: "God hates fags."

Hoping to shut him up, I said, "Better watch your step, Peter. The company has a non-discrimination policy. Everybody knows Thomson's queer, but you can't say that out loud, even if Thomson is just a guest. The policy applies to anyone on premises. You want a lawsuit?"

I was beyond tired of Peter's ranting. He knew that my sister's kid, my favorite nephew, is gay. Not even common courtesy for a coworker stopped him from trashing the gays in the name of God.

"You better knock it off," I said.

"Screw that, this is Texas," Peter said as he slammed his meaty fist on his barrel chest. "We don't cotton to faggots 'round here."

"It's policy," I said.

"I don't need no stinking policy. God's policy is my policy. Nobody's going to stop my religious freedom."

I knew he was right. Anyone that wanted to keep their job around here wasn't going to say squat. The CEO was a fundamentalist. Religion was off the table. I just wished he'd shut up, that was all I was after.

"What are you some kind of fag lover? Jesus Bill, you're not supporting these perverts are you? If they take it in the ass, they got to accept the consequences. When'd you change over?"

Now my face was red. I was hot. I wanted to argue that homosexuality is not a choice. Peter ought to know that as a scientist, but I was in no mood for his asinine arguments. Experience taught me better. I let it go. We had to go to the meeting and I was not about to let Peter's pontifications make me late again. Besides, I was interested in what Thomson had to say. My wife teaches anthropology, and as such, she's a fan of Thomson's work.

I had read about what the press called the "Merlyn's Cave Discovery" a few years ago. I never expected that we'd get involved, even though we work with archeologists on occasion. We examine soil samples or volcanic ash from dig sights for dating purposes. What falls from space compared to what Earth is made of tells one hell of a story.

We arrived at the meeting with little time to spare and slipped into our seats. I enjoyed the presentation. The artifacts found would keep many universities busy for years to come. Our part was minor. But, the last section of the presentation, which discussed the belief in aphrodisiac properties of the artifact, rubbed Peter raw.

"…And so," Thomson said, "from the surviving texts we found, a preliminary reading mind you, we surmised that the meteorite we discovered must have had some sort of special chemical properties. The ancients were apparently quite familiar with its unique qualities, though they considered it magic."

Thomson clicked the power-point and a picture of a typical iron-nickel meteorite resting in an ornate brass stand appeared on the screen.

"Therefore, we strongly advise that you take exceeding care in your examination. It may be true that the Empire had possession of it for a thousand years. That doesn't mean it's harmless. It could be the impetus of the scene we found. Proceed with caution. Any questions?"

Peter stewed. He fidgeted and had puffed in disgust every time Thomson gave an instruction.

"What exactly was this scene? What makes you think these properties even exist? Come on, now, it's just another piece of iron-nickel space junk."

Thomson ignored Peter's disdain and answered the question in a steady professional monotone.

"For one, we know that the older man, the victim, was killed in one place and his body moved. Where he fell, he bled-out. His corpse was draped over a chair with his robe hiked up exposing the buttocks—."

"He should know," Peter said, hitting me in the ribs with an elbow.

"…His mummy was well-preserved. Our medical examiners confirmed that a rape occurred, a post-mortem rape. The young man, who we believe killed him, could have escaped. The rubble release trap did not place enough material in the foyer to prevent his digging out. Our young murderer was found with his pants around his ankles, his hand in his lap and his torn and bleeding penis gripped tightly."

Thomson clicked the remote several times until he revealed the mummified body of the killer, as found at the actual dig site.

"What would cause that?" Thomson said with a dramatic sweep of his hand. "He had to be under the influence of this so-called 'spell' that we learned of in codex C-17. Something caused this boy to go insane. The meteorite is simply the only plausible explanation. Nothing in the alchemist's cave could account for this behavior."

"Maybe they was just perverted. Everyone knows how decadent them Romans was," Peter said in a steely voice nuanced with an air of vindication. The top of Peter's head flushed red as he spouted. "They was a couple of god damned pagans."

One of the VP's, Charlie Render, decided to head Peter off and called the meeting to an abrupt end. Peter and I were quickly assigned the task of the examination, maybe to spite Peter. Charlie, a confirmed bachelor, didn't like Peter. Charlie had previously obtained the approval to cut Merlyn's rock in half. That procedure was our job.

I thought about Thomson's presentation as I walked to the saw room. Thomson had pointed out old tool marks set around a deep hole in the center of this twelve-inch diameter space artifact. Otherwise, it was a typical deep brown and blue-black mottled meteorite. It looked like a petrified sponge or a piece of aerated iron slag. Thomson thought there was once a soft vein that ran through it. He proposed that it had been excavated in antiquity. Thomson rightly extrapolated that this super hard meteorite could not have been cut with any of the tools available then. A soft vein was likely. A soft core was something no one had seen in a space rock before.

I could not wait to cut that sucker open. Perhaps that was my downfall. We went right from the meeting to the cutting lab without serious thought. The sample was already there. But, of course, Peter was still pissing about being told how to do his job and he was not about to follow Thomson's suggestions.

"I'm not wearing no god damn breather," Peter said as we set up the diamond-bladed wet saw, "This is bullshit. No way this here rock got anything harmful in it. Only fags wear breathers."

I knew he'd badger me into taking mine off too, so I didn't bother with the filter mask. I didn't want to waste time arguing. The wet-saw keeps the dust down.

Wet cutting seldom produced friable material under these conditions. We set up the cut, started the saw, and went to the glass-walled observation room overlooking the cutting wheel. Cutting iron-nickel meteorites took hours. The observation room doubled as a break room complete with a small refrigerator, kitchenette, bench table and commercial coffee pot. Word was out about Merlyn's stone so half a dozen co-workers joined the vigil.

Peter could not resist this opportunity to preach. I tuned Peter out. Mindy O'Connor, our head chemist, decided to mix it up. She could make him look foolish without sparking his anger, very entertaining.

"So," Mindy said with amusement evident in her eyes, "You're saying that human sexuality is immutable and the default condition is straight only. People are not born gay or can't be forced by chemical inducements."

"Right," Peter said, "There's only one God-given sexual nature. The rest is a sickness."

"It seems to me that all people are bisexual by nature to some degree," Mindy said with her thin pixy smile. "Given the right chemical inspiration, sex drive over-rules social constructions every time. If you knew anything about chemistry Peter, you'd know that under the right circumstances, anyone can go gay, even you. Hormones are everything."

Mindy paused for effect. That was a mixed bag of bullshit pie custom designed to stymie Peter. He had a masters' degree in chemistry. His doctorate was geophysics. It was her way of calling him an idiot.

"That kid was trapped in the cave," she continued. "Maybe he didn't want to die a virgin? No, I doubt it. Something enhanced his testosterone drive. It's natural."

"Nothing queer is natural, and you can't make a straight man gay if he aren't a willing sinner," Peter responded with all seriousness. "Fags reject their God-given nature, that's all. That sick bastard decided against God. That cave was a pagan shrine."

Peter took a long sip of black coffee.

He added, "There's nothing on Heaven or Earth that'll make me do anything queer."

"So, I guess you only do your wife when messages from God tell you it's time," she said.

Peter's face turned red. He was building steam. An alarm sounded. The wet saw got hung up. That couldn't wait. This was no surprise, it happens all the time. The saw blade tends to bind up just before it makes it through. Peter and I hurried into the cutting room and manually shut down the saw arm. It was old equipment, no robotics. We started to re-set the table for the final pass when Peter suddenly grabbed my arm and spun me away from the slide table. I pulled away instinctively.

He didn't let go. He looked me right in the eyes. His chest heaved.

"Bill, I've always loved you…kiss me, kiss me now. Kiss me hard!"

I couldn't get away from him. He was twice my weight and had forearms like Popeye. As he drew me nearer, I screamed. "Lock down! Lock down!"

That's when I noticed the yellow chalky muck on Peter's lips and face. He must have been sprayed with wet meteorite slurry as he worked to free the blade. I closed my eyes and prayed for God to get me out of here. Peter pressed his lips to mine and the fairy dust kicked in.

Someone hit the lock down alarm, but no one left. Rather than follow evacuation protocol, everyone stood frozen with shocked faces pressed against the glass while Peter and I proceeded with some sixty-nine sex action on the cutting room floor as if we were veteran porn stars.

I hate to admit it, but we had an intense good time. I didn't care who watched.

It took a while for them to figure out how to stop us from screwing ourselves to death. We sure as hell could not stop ourselves. I learned why Peter is so cocksure, he was hung like a Clydesdale.

I was told the details later. Once Mindy stopped laughing, she whipped up a tranquilizing gas. Security fed it into the air purge system's fresh air emergency intake. I woke up a few days later in Houston Hospital with my hands in mitten restraints tied to the hospital bed's rails—out of crotch range. Peter occupied the same room. He was awake and restrained like me. He smiled at me and winked. In spite of a blazing headache, and my sore, raw dick, I had gained a new appreciation for Peter. So, I winked back.

Working with Peter was always stressful, but now with wholly different reasons added it will get worse. Even after all this, I'm sure he'll still be a sanctimonious dick and I'm not so sure the fairy dust wore off, I think so: I hope my transfer goes though before I find out the hard way.

**END**

# MARY COOK AND
# THE RAILWAY MEN

Seamus Lockport was proud and stiff, a man not given to dainties or dandies. In 1850, he still wore knee britches and wool stockings, same as his preacher grandfather. The bulk of his possessions were handed down from his revered sire. Black waistcoats, black britches and white linen ruffled shirts were what Amos wore from the old God monger's left-behinds.

'They isn't moth-eaten,' Grandpa had said from his deathbed so Seamus took them.

Mary hated her husband's manner of dress. A man dressed like a preacher yet proceeding like the devil was hypocritical.

"Waste not, want not," Seamus would quote when she eyed him as a fool.

No other farmer in Virginia looked as forthright or ridiculous while plowing as Seamus Lockport.

He waited in the shadows of the porch. Their Appalachian homestead was in the sun but Amos gave light no quarters. Their weather-beaten, flat-log farmhouse was bleached as gray as his good eye. He was a sight Mary thought. Underneath that black felt topcoat, which made him bigger, thicker and meaner on sight, he was stick-thin. He puffed himself up and postured imposing for a reason.

Railroad men were coming again.

On the news of their impending arrival, Seamus had Mary brush out his dirt-black and gray barbwire hair. It hung lank below his collar like last year's funeral wreath. He wore the new hat, a beaver fur top-hat, same one he took last spring when a railroad surveyor came a-calling. The fool left it behind when Seamus ran him off.

The Lockport spread was on a flat halfway up Bear Mountain, between bottom land and a long hollow that ran between mountain fingers, a likely spot for a railroad pass. Folks in Creek Bottom wanted that train, but Seamus wouldn't have it. He wouldn't split his land for any man or country. God had bequeathed this land to him.

Mary didn't think much of God-reasoning that weren't in the Good Book. She read it regular, he didn't.

"Mary Cook," Seamus called. "Bring my pistols. They're a-coming."

Mary herself was bred a good farmer's wife. 'Right and bright as polished silver,' her father used to say. She always helped others, like the Book said, or that is when Seamus let her. She was as happy as could be expected from a woman that never bore children. She loved the little children, too. Even so deprived of what helpmates children were, she forged on. Folks down in Creek Bottom said she was a stout woman, God-fearing, hard working and she was—she had to be.

She plowed and picked and slaughtered hogs and tended the smokehouse. She put up as many cans as the harvest allowed with nary a complaint and all the while keeping God's word.

At the general store, the week before, she told Molly Wells, "Good, hard work is God's blessing, it is."

But Mary did complain from time to time. Winking at Molly she went on to say, "I like hard work, I do, I oft times say, but truth to tell...I don't like hard things. Lord save me from pistols and powder and that hard Lockport way."

She didn't say more. It wasn't her place to talk about him, or his beating her, and all for wrongheaded reasons. Cherry-picked verses drawn from Lockport's dark well retreated from her tongue.

Down below folks thought Mary a sweet soul. She was anything but that this morning. She was boiling sour. His two 69-caliber flintlock pistols lay on her clean kitchen table. Seamus left them where he loaded them. She hated the sight of them. Their taint spooked her. Grandpa had killed Indians with them. Those heirlooms did murder. That Seamus loved them made Mary hate them all the more.

"Mary Cook! Bring me my guns," Seamus called from the covered porch.

Mary came through the front door dangling them by trigger guards like a pair of rotten trout. Seamus snatched them and split his long coat tucking each pistol into his wide, back belt one on either side. He wedged his coattails behind the flintlocks making his frock raptor wings.

"How many railroad men you be running off afore they send an army?" She said. "You can't chase off progress forever."

"Never mind, woman," he barked.

He lowered his voice. "I've an idea, God willing. If they don't get back to Philadelphia, why, the bosses will stop sending such robbers hereabout."

He had that look in his eye. It scared her. She had seen it before—when Grandpa talked about killing Indians. She remembered washing his bloody clothes.

"But Seamus—."

"Hush woman," he commanded. "They're in earshot."

Two upright men riding fine horses drew near. The horses were bigger and stronger than Seamus' draft animals. The men wore back-north clothes: checkered pants, matching vests, high collared shirts, brown leather riding coats, and tall, black leather riding boots. The younger man had his pants tucked in. The older man wore a bowler hat of the latest fashion and a handlebar mustache. Fine specimens, they were.

Seamus dead-eyed their holster belts and took a backward step. They both carried revolving percussion pistols. Each man had twelve shots to Seamus' one. The younger, a long-haired man, had that new-fangled Henry rifle that everybody was admiring at the trading post. It was poking out of his luggage bright as you please. Mary didn't see any pack mule carrying surveying rods like before.

The mustached man swooped back his duster. Shiny new revolvers, unlike Seamus' misfiring heirlooms, sat one on each hip with a pepperbox Derringer sticking out of his vest's watch pocket to beat all.

"My name's Tom Fix. This here's Bart Swiftwing, He's half Indian. We're Pinkerton Detectives. The Pennsylvania Railroad aims to make right all this trouble regarding the company's surveyors."

Tom Fix tipped his hat. The other hand rested on a pistol butt.

"You ain't fixing to make no trouble, are you, mister?" Bart added.

The Indian's dark eyes shone confidence. He lightly brushed the Colt's handle.

"Well, no, sir," Seamus said. "Don't mind theses pistols…A man can't be too careful. Robbers and thieves roaming the land. Won't you gentlemen come in for a meal?"

He didn't wait for an answer.

"Mary Cook, stoke the fire!" he barked. "We have company."

The Pinkerton boys dismounted and tied their horses to the porch rail. They came in and stood on edge in the front room until Seamus pulled his pistols and placed them on the pegs doweled into the stone fireplace's wall. The guns hung by their trigger guards above a chestnut mantle. Seamus' Hawking sharp shooter and a Pennsylvania flintlock hung higher above. He kept them well.

An archway led directly into the kitchen. The fireplace was open to both sides. A black iron kettle hung over the hearth above a low coal fire. Mary's Franklin stove was already lit. The stove's iron griddle was already hot. She set herself to cooking while the men talked.

Seamus had the men take the best chairs, chairs made by his hands. He told his usual tales about the Indian massacre in the hollow and how Grandfather had gunned down the chief with that Pennsylvanian rifle.

"The very one yonder over the hearth," Seamus said.

He didn't mention that he was a crack shot with it himself. Mary turned and stood aside with plates in hand.

"Mary, get them vitals set."

She laid down a mess of scrambled eggs, fresh cut pork-belly thick and fried crisp. From the cupboard, she got new churned butter, jam, and the loaf of bread that she had made that morning. The kitchen table was fully loaded.

"Much obliged, Mrs. Lockport," Tom Fix said, taking a fork in hand. "Smells like heaven."

"You have a good wife, sir," said Bart Swiftwing.

"The Lord provides," Seamus said, "as He takes away."

Seamus, like he done for the others before, made his guests feel at home.

That's how he set the trap. He had them primed like a musket's flash pan. *Overfed fish in a barrel.*

Mary felt heartsick.

Once in the parlor, he finished with his usual Indian story, the one that kept the town folks scared off and far away. He told of the Indians' ghosts in the high hollow and the haunting.

He bragged, "Was my prayers and supplications unto the Lord, I'm a hedge against spirits. It weren't for me, evil'd flood the dell like spoiled honey. Best you don't go up. Lord's my witness, some that go never come back. Others seen things they'd wish they hadn't."

"Well, sir," Tom Fix said, "I wouldn't be doing my job if I didn't go see...for the company. I thank ye kindly for your hospitality."

Tom Fix tipped his bowler hat to Mary.

"There's bad magic up yonder," Seamus warned.

"Bart here's half-breed. Got powerful Indian magic himself. Ain't that right, Bart?"

Bart cast a crooked smile at Seamus and patted his brand new Colt Navy. The two men made toward the door. Seamus saw them out.

Mary thought these detectives didn't believe Seamus. Sorely suspicious, they were. They weren't like superstitious bottom-land folks or the ragged mountain men that trapped and hunted everywhere except here. She worried Seamus' hospitality had its effect. With a good meal in them, they were relaxed and off guard. Still, Mary didn't think Seamus' usual tricks would work on them. These were sophisticated fighters, hard men and no fools.

Seamus stood on the porch until they'd gone uphill out of sight. Mary watched her husband from the kitchen archway and wondered how she let herself get tangled up with such a man. But, she knew the answer.

Grandfather had forced the marriage, an arrangement between families. A young girl had no right to question. Her parents were kindly people and easily bullied by Grandpa Lockport. She was barely fourteen. Still, after twenty-five years, she couldn't forget the murder in Grandpa's eyes. *That's what turned them.*

Since they heard more railroad men were coming, he let Grandpa's lineage full out. Mary felt weak in the knees but her heart beat stronger. He entered the kitchen and sat down to a cup of bitter coffee, just like Grandpa drank. *A good wife to a bad man.* She was sick of it.

"You want your bloody buckskins," Mary asked.

He dressed like a dead Indian's ghost to scare folks when they got close.

"Not this time," he said. "I had my fill. Time I show them fancy dandies no railroad man can take what God rightfully give me."

"Grandpa took this land," Mary said coldly. "God had nothing to do with it."

"Lord's got mysterious ways," Seamus said his voice sharp. "Shut your mouth. What knows you of the Lord's work? I'm the preacher's grandson, by God. Bring me my rifles!"

"Son of a murderer," Mary said as she fetched Grandpa's rifles off the wall.

Seamus sat and busied himself loading rifles. He had time. He knew every path and shortcuts no horse would tread. Mary thought of his remarks and fumed silently. She knew the Good Book better than him; all he took from it was justification. He used what suited him. He beat her saying it was the Lord's command. Now, he made ready to kill "for God's sake." Grandpa's rotten apple fell on fertile ground.

As Mary washed the dishes, Seamus' chair scraped the wood plank floor. She didn't turn. His boots marched out the back door. She couldn't bear to watch him go.

She got busy cleaning. She cleaned everything in the kitchen and the front bedroom though nothing was dirty. She cleaned to take her mind off Seamus. But, she couldn't wash that look in his cold, dead eyes out of her mind. She thought of all the men that went into that hollow and how many had never come back. She couldn't deny it any longer. Seamus had killed before.

In the distance, the Hawkins boomed like a cannon. A moment later, the crack of the smaller rifle sent shivers thought her.

Mary asked herself, *what's worse, the sin of murder, or the sin of letting a murderer kill unanswered?*

Mary took the pistols off their pegs—still loaded. She took the powder horn, too, and settled into the bent wood rocker at the far side of the hearth. She cocked each flintlock hammer one click and primed each flash pan. Once primed, she pulled the hammers all the way. She balanced them in her lap and waited.

It wasn't long before Seamus burst through the back door.

"Mary, get my pistols!" He shouted. "Those boys are slick, only winged him. Mary!"

Seamus set his rifles on the kitchen table with a hard thunk.

"I need to reload," he continued. "Where's my store?"

Mary had put away the powder, patches, and tin of balls.

"In the barn," she lied.

"No time! By God, Mary Cook, bring me pistols!" Seamus screamed.

"No," she said from the parlor straining to keep her voice even, "Get them yourself."

Seamus stomped into the front room. Mary pulled. Flint struck steel.

The sound was an avalanche, like a hundred boulders cracking as many trees, and all at once. A thick cloud smoked the room. It smelled of rotten eggs. Within the smoke, his form was like the Devil's shadow, a looming specter, and still standing. She had missed.

Seamus groped for the iron poker at the hearth's side. He took it and swung savagely. Mary stayed low in the chair. The blow went over her. Splinters shot forth cutting her face.

Mary pulled the other gun's trigger. The hammer fell. This time, a 69-caliber ball sent Seamus flying. He hit the gable wall so hard chunks of mud caulk rained down. The house was double full of sulfur smoke. Mary fell to her hands and knees. Eyes stinging, she crawled outside and rolled down the steps coughing and choking. She let loose her breakfast and collapsed, away from the mess, before fainting.

Mary laid there on the turf—how long only God knew. The clip-clop of a horse rousted her and she regained some sense.

Tom Fix was walking his steed. Bart was slumped in the saddle. Mary's head cleared right quick. She got up, spilling her tale.

"He tried to kill me. I wouldn't give him his pistols. Swung a fire iron at me, he did," Mary said with her lips quivering. She never cried when Seamus beat her and she wouldn't cry now. "Shot him dead, I did."

"Don't worry none, Ma'am," Tom said. "I'll go inside and cover him. You did no wrong."

Mary looked up at the half-Indian. "Hurt bad?"

"Nicked my calf is all," Bart said from his partner's horse. "Smokey didn't fare so well."

Mary never could stand idle when there was mending to do. She led Bart around back, helped him dismount, and set about tending his wound in the kitchen. The gash was full of dirt. She picked it clean and dressed it proper.

Old Judge McMinn in Creek Bottom didn't see fit to charge Mary with any crime. Especially as the County Sheriff and the Pinkerton men went back up and found bodies. One was Indian Jake the missing trapper. The others were railroad men. Some were too long dead to figure.

In court, Mary asked the judge to grant her a new name. Her maiden name she could not abide as Seamus called her that. Seamus' name, Lockport, wasn't fit to call an outhouse. With the money she got selling her property, Mary Justus lived well. She took in Indian Jake's widow, Heartfeather, and the widow's little boy and baby girl. Mary treated them like her own kin. Some folks didn't like it, but she paid naysayers no mind. It was high time somebody set right what Grandpa Lockport had done wrong so long ago, she figured. Thus she went about doing what good works further qualified her chosen name.

**END**

# STREET DUTY

O fficer Stildanko wasn't forced. He requested street duty. He didn't want it for the money and power. He came to serve the people, and he did so with or without official back-up procedures. Ignoring certain directives, of course, was dangerous. He walked the line.

Dave Stildanko thought himself a man of the people, a natural citizen's leader. His easy nature and attractive looks offset mistrust. Although he wasn't permitted to remove headgear, he did it anyway, for the citizens. Police armor hid good intentions. The people on his beat liked him for it. They trusted him...a little. He did other things for them as well, like looking the other way on the Must Carry Law. Everyone knew people had to be armed so the police could blast away at will without provocation. This did not sit well with him.

Official policy overruled rational policy. Such was police work. Headquarters recorded him on citizen-cam giving someone a break again. He wasn't wearing headgear either. Big trouble. Again.

"Stildanko, I don't give a shit about public relations," the chief said. "Doesn't matter what people want. Every citizen must be armed. Enforce the law or quit, got it?"

Once the others left assembly, the chief fluttered a fat eyelid at Stildanko.

"It's for your own good, Dave," the chief whispered. "You don't want your face shot off do you?"

The Chief wasn't a bad egg.

Next day, Stildanko wasn't on the street one hour before he issued the three warnings he was allowed. The next gun check had to stick or he'd have to pay the fine. Every citizen-cam seemed to be pointed at him. He felt the eyes of the brass through his plastic-steel shell.

*Son of a bitch. Here comes Mom Thorn.*

The old woman moved steadily toward him from a hundred yards down the block picking her way over piled trash. Stildanko looked around. There was no avoiding it. She was aiming for him and he was obligated to shake her down. He stepped behind a sedan lying on its side and ducked out of cam-view. They might still hear it, but at least he wouldn't have to get physical.

Thorn was a tough, old ruins rat. She did things her way, law or no law. Stildanko had sympathy for her. She reminded him of his dear departed mother. But she was no softie, maternal type—she ran this derelict hood.

"Stildanko, you bastard," Mom called as she rounded the burnt-out car. "I hear you been strong arming my children."

"I got to do my job, Mom, headquarters is on me. Say, I don't see any holster on you."

She never carried. Her walls must have been plastered with police warning tickets. She didn't need to carry a gun. Everybody on this block had her back. Why make a protected old lady haul iron? The law was ridiculous.

"What about it, Mom?" He said. He repeated the mantra as ordered and trained to do. "You're not safe without a piece."

"Don't you worry, Sonny," she replied. "I take care of myself. Don't need a stinking bazooka. Don't need nothing like that."

Stildanko touched his sidearm. It was a .78 caliber Cobra Giant Killer loaded with armor piercing rounds. He could shoot through a car long way. It even penetrated police armor, a necessary evil. There was a black market for used police protection. Citizens scooped it up, but not Mom. She always wore nothing but a threadbare house dress, boots and the old army coat that her late husband had worn in the Citizen's Uprising.

Stildanko maneuvered closer to the upturned car. Cameras also read brain waves. He'd keep his intent his own.

"Look Mom, I can't let this pass."

He said it with a nod toward the central cam-array.

"I got to take your thumb print and direct withdraw the fine."

He popped a thumb reader off his utility belt and held it out. Stildanko figured she had fake-print tips so he didn't check. She pushed the device away hard. She was less frail than she let on.

"I can't let this pass either, Sonny."

He was used to her subversive remarks. They were cause enough to run her in, but he never did or would. She thrust out a dirty thumb and waved it around.

"The revolution ain't over yet, Copper," she said.

She stuffed her hand into her coat pocket. Stildanko felt twisted. Mom was the glue in this hood. Her people, or 'children' as she called them, resisted carrying guns on her word. She was right. Armed citizens were fair game. Cops couldn't shoot unarmed people. Hoods like this were tricky, and his job just got harder. Hence, the need for the Must Carry law.

He should have searched her for illegal weapons. Procedure demanded that he call in the Interrogations Department on a repeat no-carry. It'd be brownie points for him, but he didn't have the heart.

"Second amendment, Mom," he said.

"Balls," she said.

Any other cop would have given her the once over. At least rob her and make her get lost, maybe roughed her up. Stildanko ignored procedure, both official and informal. He wanted a part in the growing peace she fostered, not escalate the violence. She spit at his feet. He didn't care. He considered it a small price to pay for good public relations. Stildanko lifted his face shield and retracted his neck protection. This was about trust. The armor was chafing anyway. He pulled his headgear off and dangled it on a finger by the chin strap.

"Look Mom," he said lowering his voice. "What would you have me do? If I don't get on the stick, they'll boot me. You don't want a trigger happy hard-ass down here, do you?"

####

But that's exactly what Mom wanted. Mom wanted a block full of hard-asses. Draw the cops in. That's the ticket. The street was rigged to blow. All she needed was something to bring the coppers in. Officer Do-Right was self-made bait.

"I see what you mean," she said. "We need more like you, Dave, for sure."

She raised her voice for the spy-ears. "I'll pay the fine now, hard cash."

Mom fumbled in her waist bag and retrieved a forty-dollar coin. She let it slip. It rolled between his steel legs. Perfect.

Stildanko turned and bent down to pick it up, well below camera angle. She pulled the stinger from a sleeve holster and aimed for his exposed neck. His suit alarm sounded, but too late. His head popped off like a champagne cork, like she'd seen in the pre-revolution vids.

His head rolled into a garbage pile. She picked the sidearm off his body and stuffed it into an inside coat pocket. She took up and activated Dave's headgear and pointed it so his onboard spy-cam got a good look at the body. Then, she focused the cam on Dave's head. She shuffled a few yards away, out of earshot of the suit's microphone.

"Garbage is as garbage does," she whispered into a small radio.

Mom made her way slowly to the hotel ruins. Cam-eyes followed. By the time the cops came, her children would be long gone.

"Guns, ha! Can't fix anything with guns," she said.

Mom settled into a rocking chair in front of a broken window in the hotel.

"Bombs," she whispered. "Big bombs, now that's a game changer."

Mom rested the detonator in her lap, took up her knitting, and waited.


**END**

# STALKING KILGORE TROUT

C hastity sat next to Rob, her support system, tightly gripping his hand. The antique leather sofa—actual animal skin—made her cringe. Real paper books stuffed Professor Clemens' shelves, each book older than the university and many retrieved from distant time-lines.

"The idea of killing a tree to make a book turns my stomach," she said, "Nothing from Kurt Vonnegut, either. I checked."

She doubted the existence of Vonnegut. He had to be a computer construct.

Rob didn't know anything about twentieth century literature, but Rob liked old books. As a dimensional time-slider, Rob might have come along just to see the paper books. All that mattered to her was he had come.

"Thanks for the support," Chastity said, "Every girl needs a queer boyfriend like you."

"How could I let my best fag-hag face Professor Dick Face alone? If he eats you alive where would I get another straight girl with big tits and blond hair to follow me around?"

She squeezed his hand harder.

"If I fail creative writing I won't get any more funding," Chastity said. "You'll have to find a freshman."

Rob's lips twisted. Chastity chirped a little laugh.

"I just broke you in," Rob said. "You better pass. You are as close to the real Marilyn Monroe as I can get. I could use the multi-universe time-dilator, slide back and sideways, get a sample and make a clone, but, it's not the same. Clones die too fast."

"Isn't that dangerous, sliding like that?"

"Oh, please! It's 3026; no slide traveler has died in thirty years."

Rob produced a comb from nowhere and re-slicked his already perfect black hair. He took the 1950's seriously—this week.

"Think I would do anything dangerous? Girl, you know me better," he said.

"You're the one in danger. How're you going to write a short story like Kurt Vonnegut?"

"I shouldn't have taken Vonnegut Studies," Chastity said.

A voice boomed from the inner office.

"Miss Sterling, please come in."

Together, they stood.

"No," Professor Clemens said, still unseen. "I'll speak with Miss Sterling alone."

Chastity cringed.

"Not now, Rob," the professor added, in a darker than usual tone.

Clemens' voice suggested recognition, perhaps even familiarity. Yet Chastity knew that Rob had not taken any of his classes. Chastity looked Rob up and down. That bitch! Her mind swirled. Did Rob time-slide for Clemens? Is that how Clemens gained his insight into the twentieth century? More importantly, why would Rob help him? Suddenly 'Professor Dick Face' took on new significance. Rob must have a relationship with Clemens, but not a teacher-student rapport.

Clemens had previously spent forty minutes pointing at her electronic manuscript and telling her in different ways, "This is not what Vonnegut would write." The only way Clemens could know what Vonnegut would write was if he went to Vonnegut's timeline and sat on his shoulder. Clemens was getting this stuff from somewhere. The Professor had to be sliding and if he could do it, so could she. As soon as she broke free of Clemens' clutches, she looked for Rob in the outer office. She shivered when she saw the animal hide sofa again. Worse, her time-sliding support bitch wasn't on it. She headed to the time science building and burst into his lab.

"Okay, bitch, pay up!"

Rob stepped from his holograph chamber cupping his ears.

"Girl, read the sign, no noise," he said. "You freaked out an entire tribe of Neanderthals, probably caused a religion in that space-time."

"I don't give a shit, Rob, you owe me," she said. "I agreed to your Marilyn Monroe bio-molding. You got an A in DNA morphing because of me."

"Hey, you agreed—."

"Send me to Kurt Vonnegut," she interrupted. "Real body, not a ghost visit."

"We don't do that anymore," Rob told her. "Too dangerous. People get killed. I can't do it. If I get caught, I'll lose my funding."

"How does Dr. Clemens knows so much about Vonnegut?"

"I don't know," Rob said. "Research?"

"He's had years to look over the guy's shoulder," Chastity said. "I have two weeks. Send me or I'll turn you in for sleeping with Clemens."

Rob flinched. Her hunch panned out.

Students, even doctoral students, were strictly forbidden from sexual relations with university staff. She had him by the balls and the look on his face said he knew it.

"We don't have Vonnegut's real timeline, Chaz," Rob protested. "We aren't

sure it's really him. All we have is alternate reality. Might not be his core dimension. I could only place you in the neighborhood of our best guess."

Chastity stopped to think. She had to pick Vonnegut's brain. She would only
have a few days in that dimension—not much time. Yet, this Vonnegut Studies
class would make or break her entire semester. She had to try.

"Rob, how long will I be gone?"

"Three days, tops."

"Got any period clothes here?"

Rob handed her an outfit from his collection: small black skirt, a knitted sweater that she barely squeezed her tits into, kitten-heeled shoes and a cute silk scarf.
It was his favorite period of Earth history. She quickly put on the costume. Rob
gave her a wad of antique cash. She crawled into the coffin-like time machine
and her heart fluttered despite the fact that she'd done this before. Every middle
school kid took a time trip usually to witness some gruesome assassination if they
were lucky or the signing of some document if they weren't. As a farewell, Rob
grabbed one of her fake tits, which she thought odd for a gay man, and closed
the lid. The smell of ozone filled the box. She thought it smelled exactly like an
obsolete Earth funeral home. If she had time, she would visit a funeral home…

She materialized in a dark, trash-littered alley between two brick high-rise
buildings. She gagged from the smell of piss and garbage. After the Great Antibi-
otic-Resistant Plague had wiped out half the human population, Chastity's world
had been made antiseptic, antibacterial and anti-microbial. She ran for the street
and the bright sunshine bathing it, but her shoes tripped her up making it slow
going. She was desperate for fresh air, but she found none exiting the ally. The
twentieth century was a disgusting, dirty, mad-house.

She ducked into the first door she saw and stumbled into a tiny market. She
knew about these little stores from history class and museum displays. It felt safe.
Outside was too big and too strange.

A tall, slight man with a saggy jaw-line, curled, shaggy hair, wiry eyebrows
and mustache was there sweeping the floor.

He smiled then took a moment to study her heaving chest.

"When did Norma Jean come back from the dead?" The man asked.

Chastity looked at herself in the overhead mirror. Rob had placed an emergency recall button in the shape of a brooch on the breast of her angora sweater.
She almost used it.

"You all right, Miss?" He asked.

"I'm new here," she said, feeling overwhelmed. "May I stay inside a minute?"

"Only if you buy something," a thickly-accented woman's voice said.

Chastity spun. Behind a cluttered counter near the door sat a fat, dark-
skinned woman wearing a bright orange wrap-around dress. She had a jewel on
her forehead.

"I'll buy something," Chastity said.

She didn't know anything about commerce in this timeline so she pulled half
the money, multiple green bills with tiny one hundreds written on the corners, out
of her little white handbag and laid it on the counter. The woman didn't react.

"That ought to wet her bloomers," the man said with a chuckle.

The women snapped up the cash and put it into a fold of her garment.

"Mr. Trout, keep an eye on her, will you?" The woman said.

Perhaps the little black skirt Rob put her in was too short for this century? The man looked up and down her legs.

"How could I not?" he said. "I don't think she has room enough onboard for shoplifting, unless, she intends on heisting slim-jims. But I think she already paid for her fair share."

"Mr. Trout," the fat lady said, rolling her eyes. "I'm going to lunch." She hurled herself off the stool, turned the corner and was out the door.

"Like a cannon-fired pumpkin. She can take a flying fuck at the moon, for all I care," Mr. Trout said. "Make yourself at home. She won't be back for hours. Curry takes time."

Mr. Trout pulled a notebook out of his apron pocket, took the stool from behind the counter, and placed the pad on a shelf. He sat and began writing. He quickly filled two pages, tore the paper off, tossed it into a trash can and started again.

It happened too fast, all this input crashed down on her. Within five minutes her head was spinning. It was time-shock. There were good reasons why time sliders trained for years. She wandered the four long aisles of the store trying to focus on the things she recognized from history class.

She had to work through her confusion. She pondered the canned foods, toys, bags of chips, beans, rice, boxes of cereal and artifacts she could not identify. So strange, so many items, so densely packed. Finally, she selected a long can of sardines.

"I wouldn't try it," Mr. Trout said without looking up from his writing. "Fell off Bruno's truck two years ago. Back in the war, would have been a feast. Now, not so much."

Trout ripped off a stack of pages, crumpled them and dropped them in the waste can.

"Mr. Trout—."

"Call me Kiladore."

"Kilgore—."

"Sure, Kilgore, has a nice ring." He wrote something down.

"What are you writing?" Chastity asked.

"Stories, not very good ones, I'm afraid," he answered. "This guy Vonnegut used to come here. He inspired me. Thought I'd give it a whirl."

*Vonnegut, Kurt Vonnegut!*

"Vonnegut comes here? I'd love to meet him," she said. "Can you introduce me?"

"Sorry, miss," Kilgore said. "He's off doing research, said something about India: Haven't seen him in years."

Chastity felt sick and not from time sliding. There was no point hanging around. Vonnegut could be anywhere in the world. She had to go somewhere private and push the return call, no need to shock Mr. Trout. Primitive people that see time sliders take off are often mentally affected and a slider isn't supposed to interfere.

"It was nice meeting you Kilgore, I'm feeling better," she said. "I think I'll go."

Kilgore Trout slid off his stool, gathered the bag from the trash basket, tied it off and handed it to her.

"Drop this in the can outside for me, will you?" He asked. "The boss doesn't like me working while I'm working."

Chastity went into the little foyer between doors and hesitated. Outside people swam alone the sidewalk. She could dash into the alley, but the idea of revisiting the smell…She could press the button right where she was, but what to do with the discarded paper? If she left it in the foyer, she'd get Mr. Trout in trouble. It would do no harm to take it with her. Missing garbage would not change a timeline.

She pressed the recall button.

#### 

Kurt watched the girl from his stool. The security mirror mounted on the ceiling was angled for the door and gave him a clear though fish-eyed view of the foyer.

She was quite the dish, the spitting image of Marilyn Monroe. That's what tipped him off. Nobody could look that much like the icon. When she disappeared he wasn't surprised, he'd seen such things during the war in Dresden, Germany. He chuckled to himself. This woman could pass for a goddess or siren, like a siren from Titan. Kurt had an idea. He began writing.

Kurt didn't look up when the boss returned. He was hot onto something.

"Mr. Vonnegut if you keep writing while here, you'll blow your cover. Where is that woman? I have her money."

"She's gone," Kurt said. "Don't worry about it, keep it, where she's from greenbacks don't matter." He held up his note pad. "Got what I need. I'll be back for my usual stamps, and smokes. Thanks for the use of your research facilities, and so on."

Vonnegut untied his apron, handed it to the proprietor and gave her hand a squeeze. With a wink of his eye, he hit the street sporting a shit-eating grin.

#### 

Dr. Clemens called Chastity to his office after the final. Rob must have sold her out. Maybe it wasn't him. This was the best work she had done to date and nobody believed it was really hers. Rob, always interested in retrieved artifacts, had discovered what was inside the garbage bag—a lot of short story starts. She didn't hesitate to use them.

Whoever that Trout guy was, he wrote like Vonnegut. She pulled together a pretty fair representative piece of Vonnegut's style and wrote the end herself.

After a long wait, she entered Clemens's office, took a chair and sat stiffly.

"My congratulations, Miss Sterling," Dr. Clemens said. "This is the best plagiarism I've ever seen."

"I didn't cheat, I wrote it."

"Only in part, I've read this before."

"But Vonnegut never published anything like it…"

And then she realized…She stopped herself, no point in arguing. Of course he had read it before, and not in the library of Vonnegut's known works, but as a ghost looking over the shoulder of that Trout fellow. She was still in trouble. He was allowed to time-slide, she wasn't.

"So I guess I'm done," she muttered.

"On the contrary, Miss Sterling, I've approved your application," Clemens said. "Need I remind you this is a creative writing class? Nothing is new in writing. It's all been done before and in every dimension of the multi-universe. You found a creative solution to writer's block."

"Thank you, Dr. Clemens!"

"Don't thank me. The next time I see Vonnegut, I'll thank him for you."

"But, I didn't, it was just Mr. Trout."

"'And so it goes,'" Clemens said.

She stared at him wondering why he had such a weird grin. Clemens must have made one of his cryptic jokes that nobody got. Chastity didn't care to ponder it. She had missed something but it didn't matter. She ignored the feeling. *I passed!*

She dove into thoughts of next semester as she left Clemens' office. She had heard there was an opening in something easier, something solid and non-creative. She raced off to Space/Time Physics 303 and signed up.

**END**

# UNDER THE WHITE HOUSE

The Man from Borneo, the Big Sideshow's strong man, stood near the tent's flap peering outside with inhumanly keen eyes through a slit in the canvas door.

"Don't worry folks," he said, "not even Mr. Barnum will bother us at this late hour."

He said it confidently, though not by his sideshow voice, "They know the rules, no regular folks allowed in the freak's tent when we're meeting."

"Or otherwise," said George.

The Albino Family—Clare, White Bob and their pretend son Harris—looked around with darting head jerks. They weren't satisfied, typical of their kind.

"If ever they saw one of us unfold into our true selves there'd be hell to pay," Clare said, her neck twisted birdlike, her ear touching her shoulder. "There's no chance humans would believe we are one of them. We'd be marked abominations, demons. Are you sure?"

Priscilla, the bearded woman, laughed.

"Dear me, Clare, you know I'd read a human's mind before it got a hundred feet toward us," she closed her eyes, her hairy cheeks rose with the effort. "I only see dreams. Even so, my nose is better."

Without hesitation, she lifted her blouse. She exposed her back and two rather large holes, holes like a beluga whales' were nestled there. Thick, black hair parted around each one. One porthole sucked in as the other blew out. With a sound like a bilge pump, she took air deeply. Her back flexed as if she were a railroad man driving a spike maul. She deflated and pulled down her blouse.

"Well?" White Bob asked.

"I only smell sleeping," Priscilla said. "Barnum is drunk again, the fool."

Barnum was known to wander about drunk late at night after a good take and the take here was astounding.

"Thank my makers," Harris said.

He was the youngest in this group, save George, only two thousand Earth years and impatient as a child. How clones developed persona was one of the few mysteries left in the universe.

"Go on, kid, unhitch yourself. Anyone sees it, why, I'll stomp the bloke dead," Borneo said, while pounding a massive ham-fist into his other hand. Everyone knew he was joking. He was gentle as a kitten."'I will grind his bones to make my bread,'" Borneo quoted.

He loved that new Brothers Grimm 'Jack and the Bean Stalk' tale.

The other two albinos struggled out of their Victorian covers until naked thereby exposing white, ivory smooth, sexless bodies. Their cable-thin arms and legs had been folded thrice. Once unfolded, they were spider-like. Small human bodies and normal human heads were supported by four long, thin legs and two very long, multi-jointed arms with Earth normal hands.

The seer, who used Old Hag Hilda as her stage name, set her crystal ball aside and smiled broadly, showing no teeth. A parrot-like beak projected out of her mouth. The skin mask she wore wasn't always effective.

"Goodness you clones are pretty to see," Hilda said. "Tis a shame these Earthlings have no appreciation. Damn silly and superstitious lot, I should say."

"You would know Hilda," Paul the contortionist said. "You sit with them all day long listening to their pathetic, primitive discourse."

"Now, now, Paul, they ain't so bad, really they're just a young people, and they're not far off the Stone Age," Hilda said. "One can't expect much from so new a race, so full of strange ideas. They're children."

"I can't help but feel out of sorts," Paul said. "We were their Gods, though that should never have been, and now we're two bit entertainment. Without intervention they'd have died out. Now, they jeer and laugh at us." In saying that, Paul was admitting his own failures from the early days of the mission. "The systems we placed to guide them are long buried or twisted into hypocrisy. Truly they are immature. We have a diffcrent dilemma, and I fear it is becoming urgent."

Around the tent, each in his or her way, they signaled agreement. The baby race had grown into a reckless toddler. First phase was over. The crew's retirement was ripe.

"Yes, true, their technology age is upon us," Borneo said. "Yet, still babes, children with dangerous toys, they are. I hope they survive adolescence. And here we are fixed on Earth. Past time we go."

"We mustn't give up," Clare said. "Remote monitors are about, observations are ongoing. We'll make new equipment in time. We still have our data crystals."

Borneo pushed back his long black hair. "Bad bit of luck, it was, losing that communications crystal."

"We haven't the means to call one down," Harris said, meaning a robot ship. "We can't rely on chance discovery. Archeology may one day unearth our communication device. Egypt is a hostile land—a long time in coming if ever. We need a different way. Our time is up."

"Well spoken," Borneo said.

"Harris is quite right," Clare said. "As it is, they will soon figure us witches or kill us out of some other foolishness. We can't hide among them any longer. It is time we go underground."

Everyone nodded or presented what might be interpreted as a nod of agreement.

"It's settled," White Bob said. "We go underground, but where? We can't travel outside of the circus freely, that is certain. Remember what that Hebrew did to Goliath?"

Borneo grimaced at the memory of his brother's death.

"Out in Pennsylvania they're drilling oil," Paul said bitterly. "Every place there's limestone, copper, iron, gold or coal they'll be digging. Sooner or later they'll find us."

"He's right," Borneo said. "They'll dig everywhere to feed their industrial age. Greed drives them. I don't trust going west. If ever we make it into Indian Territories, it shan't be long before they despoil that, too."

"Morons," Paul said.

Everyone became silent, each considering solutions.

Hilda watched the night sky through the tent flap's open top corner. There were lights shining on the Washington Monument. The obelisk was close at hand and nearly finished. As promised, it was done before midsummer 1884. Still spring and the project was complete save its crown of aluminum which was a new metal to Earthlings and heralded Earth's coming of age. Only the cap remained unplaced. That monument was why Barnum came. His and many other traveling shows were there for the Grand Opening celebrations. Three hundred yards behind the freak tent, in the other direction, lay the White House itself.

"You don't suppose they'll be mining anything in Washington, do you?" Hilda asked.

"Not if they don't wish to ruin it," Harris said.

Hilda took her computer and focused. The crystal ball glowed. Everyone watched. Her face was thick with concentration as she telepathically consulted it. After a time, she burst forth with cackling laughter. She was one to laugh often and well.

"Ha! Welcome to your new home," Hilda bristled.

Her beak pushed out into full view. The spine-feathers which laid flat on her back broke the harness and stood. Her frock was torn. Without clothes, she fully appeared the hairless humanoid bird that she was.

"What have you discovered?" Clare asked. Her overlarge black eyes shone with mirth, stunning against her translucent white skin.

"It seems," the fortune teller said, "three hundred feet below us are some very fine limestone caves, a large network of tunnels, and one very large cavern directly under the White House."

They all laughed now. Any human that heard it would have interpreted such a row as a cauldron of evil spirits on the boil. But no one heard. No one would hear the laser excavations either. Folks tended to keep a safe distance away from the freaks.

"If one can't hide directly under their noses," said Borneo, as he grabbed a nearby dung-shovel, "one can hide under their feet, yes?"

Over the next few weeks, after and between shows, the freaks dug. When Barnum and Bailey's pulled out after the last week and broke down to travel there was no sign of the freak's dressing tent. None of the freaks were evident. All that was left of them was a buckboard wagon and a pile of freshly placed fill dirt where their outhouse had been.

Barnum was hard pressed to replace them. All the best acts had disappeared. Washington had swallowed up the most unusual sideshows. Over the next few years, when traveling oddities came to Washington, they often vanished. It was a problem for P.T. Barnum, but not insurmountable. Once Barnum could no longer obtain real freaks, he simply phony-upped new ones and thus maintained his success.

"The show must go on," Barnum was fond of saying. And so it did.

#### 

## *160 years later*

Harris clung to the ceiling twenty feet above the monitor station. His head had rotated one hundred and eighty degrees to watch Paul and George at work. George didn't mind an audience. He missed that aspect of his former cover. George had joined them in 1487 as a jester and worked in entertainment since. Of long habit, he missed performing.

The freaks recorded and watched everything that went on inside the White House as well as the world at large. George thought observation duty fun. He had an affinity for upstairs folks, as the anthropology band called them lately. An observer wasn't supposed to acquire affection for a subject species, but as the mission was stalled inactive, such maculation didn't matter.

Paul had the ability to contort into any shape. He had long ago crawled though every wall of the White House and its out buildings planting bugs. The task at hand was seeking news of secret government-alien contact. Pirates were known to bamboozle primitives. Plus they had to maintain their own spy system. They never stopped seeking rescue-bots. Plenty were in the news. The internet was full of UFO sightings.

The White House observation system was self-actuated. It didn't require much attention. If non-Earth beings landed, friendly or otherwise, the system would alert them as the White House would be the first to know, or such was the theory.

George's official job was data transfer from the cavern to the escape pod, which was still under construction. The mission focused on gathering as much information as possible. Good fortune was that their onboard storage crystals were not yet full. However, they had amassed an incredible amount of information beside deep secrets only presidents knew.

A small rock fell and bounced off the con-table. Paul looked up.

"Oh, hey there Harris," Paul said. "How's the shipbuilding going?"

"Almost there," Harris said. "We'd be done and gone a lot faster if we had more materials. Material's a bitch."

"Back when they were doing renovations we had our pick," Paul said. "Took our fill, we did. Remember when they put indoor plumbing in, what was it, 1902? We had it made, material all over the place and nobody watching."

"Too bad they didn't have the technology then that we could use now," Harris said.

"We did pretty well for ourselves," George said. "We could live here forever if we had too, lots of room. The gardens are flourishing. We're wired. No lack of study subjects."

"I'll miss this place. I feel safe here," Paul said.

"I wish that were so," George said. "We're not safe. When archaeologists did that GPR radar on the White House lawn we were nearly caught."

The team found out that archeology study was only a ruse. There was trouble afoot.

"Like you said, it is getting harder," Paul said, "Tapping city power is a bitch. Without our thermo energy pump we'd be short. We can't get much White House juice without them noticing."

Harris hooked a stretcher cable on a ceiling carabineer and dropped spider-like. Paul waited until Harris was unhooked before he went on.

"As long as I have remote ears, I'll know what they know," he said. "We still have that advantage. But not for long I fear. Since the CIA took down the Twin Towers, they've become exceedingly paranoid."

"Right true," Harris said.

"I don't see how they'll make it as a race without intervention," George said. "It's just a matter of time and they'll blow themselves into oblivion. They're on the edge of utter ecological ruin as well. It's a grand, sad thing to watch standing idle."

"You're a sentimental one, George," Harries said with a laugh. "We've never witnessed species collapse so well before this. Anthropologists before us have only studied what was left of failed civilizations. To record an actual demise as it occurs is one in a million."

"I hope we'll get off this planet before it's too late," Paul said. "Frankly, I'm nervous. If we don't launch in a year or less, we won't get the opportunity. Things are bad up there. Someone will nuke the White House."

George hunched over his controls hiding the tears that formed in the corners of his eyes. He liked Earth humans, perhaps far more than warranted. They had potential.

"I know. I know," Harris said. "The number of UFO reports is encouraging. The universe is standing by. Nobody will miss this. 'It's the 'greatest show on Earth,' the last one."

They all chuckled at the sideshow reference.

"Once we're aloft, somebody will pick us up," Harris continued. "Our four thousand years of sociological observations has value. We'll be a sensation."

Everyone agreed. But George wasn't happy about the facts. He much rather Earth people survive—silly for a primitive species social scientist to think that way.

Noninterference was an immutable rule. Logically George agreed, but something deep inside him prevented his embrace of the principle. Humans were an infectious lot.

#### 

Two weeks later, the crew gathered for a general meeting. Something was afoot above and it wasn't good. General meetings were rare. They met in the largest cavern. It had a sun-lighting system aided by natural crystalline-infused indigenous rocks. It was the recreation area for the complex. Lovely alien and Earth plants adorned the space. Light reflected and enhanced the cave's beauty in multiple hues. This beloved place was situated directly below the White House. If discovered, it would become just another White House bomb shelter.

For now, however, it was a home away from home. There was enough room to accommodate all thirty-two crew members, from different teams, that had gathered here. George enjoyed the hospitable setting of gathered people despite the dire reason which forced the occasion. Clare, that year's crew chief, addressed the gathering.

"I'm afraid there's bad news," she said. "The situation above has become rather critical. The common public news is not an indicator. Paul's data is exacting, and best trusted."

The crowd murmured a few words then quieted. Clare went on.

"We know an over-large war will come, the AI has confirmed it. But that is not our main problem. Paul's eavesdropping revealed the White House will embark on a secreted effort for a new, deeper fallout shelter. They intend to dig to our levels. If they find us, the game is up. When so, we'll launch our data and enact self- destruct. Leave no evidence, such is the mandate."

Launching a data drone from underground wasn't a good option. The data could be lost. The small slow ship could be shot down and captured. Clare waited for the clamor to calm.

"Borneo tells me our ship won't be operational until May and it is now February. This war will happen, of course, but they know not when. However, they accelerate preparatory steps in hope of survival. Their steps are vain."

The room fell silent.

"We are not without possible success," Clare went on. "Borneo insures me that production can increase and the ship readied sooner than scheduled. The problem is that the White House is boring into our safety zone and could well cut off our escape. We need to delay them without tipping our...hand if you will. The floor is open."

Clare stepped down. Reuben stood, like George he was half-human. He suggested blowing up the White House, right now.

"That won't do at all," said Priscilla, the government studies expert. "It will be seen as an act of war. The Chinese will use such confusion to preemptively attack. It would bring on total war, not delay it."

The murmurs started in the crowd.

"Why is that bad?"

"We are safe here."

"They are doomed anyway."

Borneo stood.

"We need more time," he said. "The local space observers will move to a safe distance before we can take off. We'll be stuck in orbit and as such, a target of anti-satellite weapons."

The group murmured in understanding then fell quiet. After a time, Hilda squawked a loud, gleeful laugh. All eyes and sensors turned to her.

"We must haunt the White House!" she revealed. "Superstitious humans believe in spirits. Paul can put his bugs to work. They are capable of holograms, yes? Crawl in the walls. Make sounds."

"Yes, I can get them to do that," Paul said. "But how will that influence the president?"

"We won't stop them, but we can delay them," Clare said. "Scare workmen away. Suggest, via spirits, to the president that she must hide in some other hole."

George stood.

"Why can't we broadcast warnings to them? Go on the internet, flood the airways. Maybe they'll change direction, maybe reject their folly and move ahead into Universal Citizenship."

George slapped his six-fingered hand on his forehead and sat. Such things took centuries. Evidence of alien robot crafts was already common but Earthlings didn't accept it.

"You mean tell them the truth?" Hilda said, feigning shock in her voice. "This moronic hapless race is not interested in truth."

Everyone joined her in laughter. George looked at his eight-toed feet with deep remorse. He had the intelligence of any other off-world species. There wasn't much about him that was Earth-like. Yet, the human traits he acquired genetically were difficult to live with; he carried the human emotional spectrum. Hilda was right. His sadness deepened as they laughed.

So, it was decided. Hilda, an astute bamboozler, would lead the haunting. She and Paul started immediately. President Colleen Roosevelt and the White House staff were in for a very professional haunting, indeed.

Meanwhile, those not involved with the haunting, redoubled their efforts on the ship. Even George, a communication specialist, pitched in with vigor. No observation ship, robot or live crew, would miss his com-beacon.

"Nobody, not in this sector of space, no sir," George often said as he worked.

However much he didn't believe they would make a clean escape, he equally believed their data would survive even if they didn't.

#### 

The haunting of Colleen Roosevelt and her staff proved great sport. Paul and Hilda enjoyed scaring the most powerful human on Earth half to death. They started slow. At any talk of digging, they had probes crawling about moaning in the walls. Everyone heard it. It even made the CIA Chief, Albert Thompson, jumpier than usual.

They had footsteps follow people. The excavation contractor's workmen were dogged by fleas, bad smells, screams and aggressive spiders or centipedes. Construction slowed to a crawl. Nobody wanted to work. Warnings from the walls followed the workmen's every move. Paul went so far as to project faint but painful screams into a cabinet meeting at the mention of the proposed new underground shelter. Once, while President Roosevelt was alone in the Oval Office, Paul had every fly-drone in the house appear on her wall and spell "GET OUT." Paul's best trick was projecting George Washington into Madame President's private study. The ghost hovered over her.

"Don't disturb the graves. The dead will rise," the faux George Washington warned her. That night, throughout the White House, a whisper echoed, "leave the dead be."

But, it backfired. The next morning, Hilda and Paul learned by George's network monitor system that they had pushed too far. Haunting the workmen was effective but going after President Roosevelt directly was a mistake. She did not believe in spirits any more than she believed in UFOs. She adamant about UFOs and even refused to be briefed on Roswell.

George patched in Paul's attention call. Within minutes everyone was ready for the announcement.

"Our efforts may have failed," Paul said. "Rather than explain…George, play this morning's presidential briefing."

George played the recording. For clarification, the computer interjected each speaker's name.

President Colleen Roosevelt: "Okay, folks, I'm not getting pushed out of the White House. The American people need to know their president is steadfast. I will remain here."

Construction Superintendent Bill Johnson: "Ms. President, my men are scared shitless! Oh, I'm sorry, I mean—."

Roosevelt: "Go on, it's fine."

Johnson: "There're ghosts in the basement. It seems we're on an Indian burial ground."

CIA Director Albert Thompson: "We have no record of that, Ms. President."

Roosevelt: "That's not my problem, Bill. I want that shelter and fast. Thompson, somebody's messing with us. Don't stop until you know who and why. The enemy has technologies we don't know about. And if the workmen are scared, give everyone a hard ass marine. I'm done waiting. Johnson, you have three days to sink that test shaft or you're gone. Got it?"

George cut the recording.

"We're out of time," Paul said.

"Once the elevators' drilled shaft is started it'll hit the cavern in a week," George commented. "It's mostly limestone above. Main cave is under hard bedrock ceilings, but that won't slow them much."

"They'll drill a test hole first. They'll reach the garden cavern in a few days," Priscilla said, "and they'll send a camera. They find anything they'll figure us a spy operation."

"We only need two more weeks," White Bob said. "We may just make it yet. We need a delay tactic."

Reuben put up his hand to be heard but Priscilla, with her telepathy, answered his silent question.

"No, Reuben. we can't blow up the cavern. It will cause the entire place to collapse."

"We must dismantle the cavern gardens," Borneo said. "We'll block the tunnel to the ship launch manually. It'll take time to dig their way to the Potomac."

Everyone agreed. This would disrupt precious time for shipbuilding, but it might work. George felt it wasn't enough. The timeline was too close. Other crew members shuffled and otherwise showed signs that they thought so too. Success wasn't possible without full efforts applied on the ship.

"I recalled the bugs," Paul said.

"Shouldn't we leave a team behind to fight?" George asked. "We need more time. We must get the archives off world. We can't afford to fail."

Everyone murmured agreement. The archive was everything. The ship could fly without a finished hull. The drone program could do it. The ship's memory crystals contained the alien's collective life's work and could not be wasted.

George stood up."This is crazy, but since I pass more or less for human, I'll stay behind. Let them find a prisoner in an underground habitat. That'll keep them busy. Seal me in. I'll mess with the cams. They'll be shocked when they find me. It will slow them down."

George braced for a volley of laughter but it did not come. Everyone hushed and waited for the crew chief's response.

"Done," Clare finally said.

"What about the beacon?" someone asked.

"It's ready," George said. "Pre-programmed. When you hit 10,000 feet it'll sing every S.O.S. we know. In flight, the beacon will also automatically start projecting the archive toward home and local data bots will receive it as well. You won't need me."

There was no argument. He would not be publicly exposed and so not break the prime rule. Earth's governments knew how to keep secrets. His crewmates congratulated him and praised him until, full of human-like pride, he ventured another thought.

"Maybe I can do some good. Help stop the war."

At that, they all had to laugh.

#### 

George managed to keep the workers at bay a few extra days. He took the advice of Hilda and displayed some antics for the camera that appeared though the test hole. The workmen saw lights and green gardens and a ghost or two. Digging paused after that.

But President Roosevelt didn't wait long. Intense drilling began the next day. Messing with the camera bought Earthmen three days later. George knew they would reach him soon and so he prepared. The archive ship was ready. Its departure had been scheduled. The plan had worked. As long as that ship left the planet as intended, the data would survive.

George kept himself well back from the spot where they had sent the camera. The hole was made bigger and the bit had withdrawn. Rope ends dangled above the rubble pile.

He waited for them dressed in his best sideshow suit of clothes. His bowler hat, tweed vest, upturned collared white shirt and wool pants looked almost new considering they were made in 1880. He polished his custom red leather clown shoes and wore crepe gloves on his six-fingered hands for cartoon-like effect. He had removed the power feed and lit the room with nineteenth century oil lamps. Sitting upon his favorite rock, he leaned forward on a bamboo cane and watched as marines repelled into the cavern. It didn't take long before flashlight mounted guns pointed his way. At three-foot eleven, he wasn't the spy they expected.

"Well, hello boys," George said.

He waved his hand in a peculiar way which rippled his many fingers like a wave. They loved it in the sideshows.

"What took you so long?" he asked. "A small man gets big lonely left underground a hundred years, jeepers."

He tweaked the red rubber bulb glued onto his nose. The largest marine fainted. A few moved to crawl back up their ropes. One man of rank stood his ground.

"Lay down that cane, carefully," the marine ordered in a steel voice.

"Hey, General," he said cheerfully as he complied, "you don't have a see-gar do you?"

The officer barked and the rest of the marines swarmed in like honey bees after a blob of jelly. They grabbed George roughly and searched him. George picked the pockets of the marines while they man-handled him. George returned what he stole once the men were satisfied he was clean. The soldiers were not amused. They cuffed him, but George slipped out. Such devices could not hold him. They put nylon ties on his hands and he let it stand.

####

The President's intercom buzzed.

"Ms. President, Mr. Thompson is here. He says it's urgent."

"Have him come in."

The President just finished a meeting. She stood at the window admiring the Potomac. It was a beautiful spring day. Sight of the real world kept her grounded. Her rest was too short. She returned to the chair at the head of her conference table as Thompson entered. The CIA Director appeared exasperated.

"Ms. President, you have got to see this," Thompson said. "You said you wanted to know as soon as we made it into the cave. You are not going to believe this—."

"Put it on the monitor," the President said.

Thompson slipped a data card from a Marine's helmet camera into the desk terminal. It replayed the scene between the Marines and the odd little six-fingered circus clown they found three hundred feet below the White House.

"I don't know what to make of this," Thompson said.

"Get that little shit up here," the President said. "Make doubly sure he's not wired."

Thompson started to protest but Roosevelt waved him off.

"Let's get to the bottom of this, shall we? I want answers, and now."

The CIA director retreated from the conference room. President Roosevelt wasn't going to let Thompson control or filter this intelligence as he was wont to do. She needed witnesses. She had the receptionist call back everyone that had just left. *State secrets be damned.*

####

George found himself in the President's meeting room within thirty minutes of his capture. Things couldn't have worked out better. He stood before the President with a silly grin. The seriousness and austerity on every face in the room was funny. His shipmates would've agreed. He tried not to laugh. He glanced at the clock on the wall. The ship would go any second. He let out a breath of relief.

"We're home free, free at last," George said.

"What are you talking about?" the President demanded.

George took a bow with his hat in hand. He had removed his plastic handcuffs unnoticed and reacquired his confiscated hat.

"Look out the window," he pointed toward the river. "In less than thirty seconds, Ms. President…"George rolled his hat down his arm. "You will see a UFO escaping your planet."

"Look!" a voice yelled from the crowded room. Everyone rushed to the windows.

"A massive transmission will flood every available data bank and bandwidth on Earth, the entire history of the planet and the universe," George said. "If you like, I'll tell you why that spaceship you have at Area 51 won't fly."

"What in the hell are you talking about?" Roosevelt snapped.

Since she never listened to the Roswell briefing, she didn't know about that crashed robot probe, George knew.

But no one was paying any attention to the President. Less than a mile downrange, a shiny flying disk forty feet around hung over the river wobbling in the air while water ran off it. It made a crazy zigzag pattern toward the White House, stopped a hundred yards from the window and then shot straight up and into space.

"Told you," George said as he dropped his plastic handcuffs and Thompson's wallet on the table. "I'd be happy to tell you everything, ask away. Cat's out of the bag now, I'd say."

#### 

One year later, George sat in the President's private study as she stood by the window. She never seemed to tire of the various spacecraft that landed on the White House lawn. George thought she was at peace with herself and the world. Had his anthropology crewmates known what George had planned for his data projection, they would have stopped him and this place would have been nothing but burned ash by this time.

"Mind if I smoke, Ms. President?" George asked.

"I'm used to your cigar smoke, George. You know, as my adviser, you really can call me Colleen."

"It's hard to wrap my head around humans respecting me," he said. "I was a freak, you know. Maybe my shipmates would now think of me as such."

"You're no freak, George. You're a hero. Earth humans are the universe's freaks," she said. "Thanks to you, and that data dump you flooded us with, we'll be one 'primitive warring species' that doesn't self destruct."

George noted tears in her eyes. She paused to gather herself.

"We will change. I'm sure of it," she said. "There's no need for petty greed when you have the inexhaustible resources of the universe laid at your feet."

"There is plenty for everyone," George agreed looking past her and out the window. "I see my ride is here. I need to go."

"Sure you won't stay?" Colleen asked. "Earth needs your help. I need your help."

"Even if you're short a few fingers, you have things well in hand."

George walked slowly to the door, stopped and turned.

"Against my better judgment, my Earth human side had moved me. Faith made the difference," he said. "I can't logically explain why I broadcast the beacon so you would hear it. I hoped you would use the information constructively. Everyone else would simply let your planet to die. I don't know if I did the right thing."

"I'll prove you right, I promise," Colleen said. "Faith in us will prove well. I hope faith is not just an Earth human trait."

"I hope that, too," George said.

George smiled. Earth human traits were rare in the universe. Perhaps the experts who slated this civilization doomed to die were wrong. Perhaps the universe needs what Earth has to offer. Maybe Universal Citizenship's way to the next phase of evolution was hidden within humankind. George turned and hurried on to his transport with another rare emotion in his heart, a treasured seed, the one called hope.

**END**

# INTO THE LIGHT

Jimmy's was a typical New York City neighborhood bar, where they all know your name but they don't know you. Arney Bailey sat on a rickety bar stool trying to get drunk without success. Whiskey didn't have taste anymore. Arney looked around, but there wasn't anything worth seeing. Nine in the morning, there should have been something bright, something less cave-dark to lighten his soul. Dirt-brown nicotine covered everything like demonic shellac. Jimmy hadn't painted since before the smoking ban.

By the door, knives of light stabbed though greasy blinds enhancing the grime caked on the window table. Arney spun on his stool and put his back to the slivers. He wanted nothing to do with it, reminded him of his mother.

Bellevue said she got knifed in the subway. He made it to the hospital just in time to watch the lights in her eyes click off. He felt like his light had blinked out too. He didn't get to say goodbye.

"She say anything?" He asked the nurse.

"Gold tooth," the nurse said, "and something about look for the light."

The sudden parting of the red drapes that shrouded the back room shook Arney from his memory. Jimmy emerged with a case of beer, sweat glazing his Q-ball head.

"Hey," he said with his usual fake clenched-tooth smile. "What are you doing still here? Isn't you going to work?"

Arney was supposed to go back yesterday. His bereavement time was up."- Fuck it. Not going in. I got better plans."

"What're you stupid? Plans shit," Jimmy said. "You told me yesterday rent's gone up. How you gonna make it without your mom's social security check?"

Jimmy started putting beers in the stainless cooler. Even that cooler was dull. *Stainless, my ass.* Jimmy talked on. "Holy Mother of God, you were just bitching about overtime and what you got to do to make it. Sitting here isn't getting you overtime."

"I don't know," Arney said. "Maybe I got a better plan."

Arney hunched over his rock and rye and stirred it with a yellowed World's Fair swizzle stick. It had 1964 on it in red letters, red like old dried blood.

"Nothing changes around here," Arney said.

"Plan, plan," Jimmy asked, suddenly suspicious. "What kind of plan? What kind of shit are you talking?"

The bartender's smile turned sour. Jimmy was a retired cop, still pretty sharp. He didn't miss much. Jimmy was hard candy. Never gave a break, except maybe to break a man's jaw for not paying, but deep down, Jimmy had a soft center.

"I'm cashing out. No point going on. I mean, I can't afford shit. Got no family left." Arney crossed himself thinking of Moms. "Hate the job. Got no woman. Can't get ahead. Can't get even. I got nothing."

Arney sucked down his drink and set the glass down in one motion. "Only way I'm getting out of this rat-hole life is in a box, just like Moms," Arney said. "I'm up to my ass in shit. I even owe you. My tab's got to be a hundred bucks."

Jimmy laughed nervously. "Look now, don't be an asshole Arney," he said. "It's not worth it. Sure, things are hard but life is worth it. You got to look for what's good."

Jimmy pointed at the knives of light slashed across the window table. "Look at that, like the gates of St Peter. Look for the light man. It's everywhere. Open your goddamn eyes!"

"Ain't no light for me, Jimmy."

"Bullshit," Jimmy reengaged his barkeep smile. "Light is where you make it."

"Just what I need, a fuck'n barroom Gandhi." Arney laughed despite his mood.

"Tell you what, check this out," Jimmy said. The bartender turned and grabbed a cigar box. He pulled out Arney's tab. "I'll prove it, good shit happens when you can't see it coming."

Jimmy ripped Arney's tab and tossed the fragments into the air. Pieces of white paper fluttered onto the dirty, green-tiled floor. *It's like snow, the only time things are white in the city.* He loved snow as a kid. Walking in Central Park on a clear winter's night with Moms after a big storm came to his mind. He almost heard frozen snow crunching under his cheap sneakers. Power was out so stars dotted the sky that night like them bits of white paper now.

"Good shit happens, man," Jimmy said. "Merry Fucking Christmas!"

Jimmy beamed a real smile, something Arney hadn't seen before. He looked away from Jimmy's yellow teeth and at the scraps of paper. It was a minute before he could speak.

"Are you for real?" Arney said.

"I am, fuck'n A, right?" replied Jimmy. "Only one hitch…" His tone changed quiet and serious. "You better not tell a soul. Not a goddamned soul," Jimmy said. "I don't want my reputation all fucked up here." A sly smile crossed Jimmy's face.

"Damn," Arney said. "Thanks, Jimmy. Shit. I better go to work. Those subway cars don't run right without my ass warming a seat."

"You got the spirit," Jimmy said. "Remember, not a word."

"Not a word," Arney said as he slid off his barstool.

He heard it and saw it, but deep down, it didn't take. Things weren't turning for real. Maybe Jimmy was drunk. Arney walked the dozen steps to the door off balance but sober enough. Opening the door, Arney got eye-stabbed by brightness. It felt like a mugging by nature. It was unusually sunny in this concrete canyon. He staggered a few yards along the sidewalk while struggling with his adjusting eyesight.

"Look for the light," he muttered. "Bullshit."

Something knocked half-blind Arney off his feet.

"Jesus!" he cried out. "I ain't got no money! I ain't got nothing."

The expected mugger didn't answer.

"Oh my God," a frantic female voice said in a distinct Manhattan accent. "I am so sorry. Are you all right? Should I call 911?"

His eyes adjusted and he saw a Yellow Cab door wide open. A plump but pretty brunette had swung a long, thick wooden pole, the kind rich people hung their drapes on.

"What the fuck?!" Arne exclaimed.

"I'm so sorry! Really, I didn't see you. I just turned around and—."

"Jesus, lady. Take a chill pill," Arney said. "I'll live...for now."

"Let me make it up to you," she pleaded with watery eyes.

Arney rubbed his balding head.

"Goddamn," he muttered. "I got a fuck'n knot the size of a golf ball."

Arney gave the woman his best native-New-Yorker dirty look. As he glared, her tears let go and makeup streaked down her cheek. Just like Moms when he graduated high school.

"How can I make it up to you, sir?" she said. "I feel so bad."

Arney believed her, but he wasn't one to give up easily.

"Shit! Now I'm late for work," he said.

He wasn't going to work. He was going home. He wanted to get Moms' pistol. It felt good for a second making her feel shitty, but he felt bad about it, too. Her voice sounded like she really cared. She didn't hand him that phony, condescending crap he usually got. *Nobody cries for a stranger in New York.*

"Please, what can I do?" she asked.

"Look, it's ok," Arney said, regretting his malice. "I got to go. I got shit to do."

"What about a doctor?"

"I got no money for doctors, lady, Christ!" Arney snapped.

Her good will was something new to Arney. Foreign turf always put him on the defensive.

"Let me pay for the doctor's visit," she said.

"I can't. I got shit to do," he protested.

She dug into her purse and retrieved three new one hundred dollar bills. She placed them in his palm and rolled his fingers over them. "Here," she said.

Even more perplexed by her behavior, Arney started to say no but she cut him short.

"Take it, I insist."

With that, she got into the cab and left her curtain rod in the gutter. The cab took off. Arney stuffed the bills deep into his front pocket. He only used his wallet as a prop. If anyone robbed him, they'd get a couple of twenty-year-old condoms and a stack of dead lotto tickets.

*Must be my lucky day,* Arney thought. *I decide to off myself and the fuck'n sky opens up. Fuck it I'm still doing it.*

Despite his plans, he felt hopeful. He walked past his building, toward his regular subway station and forgot about the gun. A block past his place, Arney snapped out of it. He formed a new plan, a better one, one with a statement. He'd jump off the platform in front of his regular train, the one he took to his crappy sewer laborer job every day.

*That'll show them. Nobody on my car ever noticed me. Fuck them. They'll know my name after today.*

He strengthened his resolve. He didn't get twenty yards when the woman on the corner, the one he saw most days selling flowers, called to him. Her mom wasn't there, which struck him as unusual.

"Hi, Arney," she said in a sing-song voice.

This stopped him dead in his tracks.

*How did she know my name?*

He looked at her, not for the first time. He always thought she was a looker. She was pretty and thin and small, even as Asian girls go, and about his age, thirty-five tops. She had shiny, long, black hair and an infectious, bright smile. The sun glistened off her white teeth.

*Nicely put together and too good for me.*

He glanced down at his over-sized belly. He ignored her and walked on.

"Don't go, Arney," she said. "Please."

*What the fuck does she want?*

He decided to stop and talk to her. He never had before. He had nothing to lose. *Moms can wait for company a while longer.*

He stepped closer to her. "What the hell," he said. "I 'm not in no hurry to-day." When he reached her he asked, "hey, where's your mom?"

"She passed two weeks ago. Cancer," she answered. Her brightness dialed down but she didn't look sad. Arney's chin fell.

"It's okay, Arney, she was sick a long time. Life is for living and…I'm still here."

She cooed a little as she said the last part. He spent twenty minutes with her. What started as a bother became a dreamscape. No woman ever paid any attention to him in this protect-your-space city before. It turned out, she had been asking about him. She said she figured him a nice guy, always goes to work, walked with his mother everywhere. When he wasn't working, she noticed that he was alone, and she liked his looks. That flabbergasted him the most.

"Get out," he said, "I'm some short, pudgy white guy, not some Tom Cruise!"

"I don't like Tom Cruise," she said. "He's phony, you're more attractive be-cause you're real."

Arney felt his face turning red. No one ever said anything like that to him before.

"Dinner sometime?" she asked.

"You want to have a date?" He could not believe his ears.

"Sure. I'll cook. I'll make an authentic Chinese dinner, not like that crap at Lo-Wangs." She pointed across the street.

Moms always said, "'If a girl's serious she'll cook for you.'" He forgot his suicide plans for the moment."Okay," he said. "I'll stop by after work. About seven. Okay, Sue-Lee?"

She smiled an oasis of light which bleached out that dirty brick wall behind her. "Call me Sue. You have nice eyes." she said. "I'll meet you in my lobby." She pointed at the Brace apartment building down the block.

"I got nice eyes," he said. "Go figure." Arney waved as he walked off toward his regular subway station. *Holy crap, three good things all at once.* He felt juiced. *Jimmy's right, you never know when shit turns around. I ain't jumping in front of any goddamn subway train today, fuck that!*

The oppression of the city fell away like the old plaster he scraped off sewer tunnels. He never felt so light. His normal slogging steps became a springing gait. He heard himself whistling a song as he walked the last block. He laughed at himself. His face must have radiated like a star. People smiled or tipped a hat as he passed by and that never happened before. For the first time in years, he felt alive, but also, altogether different. Everything shone in his footlights and everything lit was good. Just before he entered the J-train stairwell he looked up. The sky was bright blue. A spike of light was on him. He felt like the sunlit stained glass angel windows at Saint John's.

"Thanks God, thanks for keeping me," Arney said pausing at the subway stairs. "I'm not leaving. Things are turning." At the bottom of the stairs was the regular pan-handler. Arney felt so good, he walked up to the man and talked with him, wished him well and gave him a few dollars.

"Why you give me money today, man?" the old man asked. "You never even looked at me. Hell, you don't look at nobody. You hit the lotto?"

"Something like that," Arney said, walking away happy.

He looked down the platform tunnel and saw that the far end was oddly well lit for a change. It was always dark on that end, the lights were always out. Maintenance must have put in bulbs.

"Where you going, Mac? It's dark down there," the transit cop said.

"Following the light," he said as he passed.

"Crazy bastard," the cop replied.

His words echoed down the tube. Arney headed to the far end, the place where the lead car boarded.

*I'm number one today so I'll ride the first car.* Arney walked away from the cop on concrete clouds. *Nothing can hurt me today. I'm into the light.*

He arrived and waited a yard from the edge of the platform. As the train approached, somebody pressed his back while a hand groped his wallet pocket. The man came from the shadows.

"Hey man, spare some change."

Arney was about to say he didn't carry money in his wallet, but couldn't spit it out. The knife plunging into his left lung took his breath. He twisted around but only saw eye-whites and a gold tooth set off between filthy teeth.

The train was closing. The bum pushed him toward the oncoming by jacking the blade. Too weak to fight, Arney collapsed falling face-first onto the edge of the platform. The killer and his knife sailed over Arney's head and crash-landed on rattling steel rails. Arney was half hung over the platform and dazed but the train's light blasted him awake.

Just as the killer sprung to his feet, the tunnel lit like a flare. Moms' face was the headlight, a laughing shooting star. Arney rolled away. The train plowed the mugger. Blood and a gold tooth flew past Arney's face on the impact. When the transit cop ran up, Arney was lying on his side and could swear he heard Moms laughing. But no, that couldn't be.

The cop told Arney later at the hospital that he had heard a woman celebrating over the screech of that subway car's breaks. The car had overshot its stop or the mugger would have survived. Arney told the cop he was nuts. Sue Lee, holding Arney's hand, said she wasn't so sure.

**END**

# THE FIRST GREAT SUPER

Super Jake hobbled into the physical therapy waiting room and didn't get the chance to sit. Nurse Gina, clipboard in hand, came through the metal door leading to the interior. Jake recognized her from last year's round of visits to the clinic.

"Jake, Jake Worthy," she said with a broad, white-toothed smile as she looked down at him.

"That's Super Jake," Jake replied, puffing out his pigeon chest. It wasn't easy. His four hundred years of crime fighting had taken it's toll.

"Of course," Nurse Gina said with a pert tight-lipped smile, "Right this way, please."

Like most people these days, the nurse was about seven-foot tall. She would have made a fitting adversary back in Jake's day. Now, he struggled to keep up with her. Her legs pumped like a well-oiled locomotive. But Jake wasn't jealous. Supers don't get jealous.

He was five-foot-six. Although he was shorter and stick-thin before Comet Bleb passed the Earth making him into the world's first superhero, he never did grow much. That didn't bother him. He gained massive muscle power and amazing healing powers before anyone else. Nobody could match him, back in the day. Too bad his bald-on-top head stayed that way and he still required glasses. Actually, he looked rather like an accountant, coincidentally his old profession. Jake still did people's books, just for fun. It helped keep his mind sharp.

Jake fell far behind Gina, but she must have sensed it. She stopped to wait.

"Large facility you guys have here," Jake commented a little short on breath.

Nurse Gina replied with a kind smile. This girl was a smile machine—was that her special power?

She led Jake on a bit farther. She went slower, but continued with a spring in her step. If Jake walked like that he'd have taken off, or at least bound over a building or two, or he would have…in the old days.

They entered the workout room with a section of exam tables in the rear. It was like before. Every time Jake returned, it was the same routine. Gina would fill out the questionnaire and a physical therapist would come in, read it, devise and schedule a series of therapies to help Jake with his often-broken, always-mended, tired, old bones.

"How are you feeling today, Mr. Worthy?" Gina asked.

"Fi...fin... fine." Jake stammered as he jumped onto an exam table that was three-feet too high for him just to demonstrate he still had super powers. Jake cried out on landing, however. He worried that he had broken his hip, but it was just an old injury acting up again.

Gina didn't notice and went on with her questions, none too difficult. Most things were the same. She filled out the form with diligence plastered on her pretty face. This girl took her job seriously, just like Jake did, back in the day.

"I hope you've been doing your stretches," Gina said.

Jake didn't do his home therapy, but he also didn't wish to disappoint her. His lips quivered which started his jaw going and teeth chattering. He just couldn't spit out the white lie that formed inside his mind. *Of course Gina, I always do my job.* The more he tried, the more his teeth chattered. Gina smiled knowingly.

"That's OK," Gina said, handing his chart to a young girl in a blue scrubs uniform. He didn't know Gina's coworker. "I'm sure you've tried your best. You're a good egg, Mr. Worthy. This is Sally, she's new. She'll be working with you, OK?"

Gina didn't wait for an answer. She vaulted over to the appointment desk in one leap and began a conversation with someone else. Jake lowered himself gently off the padded table. His new therapist was a pretty girl and she hadn't heard his stories yet: Good.

Sally was tallish, but not as tall as most. She sported a cute pixy blonde haircut, a button nose, and just enough freckles on her cheeks to play connect-the-dots. Super Jake decided to impress her.

"You know," he started, "I was...er...I am a super hero, you know, back in the First Days." Jake's voice rose with power. "Bad Bart was the one that twisted my leg around backwards. Of course, I healed, but, at my age...Even Supers get old. It's catching up to me."

Sally smiled demurely. She patted a low work-out table. Jake knew to climb up and lay back. Sally grabbed a stool on wheels. Jake rolled his exercise suit's nylon pant leg up. She took his leg and moved it, bending his knee, feeling the movement of bone and muscles.

"Bad Bart got the worst of it, yes sir," Jake said. "It was in our fifth and final battle, I swung him so hard his arms tore out of their sockets."

Sally looked at him with a pained look and shuddered.

*Oh, great, I've upset her. People don't like hearing of violence, not like back in the day.*

"I think we'll try some mild electrical stimulation to get these nerves firing before we put you on the stationary bike," she said.

Sally pulled the stim machine closer and attached suction cup electrodes onto his leg.

"Bart's okay now," Jake said. "He mended his evil ways. We are best of friends.

I even do his taxes. The arms didn't grow back, but he says he likes the robot arms just fine."

Sally nodded. Maybe she did have some interest.

"Back in the day, it was not easy being a Super," Jake said. "Bad guys were everywhere. Some people caught that cosmic ray just right…That changed later with the second wave, but in the beginning every disgruntled postal worker became an evil villain…"

"Yes, I've studied that in college," Sally said.

"The world was in turmoil back then." Quietly Jake said, "I kind of miss it. Not the violence, the sense of purpose."

With some rubbing alcohol and a cotton ball, Sally removed the suction cup gel from Jake's leg. "That should do it, Mr. Worthy. Ready for the bike?"

"If you hook that bike to the power station, I could power the entire town."

"I'm sure you could," Sally said and slid the nerve stimulation machine into its proper place."You know how to use the bike's timer," she said looking at his chart. "Let's do fifteen minutes, OK."

Jake completed a series of exercises under Sally's supervision. On the next few appointments Jake would have a fresh ear for his stories and that was a good deed opportunity. The exercises Jake could do on his own he'd do like he always did before, of course. Supers did their duty. For Sally, Jake was an example of living history. He'd share more about the bad old days next time. Jake would have relished the chance to speak with his heroes, back in the day. Sally's bright blue eyes and sidelong smiles pervaded as he spoke and so Jake knew his services mattered. He mattered. He still had a positive effect, a contribution to make.

After his workout, Sally asked how he was feeling. Jake didn't need to lie. He filled his lungs with air and proudly announced that he felt glorious. Although he was a bit sore, and the old leg pained him.

"I'm so pleased," Sally said as she walked Jake to the door.

She wasn't lying. He could tell. She was a girl that enjoyed her work. Jake admired her good attitude and her desire to help people. *That's a Super quality if ever there was one!*

"Good job today, Mr. Worthy. I'll see you Wednesday."

"Indeed," Jake said. "If you ever need your taxes done, I'd be happy to do them. No charge."

With a good-natured pat on the back, Sally bid Jake goodbye. Jake left the clinic without his feet touching the ground. He felt like his good-old-self, Super Jake, caretaker of the down-trodden, protector of the weak, in service to the people, by God. Jake made sure not to engage his super hearing as he came out of the building. Super Jake respected people's privacy. Jake felt so good he got himself into the medical-transport bus without any help.

####

Sally leaned against the door jamb as Jake floated across the lobby. She heard

Gina approach from behind.

"How'd it go with Jake?" she asked. "Did he bore you with his Bad Bart stories?"

"No," Sally said. "He was cute. I felt sorry for him. He seems lonely."

"A bunch of us are flying to Madrid for dinner, care to join us?" Gina asked.

Sally used her X-ray vision to watch Jake hoist himself onto the medical transport van.

"Thanks, but I can't," Sally said. "My flight suit is at the cleaners. I hate flying without my cape."

Gina nodded. "Resist the urge to stop at the Old Super's Home," Gina said. "You can't befriend every old Super that comes here."

"That wouldn't be professional," Sally said, "but I do need help with my taxes…"

"He's good with numbers," Gina said with a knowing smile.

Jake's bus left and a new van appeared.

"Looks like Water Woman's here for her breathing treatment," Gina said. "See you later, Sally."

Water Woman was a dastardly villain once, but now she was nothing more than Mrs. Trout, a hurting old woman, a human being in need. Sally gave her the best of care, just like any other evolved human being would. Coincidentally, Sally's fish pond needed attention and Mrs. Trout volunteered to look into it.

**END**

# DEATH BY LAWNMOWER

Egon of the planet Lepron waited at the edge of Rendlesham Forest in the United Kingdom of the planet Earth. He stood inside a man-bot which sat upon an old stump three feet above the ground. The UK/US Joint Military Security Team from Bentwaters AFB made this stump when they slaughtered a perfectly fine tree while searching for evidence of a UFO landing in 1980. The humans found no evidence, although the spaceship was real. Egon pitied the tree.

The robotic scout ship which grazed the treetops sought his Lepron Mercenary Unit or for a sign of Lepron's enemy. The probe didn't find anyone, as the 'lost' Lepron battleship crew intended upon their disappearance.

"Ah, shag it," the plastic face of the man-bot said.

From within, Egon opened his man-bot's jacket. The chest split and swung open like a barn door. Egon climbed free.

"Bloody hell, hot in there," he said.

Egon stretched his legs, which didn't reach the ground from the stump. He would have looked like doll except dolls don't wear two-thousand-dollar handmade Italian suits or wear pig-bristle beards without mustache. He wore his suit and his twelve hundred Earth-count years well. As a creature just coming of age, he naturally enjoyed looking good. The man-bot next to him appeared less well and less human. It wore the same suit as Egon, but the clothes fit it poorly. Its fake skin wasn't up to par and the machine was still dusty from storage.

Even without the man-bot's enhanced vision, Egon saw Professor Black's barn plainly. It bordered the former military instillation, farther over a rise is where Bentwaters had been decommissioned, economics being what they were. The base was converted into a satellite campus of Oxford University.

The farm, the only one near, was privately owned by Egon's human friend

and business partner, John Black professor of space anthropology who special-
ized in space habitat studies.

Black invested the Lepron's assets. He was the perfect human contact. Black's
low status as an American at Oxford made him amiable. Egon liked the arrangement for reasons his Lepron crew didn't know. Oxford had a space drive systems
engineering and space technologies research facility. Egon needed access to it.
*My ticket off this backwater planet.*

These dense woods, still property of the government, served the Lepron crew
well. It was an ideal place to hide. The locals feared the forest's fairy hills and
strange lights.

*Where better to hide a Lepron starship?* Egon thought as he looked at Black's barn.
*Right under their beaks, mate.*

Egon heard Omer coming from the deep woods. Omer normally danced si-
lently though the tree tops. The old reprobate was good with an anti-G belt.
However, today Egon's shipmate was lugging an ungainly leather sack. Omer's
G-belt whined and strained with the weight. Even an Earth human could hear it.
Egon didn't need his auditory enhancer.

"Like a bloody army of monkeys coming," Egon said.

He enjoyed mocking Omer.

"'E's a stealth scout that Omer 'e is, if I ever knew one!" Egon said in imitation
of Omer's accent.

A minute later, Omer dropped from the trees and hit the ground with a thud.
Lepron was a high density planet and Omer was pushing two hundred stone
despite his Earth dwarf height.

"I hea'd ya, ya bloody twit," Omer said, wagging a finger at Egon. "I'm old
but my hearing's sharp as the points of your ears!"

Egon looked down his pug-nose at Omer who wore standard Lepron military
garb like the other crewmen such as a green knee-length tunic, green or brown
tights, a thick, standard anti-G belt with large gold buckle, pointed green felt
shoes and a tall, pointed, green Robin Hood hat. Omer's hat was ringed with a
thin black belt and a wry gold buckle, which wasn't a buckle, it was a Navy issue
communications module.

"You look ridiculous," Omer said. "Wear a proper uniform will ya."

"I'm civilian," Egon shot back. "I don't have to. My contract's run out."

Omer's fat cheeks flushed red to match his bulbous nose. He was a stickler for
military rules, unless the rules applied against him.

"That may be, cabin boy," Omer said, seething. "Dress as you will, but you
better be wearing that man-suit before the human gets 'ere or ye be in violation."

"Violation, bloody hell," Egon said. "We're not at war. You guys killed the last
Gorgon two hundred years ago. And, I didn't sign on for a seven-hundred-year
tour. You got me stuck here. I'm not a cabin boy anymore. I'm your civilian
expert on economics and human affairs, remember?"

Omer glared at Egon. "Ya may be good at book learning, but you're...
expendable. You're no military man. Ya don't even bugger!"

Egon shook his head. *Old conflicts never die.* He was the only straight man onboard a ship full of homosexual warriors. If Omer could sling mud so could he.

"What you guys are doing isn't right, and you know it."

"What ya don't like us buggerin'?" Omer said.

"I'm not against buggery. It's Navy tradition, but I'm for women and I'm of age! And I want a female, a wife! Keeping me here's not right. My contract ran out a hundred years past."

"Your contract lasts as long as there's war!" Omer barked.

Egon jumped off the stump. "There is no war!" He shouted.

Omer laughed. "There's always war lad, and the Captain decides when we stand down. The Captain run's war rules, so war it is! 'e is a sayin' so."

Omer always won this argument.

"Bunch of blarney," Egon grumbled. "It's money. You guys are making a gold pot here. The longer we stay, the less you fight and the bigger your pensions."

Omer's thick upper lip rose bearing yellow teeth. "Better watch yourself, lad. That sounds like mutiny. One more wry bit of treason, and I'll cut you open me-self."

Egon crossed his arms. "You got nothing on me, buzzard," he said. "I know regs as well as you."

Omer's face flushed crimson."We'll see lad, we'll see," he muttered.

Egon climbed into the man-bot. He paused before sealing the cockpit and said.

"Better get going, sharp ears. I hear the professor coming." Egon shut the door.

Omer huffed and grunted while placing the green leather bag of gold beside the man-bot. He knocked on the man-bot's chest and said. "Invest it well or suffer the interest!"

Omer bounced into the trees and disappeared with chilling military skill. The man-bot rose and paced the clearing. A few minutes later, Professor Black arrived. He looked at the man-bot and shivered.

"Would you please get out of that thing? Don't you know it is quite disconcerting? Your mannequin is not at all convincing."

The man-bot returned to its previous place and swung open. Egon climbed onto the stump. He jumped, flying ten yards and landing near John Black, who stood hunched with his skinny chicken neck thrust forward.

"Ship's crew is too blind to see it. This thing's completely run down," Egon said as straightened his clothes. "Did you overhear that conversation, Professor?"

"Yes, I did," John answered. "The sensory enhancement device you designed for me works splendidly."

John grabbed the thin snakeskin belt around his waist, lifting it by its large gold buckle. It was functional but not exactly fashionable. Large and bright didn't work on John's boney frame. *No wonder he's a virgin, peas in a pod we are.* John's loose mud-brown suit, white shirt, and black bowtie were girl repellents and that mismatched buckle didn't help. *Hide in plain sight mate, that's my lad.*

"I heard you from my barn," John said as he pointed a gaunt white thumb over his shoulder. The barn was more than a kilometer upland.

"So then, here's the gold for the drive-core catalyst. Take money out of your account to cover the value, invest it according to my email."

"This is it. Our drive system's ready," John said with a mix of worry and excitement in his voice. "We can launch anytime. All I need is a wife and I am ready to go..." His voice trailed off.

"How did you get pure gold?" John asked. "I can't find any on the market, and I can afford it."

Gold was hard to come by. The Chinese had been buying it up for years, until recently. Egon felt his cheeks flush. He shouldn't say, it was forbidden but he had to say something.

"Leprons live for money," he said. "We have a hull full. A lot of good it'll do them once we're gone."

John gazed to the sky. "I'll load my silver and jewels. I have hard commodities."

"Don't bother. Fact is," Egon said. "Such is common. Gold's used for the rainbow drive, so that's valuable it is, but no more than other ores. Information is the only universal commodity. Aye, and we have servers full." He rubbed his hands together. "Let them hoard hollow wealth."

"If a nuclear war breaks out between China and America," John said, "Nobody's wealth will mean squat."

"It's not so much if," Egon said, "but when, and soon, to be sure. It helps us."

John trembled.

"No worry mate, nuclear weapons cannot be used," Egon said. The possibility of leaving improved Egon's mood and dulled his caution. "I'll tell you a wry secret; Leprons have a satellite network that'll disarm any warhead launched. Aye, the crew can't make money on a dead world."

"What about the Captain? Is he retarded?" John asked. "The world's economy is collapsing. The oil's almost gone. We may very well blow ourselves to kingdom come over the last few drops."

"Human wars come and go. You're a resilient species," Egon said. "Captain's betting on it. The longer we sit the more pay we get. As far as Command is concerned, Spaceship Hunter is chasing Gorgons. Pensions accrue until the Hunter reports or found wrecked."

"What in heaven's name is a Gorgon anyway?" John asked.

"Military secret," Egon said, coming to his senses. "If I tell, I'm dead."

Egon put a hand to the side of his head and cocked a pointed ear. He looked about with eyes wide like a staring garden gnome. The smile on his face was for focus and would look funny from a human's point of view. John knew better. Counter surveillance was serious. Egon, satisfied no one was within hearing range, continued, but lowered his voice.

"Leprons are warriors for hire. Our economy is military. The Gorgons went rogue and attacked shipping lines. We were contracted to hunt them. Some hid on Earth. You've seen them."

"How?" John said. "Didn't you say they were dead?"

"More ship's secrets."

John always asked too much, but Egon's good mood made him talkative. He paused and listened once more before continuing.

"When you see St Mary's Cathedral's pediments you're looking at them. The best gargoyle statues aren't stone but corpses."

John's white skin turned paler.

"Jcsus," John whistled between the gaps of his front teeth.

"Jesus was before my time," Egon joked.

John's forehead furrowed. "If there's more out there, I'm not so sure I'd want to go with you."

"It's the lack of a wife, why you hedge," Egon said with a laugh. "Shanghai one!"

Escape was close at hand. He could not help but add a wry bit more jesting. "And by the way, John, aye…them Gorgons, they ate people. That part is true enough."

John stiffened and it wasn't from the damp English weather.

"Rest your doubts," Egon said, "Best be making up your mind and quick about it mate. Time is short. We'll be leavening. Load that core today."

#### 

John was in no mood for the alien's Vaudevillian humor. He was struggling over whether or not he was doing the right thing. As launch became a reality, his reservations grew. Life in a starship with a small man that made bad jokes was wholly unappealing. Thus, he did not respond to the Lepron. Instead, he stood like a stone, not hearing, sweating in the cool, damp air as he considered leaving the Earth forever and without a wife. The idea he had in mind might change the wife part and why not have a few? He pushed that creepy thought off. The technology he had at hand could change everything on Earth. *Why should I share it?* There was much to consider.

"I better get along," John said. "I teach in twenty minutes. I'll see that our paper trail is viable. I'll load the core today."

"That's my lad," the alien said.

John turned and looked toward his farm. Beyond it, out of site, was the Oxford satellite campus. He missed the farm already, but he wouldn't miss Oxford.

He picked up the leather bag, hoisted it over his shoulder like a sack of potatoes and made for the barn as stiffly as a man-bot and nearly as hollow.

"Don't worry, mate," Egon called cheerfully, "there's time to find you a lassie."

'Find you a lassie,' rang in his mind. John wasn't so sure he had the balls for it. He dropped the sack of gold at home, marched up the hill and entered the astrophysics building. The walk had refreshed him. He redirected his apprehension along the way toward the positive prospects of his future. *Think of the possibilities.* But was he trading his scientific interests for humanity's needs? No, they'll be alright or so he convinced himself.

He headed for class daydreaming of space travel. Upon the thought that he was actually about to fly off, his concave stomach produced a twisted knot. Space travel was what he always wanted, but, not alone, not forever, and not without a wife. He had placed personal ads to no avail. He was no prize, granted, but he had substantial money, three masters and one doctorate. Someone would bite eventually. But they were launching and he was out of time. The drastic contingency measures that had hatched in the shadows of his egghead were the only way.

He traveled the universe inside his head without seeing his real surroundings until voices unseated fantasy. Department Head Bob Thompson and Dean of Students Charlie Steward were down the hall like binary black holes sucking up his light. They drained his energy daily. He cringed. His heart pounded harder with each step. Coming near, he ventured a greeting.

"Hey there, guys. How's it going?"

It never came out right. They looked at him like he was an uncouth Viking invader and proceeded to ignore him. Their contempt was habitually blatant. He kept walking.

"Sorry guys no time to chat," John said. "I have class."

John wasn't liked by the staff, administration, or anyone else for that matter. A handful of students pretended to like him, only because he paid them. Egon was his only friend. He didn't know why everyone despised him so he generally avoided people and especially his academic peers. They often rolled their eyes and sneered condescendingly at him, not bothering to hide their disdain.

*That's okay,* John rationalized. *I'm leaving this planet anyway.*

The knot in his gut tightened. Maybe they'd like him if they knew him better. Maybe he should find out what his offense was. What did they think of him? He suddenly realized he had the technology to know. He touched Egon's obnoxious belt buckle.

"What a bloody twit," Bob said. "Why must we put up with that American abomination and his misfit ways, he is just so, so—."

"Unorthodox," Charlie interjected.

"Crude, I'd say," Bob said, "But, certainly that, too. He doesn't belong. This is a space engineering campus. What's anthropology to do with it? His work has no application. His insufferable experiments are unnecessary."

"Black's subject is years before its time, granted," Charlie answered. "Yet, his endowment makes his course study profitable."

Charlie Steward was obviously more interested in financing than students or fields of study, that aspect of him was well known.

"Black's eccentricities support this institution," Charlie continued. "No other university has a sophisticated spaceship simulator and it didn't cost me a bloody shilling. Did you know his property goes to us should he expire? Misfit or not, Oxford likes his money."

"Damn American," Bob said. "Bloody foolishness."

"He's harmless," Charlie said. "Besides, his Space Living Lab is popular, an elective that complements hard science. He paid engineering students to construct it. Students need cash."

"You like his money," Bob said.

"Of course," Charlie replied, "but I don't have to like him. He's a pathetic bachelor."

"You suppose he's gay?"

"Not the way he eyes co-eds," Charlie said. "Too inept to land one, poor devil."

"Inept or unattractive?" Bob asked.

John touched the hearing enhancer and tightened his belt along with his resolve. As the voices faded, so did his doubts about leaving the planet.

"I heard enough," John muttered to the universe. "Where I'm going, I'll be quite popular with the ladies. Oh yes, indeed, they will be quite captivated."

He unlocked his classroom determined to forge ahead. The students filtered in, mostly one by one, a few in pairs. Feeling self-conscious, he tried not to look at the ladies as they entered. *Am I that obviously in such desperate need of a woman? Even that stuffed shirt Thompson sees it.* He checked his email while the class settled. M*aybe someone responded to my personal ad.* An email from Egon357 was waiting.

"John—Our satellites show the Chinese are breaching borders right now. This is the opportunity we need. The powers will soon be busy fighting the oil war. It has begun. Get the ship ready. We leave two p.m. tomorrow."

John swallowed hard. His oversized Adam's apple bobbed like a cork in rough seas. He slouched behind his laptop collecting his thoughts.

"We're leaving. I hope he brings the launch code. We can't fly without it."

John realized he was talking to himself and looked up distressed. But, as usual, the class paid him no mind. They were busy chatting. John took out his hanky and wiped a bead of cold sweat from his tall forehead grateful nobody noticed. *I must not blow it.*

Over the years, to safeguard his activities from Egon's spying shipmates, Egon had encouraged John to study acting. He did and learned the craft. He played the part of a harmless wallflower on campus but it wasn't difficult. It was good cover. His covert activities weren't detected. He naturally looked the part. And to be honest, he didn't need to pretend much but now he needed to act and well. He taught the lesson with a racing mind and wild thoughts that didn't show. With the hour almost over, his plan jelled.

"I made a change."

He paused and tried to still his trembling hands.

"I want to run the all girl flight sim tomorrow," Black said. "Team three report to the simulator at one p.m. tomorrow. The rest of you monitor it from your computers starting at 2:30 p.m. This is your seventy-two hour lock-in, ladies. Bring everything you'll need. Once we lift off, no one can leave until the experiment is over."

The class groaned about their ruined weekend.

Professor Black's experiments were designed to see how confined spaceship crews worked together in various combinations under stressful conditions. His intent was to develop social protocols for deep space. Aspiring astronauts and engineers knew Professor Black's simulator was the ultimate gamer's dream and the most realistic simulator ever. No one cared about his class but everyone wanted sim-run time. There was a long line of volunteers yet only three students served at a time as onboard crew during an experiment. Team three didn't appear overly unhappy to John.

Simulations got old fast for the rest of the class whom were relegated to monitoring the experiments and recording everything inside and outside the barn. In turn, each crew spent three days in the simulator. It was understood: Don't expect routine. The simulator randomly chose problems. The only saving grace, between drills, they had satellite TV and a working bathroom replete with sonic shower. Leave lock-in and you fail the class.

The simulator fit tightly inside John's vintage pole-barn with minimal room between the ship and the barn's twenty-five by forty-five meter stone infill walls. Only John's riding lawnmower and his garden tools fit in the space left in front of the ship.

As the class filed out, Professor Black called to Willy, a media arts minor. "Willie, I'll have a word with you."

The class dissipated. He waited until the room was empty. Satisfied John went on.

"Is your disaster program ready for the simulator?

"Yes sir," Willie answered. "Best one I ever did, so real it scared fuck-all out of me."

"You're sure no one has a clue what we wrote?" Professor Black asked.

"Not a bloody soul. The script and special effects are safe on your server. Bloody lot of data you have, Professor."

John handed Willy an envelope stuffed with cash, he had doubled the usual amount. The kid needed the money and was always looking to make a buck. Willy stuffed it into his computer bag. John liked him. He was the only student John allowed to have access to his massive computer system. John built it himself with input from the computer science department.

"What's with all that data?" Willy asked.

"That's not just scenario stuff," John said with pride. "The complete plans for my ship are in there." John thought of his history, arts and sciences information hoard, the essence and mechanics of the Earth itself. "Everything you need to get off the planet is right there."

Willy looked blankly at Professor Black. "Right, Governor," the young man said.

Black almost said too much. "Right," Black continued. "This team has not been in yet. They must believe it's real."

"It will blow them away, it's killer," Willie said.

Black raised an eye brow.

"Sorry, Governor. Bad choice of words."

"Thanks, Willie. Make sure you load the program before the day is out."

"On it." With that, Willie left.

"Not a word," Professor Black called after him. "And don't forget, you're cutting my lawn tomorrow."

####

Egon walked the man-bot into the forest far from the starship. For security, he parked it in a hidden shelter, a fairy hill that served as Egon's base of operations complete with living quarters and untraceable computers. As long as Egon fulfilled the Lepron's greed, they justified his freedom of movement and birthed his hope. Being the only straight one on an all-homosexual ship didn't bother him. Being the only single person in this 'everyone's married' environment of Earth did. Loneliness wasn't fun on any planet. *How did I get assigned to this crew?*

Egon shed the man-bot. He started his computer. He typed out emails as he watched the human news, all the while keeping a half-eye on the Lepron's satellite feeds.

"Bloody hell," Egon said. "This is our window."

He wrote to John. Egon had just hit send on the email when the dragon-tight grip of a Lepron hand slammed onto his shoulder and violently dug into his flesh. The force spun him around in his chair. He faced Omer and Omer was none too happy. Two MPs flanking him grinning with blood lust.

"Ya gone too far now, cabin boy," Omer growled. "I heard what you said to the human, giving ship's secrets. Tis treason. Away wit' him, lads."

"What secrets?" Egon demanded.

"Told em about us!" Omer sneered,"Tol em bout Gorgons."

Egon's heart raced. He wondered how much they had heard. Ruin fell around him like plasma fallout. *All is lost!*

"Whatever that bloke knows, 'e won't be knowin' it long," an MP said.

"We'll deal with him, aye, but first you, cabin boy," Omer said with a toothy smile.

They took Egon to the starship in chains and tossed him into the hold like a sack of blighted potatoes. Landing on piles of hard gold didn't soften the impact. Ship's court would hear his case next morning. Wartime regulations required fast response.

By nine A.M. ship's officers gathered at the Captain's table as required. Egon was brought in at half past noon. He was bound in tenth century iron shackles, irons made for human children by Arabian slave traders. Earth-made binders were a bad omen. They were disposable.

The Captain, red-faced with anger, eyed Egon.

"We have passed sentence on ye," the Captain said. "We find ye guilty of treason, what say ye?"

Egon looked into the Captain's eyes defiantly and said, "You can't do this. As a civilian, I can't be tried this way. I demand home courts."

"We're at war, mutton head," the Captain said, "and you're under Navy Command."

"There's no war!" Egon seethed. "Human wars aren't ours! They don't count. The interstellar news announced the defeat of Gorgon hundreds of years ago!"

Omer slapped Egon. "Ye will show the Commander respect!"

Egon licked blood from the corner of his mouth. *Commander he thinks he is now.*

"No one sees what I see. Probes cannot think," the Captain said. "With the humans sighting UFOs, Navy probes can't stay long enough for a proper scan.

How can they find the enemy? They can't even find us."

"By your design," Egon retorted.

The Captain stood. With hands planted flat on the table, he leaned toward the prisoner. "I'm in charge here," he said. "I say when the war has ended. Gorgon signs are still about. I don't need explaining it to you."

*Gorgon signs my ass.* Egon had to say something, if only to cover himself on ship's records.

"Carbonized Gorgons don't count."

"You served well as ship's comptroller," the Captain said. "We thank 'e for the wealth ye made us, but ye gone too far."

"You fool!" Egon yelled. "I am more than the money-man! You need me, especially with a war coming."

The Captain laughed. "We have spies in every land. The war's partly my doing. A Gorgon sits under the White House and I will draw him out. We invest in the Asian market for a reason. China will disarm the rockets without us, even wry ones. Warheads won't explode. Best, we don't have to use our own."

Murmurs of approval circled the table. Egon realized—his shipmates had fixed the unfolding Earth war. It was illegal as hell and he was a witness. *They'll make a killing.*

"Only a Gorgon mind can explain the doings of the Americans this past hundred years, and it will pay, oh yes." The Captain said. "There will be war, but the Americans cannot win. The Gorgon War continues."

"We're not supposed to interfere," Egon muttered.

The MP slapped Egon again. He fell like a bag of rocks. His iron restraints crashed loudly on the plastic/steel floor.

"You be no one to tell-in' the Captain how to wage war."

"Hypocrite," Egon spat blood at the Captain's feet.

The guard kicked him.

"I've 'ad my fill of insubordination," the Captain said. "No one bloody well questions me in war time. Ye have no defense. I pronounce sentence."

The guards pulled Egon up, forcing him to stand on shaky legs. The Captain struck an old iron tinker's hammer on the metal table.

"Death to you, Egonoperin," the Captain proclaimed. "Death by lawnmower!"

Omer, with a stern face, read the final proclamation aloud.

"Egonoperin shall be tied to a stake in the tall grass of the Black farm this afternoon and will meet his doom by the blades of the grass-cutting tractor. The farm and the tractor bought with Lepron funding shall be the implements of this traitor's death."

"So be it," the Captain said. "Take his belt and devices."

The guard presented his gear to the officers at table.

"Where's your backup sensory enhancer module?" the purser demanded.

"Lost it," Egon said. This was a great offense. *Let them chew that.*

"I see we've made the right decision. Take him away," the Captain ordered.

####

Professor Black waited at the barn doors. Five co-eds were on the downhill path from campus. *Where was Egon?* He switched on the sensory enhancer but the co-eds' chatter stole his attention. From teaching class, John knew each voice.

"Is it only me or did anyone else notice that the five hottest girls in school are all on this team?" Natalie said.

"Get real! 'e's no Don Juan. 'e's a geek," Rebecca said.

"It's a computer personality drawing, right?" Natalie asked. "He shouldn't be able to fix it. Still, I wouldn't put it past him."

"It's based on psychological profiles," Rebecca said.

"Assigning based on looks is way creepy," Debbie said.

"I wouldn't bed him if he was the only guy in the universe," Natalie said.

The girls laughed. Embarrassed and unsure, John's doubts suddenly assaulted him again. He turned away, toward the fields below. His resolve was waning. The enhancer scanned the tall grassy fields bordering the woods.

John absentmindedly noted Willy on the John Deer lawnmower. When Willy approached John's enhancement range, a volcano exploded in his ears. He quickly projected over the lawn tractor and into the woods for relief. Something sounded wrong. Voices were coming from the woods, a place no one should be.

*"Who was Egon talking with?"*

John strained to hear, but they were out of range. The girls were nearly at the barn. He switched off the device.

"You're right on time," he told the girls.

"Wow!" Heather exclaimed. She looked into the open end of the barn where the starship gleamed. "That thing's so real," she said.

"Give me a break," Natalie said, dropping her back pack. "It can't actually fly."

Everyone laughed except for John. He stood there shivering in the rare warm sun. Regaining some composure, he led them into the barn and to the ship's main entry.

"Well, Heather, that's the point," he said in his strongest Professor Black tone. "It needs to look and feel real."

John kicked one of the hydraulic rams that made it move. Massive cables swarmed around the motion cradle's frame base like snakes guarding a viper pit.

"It's like real flying," he said. "You'll be convinced."

John gave them an outside tour which didn't take long. They boarded. The first ten meters of the thirty meter cigar hull was the simulator flight cabin and living space. The cockpit was at the tip nearest the barn doors. The flight control compartment and recreation area was just behind the pilot's chairs and held five work stations. Further aft, behind a bulkhead door, were the crew bunks and the bathroom. Aft of the sleep quarters was a closed and always locked bulkhead door. It was marked 'Captain's quarter,' otherwise known as John Black's office, and off limits.

"Any questions?" John asked.

"What's this big hatch here in the middle of the floor for?" Debbie asked.

"The engine room, you might say," he explained. "That's where the equipment is, hydraulics and the like, it's a greasy mess. Go down there and you'll ruin your clothes, you won't will you?"

All the women nodded agreement. They were space engineering students not truck mechanics.

"Okay, then, stow your gear and prepare the ship for takeoff," John said, "Just like we practiced in class."

John looked at his watch. It was almost two.

"We are supposed to have ah…ah…mmm…a guest observer. He's late. I'm going to check for him. Man your stations and do not launch until I'm onboard. I won't be long."

"Great," Natalie said. "The fun begins."

The ladies all groaned. As he backed down the gangway stair, he heard someone turn on the television. John smiled.

"How predictable, perfect."

He dismounted the entry ladder and walked a few yards to the barn doors. He saw no sign of Egon. Egon was never late. He looked at his watch, five past two. The only thing John saw was Willy on the lawn tractor running an oblong loop from the fence line bordering the forest road to the house. Willy was making slow progress. He had to get off every few minutes and move a rock. Ten minutes went but, still no Egon and no launch code and no way to activate the rainbow drive.

Suddenly, he noticed the grass parting in a line. Several Leprons walked in file. Curious, John switched on the enhancer. Rancorous laughter assaulted his ears.

"'Tis a fitting end for him," said a Lepron voice.

Harsh insults toward Egon rang in John's ears followed by more laughter. John adjusted the volume.

"Aye," another said. "Death by lawnmower, the Captain is creative."

A chorus of horrid laughter followed, then the sound of chains and finally Egon's voice.

"Don't be fools! Killing me is pointless. You need me—."

A blow followed and a grunt of pain. The line stopped in a spot of extra tall grass. A hammer hit steel.

"We don't want that lawnmower kid warned, gag him," someone ordered.

"Give me my last words then," Egon said.

"The dead shan't speak. Stuff him, lads. Tie 'im right."

A few moments passed. Something terrible was happening.

"That'll do, lads. 'e's quieter, eh. Let's go."

"When that tractor meets you, only crows will know the pieces."

A column of tall grass parted and moved toward the woods. The lawnmower was only minutes away from crossing that spot.

"I must do something," John said out loud. "I need that code."

He had almost forgotten that Leprons could hear at a great distance. He adjusted hearing capacity to Lepron normal. John stuffed his fist into his mouth. Seconds passed.

"Omer, where to…"

The voices continued. It didn't seem like John was heard.

"Yonder," Omer said. "We'll wait at the clearing. After the sentence is done, we'll ambush the Professor. 'E's supposed to meet the dear departed this afternoon. It'll be his last day on Earth."

*That may be true but not the way you think; not if I can help it.*

The lawnmower turned one hundred and eighty degrees and headed back toward the barn. It passed only a few rows from Egon's position. John stepped back, out of the line of sight of the clearing, and waved a gas can frantically at Willy. The lawn mower finished the row, and abruptly turned uphill toward the barn. John's knees went weak with relief.

"What's this, eh?" a Lepron voice said in John's ears.

"'E must be needin' petrol. Not to worry, lads. 'E always finishes the cutting."

John switched off the enhancer. He grabbed some burlap sacks and a pair of overalls from the hooks on the barn wall. He put on the overalls as the tractor slowly made its way to the barn. Next, he picked up a wheat sickle and ran to the pig pen behind the barn.

#### 

Egon struggled against his chains, but it was no use. He could not get the leverage needed to break them. He was suspended off the ground so he could not use his legs to dislodge the steel stake to which he was chained. He counted the minutes between lawnmower passes. Then, the killing machine ran to the barn. Hope sprang, but before long, the mower returned to its monogamous path. With every pass, the machine got closer. Over the roar of the motor, he heard the death squeal of a struck rabbit. He was pelted with blood, fur and grass. Then, a heavy thud was felt. The din of the mower receded.

That was close. The blindfold prevented seeing his doom. Then a body at least his size hit the ground just behind him. Wet, sticky hot liquid splashed the back of his legs. Had the mower run down a wild boar?

*I do not die alone. One more row. Sad to die young and worse dying a virgin so far from home, but at least not alone.*

The lawnmower rounded behind and headed directly toward him. In spite of the blindfold, he closed his eyes as death approached. The last thing he knew was a tremendous crash. Blood, chains, stone and guts flew about like the inside of Hell's own blender.

Then all was still.

#### 

Four Leprons stood on a stump watching the tractor.

"What's this, lads?" the MP asked.

"The bloke's off the mower, seems 'e 'it something, stalled it, 'e did."

The Leprons laughed. The mower hitting a steel stake had surely stopped it.

"Broke its blades did he? Tis a pity, waste of good machinery," Omer commented.

"He's looking under the thing," the sergeant-at-arms said. "If that lad has questions about the body, we got ta kill him, too."

"Don't seem so," Omer said. "The bloke's not in a panic. Looks 'e's kicking the tire. E's hot that one."

"Poor bloke," the lowest-ranked Lepron said. "'E's busted the Professor's machine. Look, 'e's putting parts on the carriage. Must be bringing home the proof."

"He's leaving," the MP said. "Can't cut without blades, aye. What of Egon?" The MP brought up his field glasses. "I see body parts. There's blood, plenty of it! Can you smell it, lads?"

The group held their red noses to the air but the wind was wrong.

"That's the spot, mates. Egonoperin is dead and 'e took the lawn mower with him."

"Professor will not be a'needin' it anymore anyway, eh, lads," Omer said. "Soon as 'e comes 'ere 'e won't be needin' anything but a hole to rest his bonny bones."

The group laughed. They relaxed and sat on stumps. A few brought out long pipes and made ready for the wait. The Professor wasn't due. It wasn't the trader's usual hour.

"Omer, you think we should take a better look?"

"No, lads, we'll have a look after we deal with the Professor," Omer looked at his gold Rolex pocket watch. "It's half past three. Egonoperin ain't going no wheres…eh."

####

John looked at his watch as he slid off the tractor. " Past three already, balls!"

He took off the blood soaked overalls and tuned on the enhancer. He stuck his head around the corner of the barn door. Leprons were talking in the clearing.

"We ought to have a look, mates. Let's see the body."

John quickly lifted a bloody burlap sack out of the lawnmower's rear deck. The sack moved and moaned as he hauled it over his shoulder. He boarded the ship at the rear gangway and felt the vibration of the running engines as he climbed the steps, a lot of good it would do without the code. Once in his quarters he gently lowered the sack and pulled the fabric away from Egon's face.

*Still breathing! Good!*

He patted the Lepron's face. He removed the shackles. They were designed so the wearer couldn't reach the catch and didn't require a key.

"Egon! Egon! Come on, buddy," John said frantically. "Wake up! We got to go! I need the launch code! Goddamn it, we're out of time!"

Egon mumbled something about blarney stones.

"We're screwed. Come on, Egon."

He could try the old codes or have the computer run random numbers. He raced to the cabin, burst through the door and the girls greeted him with a chorus of screams.

"Oh my God, you're covered with blood!"

John looked down. The blood had soaked past his coveralls.

"Pig's blood. One of my pigs got out and it got caught in the lawn tractor."

The girls' eye makeup had run like rust on an old iron ship. They had been crying, The TV blared. A newscaster was on screen. A BBC newsman was on and looked haggard and he was talking fast.

"Just two hours ago the Chinese had begun marching, pouring over borders, reminiscent of the German blitzkrieg of World War Two," the newsman said. "The Chinese are making an all out attempt to capture the Middle East oil fields. The Caspian oil platforms are now surrounded by Chinese military vessels. Another large Chinese force is running for Kuwait…wait…This just in. The US has armed its missile defense system. Gill, what do you make of that?"

"As I see it, Shawn, the Americans do not have a large enough conventional army. They are bogged down in Iran, Jordan, and Iraq. American forces have all but been overrun. It appears that rockets have been launched, launched from nuclear armed American submarines."

John tried to ignore it. He had to crack the launch codes.

"We pause to bring you this bulletin," the television said. A new announcer appeared on the screen.

*Damn. Willy did well, but I don't recall that sim.*

"We have just heard from the President of the United States."

A live press conference popped up. Sarah Buchanan appeared as the newscaster faded.

"We will not allow this aggression to go unchecked. We have a duty to protect our allies. I have authorized a limited nuclear strike. Israel is under attack."

The flabbergasted crew gasped collectively.

"Oh my god," Debbie cried. "They can't launch nukes!"

They all started crying and talking over each other. John rose.

"Man your stations," he commanded. "This is not a drill!"

The girls looked at him like he had three heads.

"What are you talking about?" Heather yelled. "The world is at war and you want to do this stupid space class!"

"Shut up! Just shut the fuck up!" John screamed. "Debbie, switch on the outside cam number three. Do it!"

She was so shocked by John's uncharacteristic outburst she obeyed.

A horde of Leprons, armed and grim-faced, marched across the freshly cut grass. The girls were mesmerized. The green-clad men reached a bloody spot in the grass. They sputtered and pointed toward the barn.

"See that," John said harshly. "They're coming here next and they will kill us! Nat, magnetize the hull."

"But professor it doesn't really…"

"Yes, it does!" John screamed. "Do it. Do it now! It will deactivate their hand weapons and give us some time."

"Oh, I get it…it's all part of the test," Nat said, but her voice quivered as if she wasn't sure. "Yes, Captain."

On the surveillance screen, Leprons ran toward the barn. The girls could not tell the size of the soldiers. The camera shot gave them no sense of perspective but it was plain that these men were dangerous.

"Are we ready to launch?" John squeaked.

"Ready, Professor," Heather said. "We only need the launch code."

From the rear of the cabin, a male voice thundered, "John, punch in Egon357."

They all turned. Egon stood there, naked with blood and grass splattered all over him. His dick was human sized. He looked like a horror movie doll except Egon was quite alive and the caked blood smelled like iron. The girls screamed. Two fell to the floor in a faint.

John ignored the pandemonium and pecked frantically at the command keyboard. A terrible, loud clang coming from outside jarred the hull. John switched on the barn monitor. A two-foot-tall green-suited man wielding a great maul hammer drew back. The handle was longer than he was tall. The stranger swung mightily and the ship rang with the blow. He was swinging for the door's hinge. John felt like a fish trapped inside a steel drum. John yelled for Natalie to launch. She looked blankly at the screen.

"I don't believe this," she said. "This is crazy."

John clamored over one of the prone co-eds, yanked Natalie out of the navigation chair, and pressed the launch button. The monitor showed another mighty swing but the hammer missed. The man's pointy hat flew off as he almost fell into the equipment pit. He rolled onto his back away from the pit's edge and shook a clinched fist at the sky. Three others like him ran to his side with strange guns drawn. Roof timbers fell around them.

They seemed to point their weapons at the camera. John hit a button. The ship jumped. The monitor looked down at John's farm from a half mile up. The barn's roof was in ruins but the walls stood and there was movement within. John stared at his barn in disbelief. He loved that old building.

"Hit the gas, John!" Egon yelled."Not out of range."

The ship accelerated again and this time the G-force pushed everyone to the floor except John. He was thrown into a molded chair. Within seconds, the ship was in orbit. All was suddenly calm and motionless.

"We're safe," John said. "We're in space."

"Professor, we were watching the news," Heather said. "Oh my God, the Americans are nuking the Chinese."

"You can't be serious," Natalie said. "This is all part of the test. It's a crock. We can't be in orbit. We have gravity, and that thing back there is just a robot. Snap out of it, girls."

"This is not a simulator," John barked. "We can't do anything about the war in the Middle East."

John pressed a switch and a side window bubble shield recessed into the hull. "Look for yourselves," he pointed at the window.

The girls gathered around and peered out of the starboard observation portal. Egon joined them.

"Sorry, lasses," he said. "I'm not a robot."

"I think I'm going to be sick," Natalie said and fainted.

"I swear this is so not real," Rebecca said unconvincingly.

"Be thankful it's real," John said. "You don't want to be down there right now." He gestured to Egon. "And this is Egon from the planet Lepron."

Heather laughed nervously. The other girls gawked with open mouths. Egon stepped to the front of the cabin. "Happy to make your acquaintances, lassies," he said in a thick Irish brogue.

Everyone stared.

"I best be getting cleaned up, then," he added.

Egon left. Natasha switched the TV back on. It had blacked out during lift off. They watched in stunned silence as footage rolled depicting nuclear explosions, newscasters yelling about unspeakable destruction and radiation, satellite views showed large parts of the Earth engulfed in fire storms, and then the screen went black. Nat switched channels. It was the local Suffolk cable news, the real one.

"Less than one hour ago, a spaceship apparently launched from a barn on Oxford University's space studies campus, Bentwaters. The famous simulator housed there was in fact a real flying craft. Security cameras at the main campus caught this on tape."

A video of a large cigar shaped object pushed through John's barn roof. The stone walls remained in place as the craft rose above the farm, once well cleared of the roof it hovered a second before shooting straight up. The camera followed. The ship hesitated then shot away and disappeared entirely. John switched the TV off and started the communications monitor. They watched quietly for the next twenty minutes. It wasn't a news feed, John explained, it was an NSA satellite tap. Nuclear explosions rippled over the Earth. Mushroom clouds filled the screen. Egon returned dressed in slacks and T-shirt. When John flipped back to broadcast TV, the air waves were dead.

"Let me out! Open the door!" Natasha cried. "Fail me. I'm done."

"I can't open the door," John said, "This is real. There is no air outside."

Debbie sobbed. "I want to go home."

Egon walked to the front of the cabin.

"I'm sorry, lassies. But home is gone. Time to look to new inhabited worlds."

Egon set course for a neutral commercial world and explained as much. Egon wanted to go home, of course, but not until he discovered the lay of things. Finally the women, tired and distraught from a long emotionally disturbing day, and feeling defeated, depressed and overwrought with remorse, went to their bunks and fell asleep. Only John and Egon remained on the bridge.

"That's a hell of a simulation you put on," Egon said. "The war is real, sure enough. But how did you come up with that footage? There weren't any nukes."

"Film minor student," John replied.

"Sly," Egon said, "but why? They can't escape."

John leaned toward Egon. "You don't suppose these girls would warm up to me if they knew that they had been, as you called it, shanghaied," he said quietly, "or if they thought they had a planet to go home to?"

Egon clicked on a monitor. "You'll do well in the co-op," he said.

They looked together at a perfectly beautiful planet, the Earth, at a great distance, shown like a precious gem.

"You had better dump all that simulator junk," Egon said. "By the time they wake, we'll be a standard light year out and out of TV range. They won't be the wiser."

"Already done," John said.

"I won't be the only one getting laid, eh mate."

"I need to repopulate the human race," John agreed.

"You wiped your ground server's data, right? Ships plans?" Egon asked.

"The ship's computer sent the command when we launched. My back-up server's on the ship's network. I uploaded the entire Oxford library weeks ago. We have all the data that's fit to sell or trade. No worries, partner."

Egon grinned broadly, "Right, partner. No worries."

#### 

Charlie Steward and Bob Thompson were standing outside having a smoke when they heard a tremendous crash. Professor Black's simulator had crashed through the roof. It hung above the farm, eye level to them on the neighboring hill. It shot up and away like a streaking missile.

"Bloody mother of God!" Bob exclaimed, "Did you see that?"

"I don't believe it," Charlie said. "Now, he's gone too far. He's bloody mad."

Bob and Charlie ran to Professor Black's lab huffing and sweating. The two men burst through the door out of breath.

"Black, where are you? Black?!" Charlie cried.

Charlie stopped short a few feet into the room. Black was not there. A student, Willy Logan, was at Professors Black's desk staring at Black's computer monitor. Willy wore grass-stained overalls with safety glasses on top of his head.

"What's this?" Charlie demanded as he walked to the desk, stepping into his role as dean. "Where's Black? Why are you here?"

"You've got to see this," Willy said. He didn't bother to look up.

The two men stood behind Willy. Looking over the student's shoulder, they watched as Willy replayed the digital recording. It was one of Black's observation cameras. It showed what Bob and Charlie had just seen but from different angles on a split screen.

"We saw," Steward said exasperated. "What's the meaning of this?"

"See, 'E bloody well left the planet!" Willy said astonishment in his voice. "That bloody thing bloody well flies!"

Willy took a deep breath. The boy calmed himself before explaining that Black had flagged him down—told Willy he'd finish cutting. He sent Willy up to the office to pull the CAT cable from the server. Willy understood the CAT line to be a backup hard-wire link for the simulator. But it was more than that. Professor Black was adamant. He had told Willy it was an emergency.

"I had the feeling," Willy said, "Mr. Black just wanted me gone. I took the hint. He didn't need anything on the server. I had gotten distracted so it took a while before I got around to pulling the wire. It was plugged in, like he said, so I pulled it."

Willy stopped, pulled off the safety glasses and raked his fingers over a ridiculous spiked hairdo.

"Got it a split second before the ship took off," Willy said. "I think I launched it. If I'd known that, I wouldn't have pulled the bloody wire."

"What's this?" Charlie said, pointing to an icon on the screen.

"Oh that? That's the simulator file. Popped up on the desktop by itself when the bloody thing took off. Everything else was deleted before I yanked the CAT. The whole server's wiped clean."

"Email that to me, will you my good fellow?" Charlie said. "I think Oxford will soon be in the spaceship…ah…simulator business. Good of Professor Black to leave us this endowment."

"Jolly good fellow," Bob said respectfully as he rubbed his hands together like a greedy leprechaun lauding over a pot of gold. "Good show, that."

The two men left.

#### 

Willy didn't like the sound of those two. They always treated the Professor like crud. Good old Professor Black took good care of Willy, he did, while the school wouldn't give him or Black a rat's ass for tea. Willy was never one to pass up an opportunity to earn a pound and the Professor was generous to a fault. Willy figured the good old gent wanted it this way. Professor Black hated Dean Steward. So, Willy emailed the construction file to himself. Then, he deleted that file from Black's computer.

Willy got up and went home. Booting up his personal PC, he found Professor Black had emailed Willy instructions about accessing the good gent's Swiss bank account and with certified permission to do so. Willy singed in. It was a fuck all lot of money. With so much money, and Black's construction file, Willy went on to launch Earth's first successful private spaceship business.

**END**

# STORYVILLE 1890

French stood sidelong at the ebony-wood bar twisting his handlebar mustache between deep drags on a mint cheroot. He ignored the hoots and catcalls of his patrons. The Booty Sisters had just stripped down to bloomers. In Storyville, that act was common. It wasn't what brought customers in, the Sisters of Sappho show was. That's what made him rich, but it also marked him.

Macintyre was due. French checked his pocket watch then looked up as the double swinging doors banged inward. The band didn't flinch, but French did. The local corrupt bobby waltzed in twirling a blackjack on his finger like he owned the place. French had the urge to pull his derringer and stick it in his jacket's watch pocket with hammer cocked. It was an old ball and cap but it still shot well. French could take him, nobody would care, but one bad city cop was better than an army of Pinkerton detectives with their hands out. So, French stowed the thought and downed his glass. Macintyre sashayed over and put a leg up on the brass rail as he tipped his bowler.

"Whatta you say, Frenchie, keeping it clean?"

"You got eyes."

The half-naked sisters ran off the stage. The crowd stamped their feet. That was the trick. They weren't real naked or the cop bribes would be too steep. French couldn't afford that much. The band stopped. Hats flew into the air. French was obliged to wait until a house of roaring drunks ceased slapping tables and whooping.

"You seen yourself, Patty. All is right."

"The lads approve, they do."

"These girls ain't even the lesbian act," French said proudly.

Macintyre blushed on the word 'lesbian.' Things were wild in New Orleans but not that wild. If French had real lesbians on stage, they'd run him out like a carpetbagger. A man could do anything he wanted with a woman in Storyville, for the right price, so long as it was a man and a woman doing it. It was a Catholic town after all.

"That's why I'm along, Frenchie. You best not be breaking rules as I hear it."

French didn't like his tone. The asylums were full of women that took perverted liberties while such men that went buggering for one another didn't live long enough to be claimed insane. Macintyre wouldn't mind sending his girls to the loony house, either. French wasn't stupid. Sure, he hated the sergeant but he'd never show that hand.

French flashed a gold-toothed fake smile. Macintyre was a sharpshooter during the war and the killing lust stayed on him. He mostly took it out on queers and beggars, but French wasn't taking any chances. He wished he had that pepper-box pistol close to hand. French cordially slipped the Irishman his due, a little package slid along the bar rail. The cop scooped it up and stuffed it inside his double-breasted jacket.

"Ben," French called the barkeep. "Give our friend here a drink. Whiskey, the good stuff."

It was the usual offer and usually refused. If anything, Macintyre did his job sober. Half drunk was no way to do police work, that'd get him shot quicker than spit. A lot of people hated Irishmen. But today Macintyre didn't say no.

"Don't mind if I do," he said.

He signaled Ben for the drink, waving a big ham hand with flat knuckles. Ben slid the drink slickly along the bar. Macintyre caught it, downed it, and wiped his sweaty brow with a grey sleeve cuff. He was usually cool, even summer days. Something was eating him.

"What gives," French said.

"Mayor's upset. Seems some church ladies on Market Street heard rumors, wrote the Father who told the Mayor. He asks me, the Mayor, 'Patty will you go to see?' I says, 'You're keeping it clean, and that'll be so or there'll be trouble to pay.' Understand, Frenchie?"

French needed another drink. The show wasn't as clean as it should be. Macintyre never stayed around to find out, he was too straight-laced. French figured he had better put Patty in a better mood and quick. He nodded at Ben to bring another round. The little quadroon boy he had was already uncovering the footlight candles. Under the curtains he saw bathtub feet slid into place. The set was in place. Not enough time remained to get Patty Macintyre drunk.

The piano struck a raucous cord, the brass jumped in and a popular ragtime song filled the hall. Even the whores on the balcony and their boatmen customers leaned over the rails to watch. The song was near finished when the band leader hopped onto the low stage and raised his hands. The band paused. The crowd hushed. French heard a spittoon ring.

"Ladies and gentlemen," the hawker said, tipping his hat to French.

Russell must have warned the girls.

"Without further ado, I present to you, all the way from the Island of Lesbos, by way of France, the lovely, Sirens of Sappho!"

The main curtain split and slid back. Gauze drapes had been placed in front of the bath tub. The house thundered. French almost collapsed with relief.

#### ####

Stasha saw what she had expected when Patty came in. From backstage, she eyed the bobby-cop with contempt. Her letters to the priest had had their desired effect. Her humiliation would be less for a while. In Russia, she was a ballerina, respected and adored. Then, when her patron tried to force liberties, she shot him dead him and ran for England.

"Drape the veil between columns, hurry," Stasha ordered her stage helpers, backstage she was boss. "Leon's opening the footlights."

Her performance partners, Lizzy and Melba got into position. Lizzy, Stasha's favorite, spoke over the disharmonious rattle-can music, if it could be called music at all.

"Miss Stasha, should I read the dirty parts?"

"Not tonight, Sweat Pea, the police are watching."

"What should I say?"

"Make it up. Insert your own words as you may, you are a clever girl."

Lizzy was smart but she was much more. She was fair and pretty yet strong like a Russian peasant girl. Stasha had Lizzy wear the modest costume, not the usual but still not too restricting. It was molded after a short Roman toga, not that these people would know that. Lizzy wore no corset, nor bloomers. Her ample breasts swayed freely side-to-side in loose-fitting linens. Nude but not nude, no one could complain and it wasn't too short.

The curtain slid away with a swish and Lizzy stepped out from the left wing, strode to and fro on her milky long legs. She took the stage with breasts wriggling like Mississippi catfish crossing a mud bank. The men roared until she stopped and unrolled a phony scroll, blocking her bosom. The one legged drummer was ready at his snare—both he and the drum were war relics. He smartly rolled his Confederate sticks.

"A poem of Sappho," Lizzy cried dramatically and the audience quieted.

Of course it wasn't really a poem of Sappho's, Stasha wrote it herself. Sappho was a ploy to sell an 'educational and cultural performance' as the handbills proclaimed it. Scholars in Europe had long hailed the ancient poetess as genius and Stasha agreed. Sappho was generally known, but few Americans understood that the work was incomplete. Just fragments of the famed lesbian's work existed. The audience only had the reputation of Sappho's poetry to go by and that was all Stasha needed.

As Lizzy read, Stasha floated on tip toes across the stage from the left while Melba came in from the right wing. Melba, a pretty African girl, was the perfect contrast for Stasha's tundra-white complexion. That aside, Melba had other, more desirable qualities not seen on stage this night. The two danced the routine together stage forward with light touches and caresses as Lizzy described within poetry what the two players supposedly felt.

"Her neck was that of a swan, her bosom called for m...myrrh," Lizzy read.

'My lover's kiss,' was the actual line, but Lizzy called it the spice myrrh. She'd get spice later. On cue, Stasha pulled in and stroked Melba's neck lovingly. She let her hand 'accidentally' caress Melba's pert nipples as she improvised applying perfume. Melba's nipples looked hard, but it was a trick sewed into the fabric.

The men cheered, slapped the tables and stamped their feet. Various similar words and happy accidents were put forth for five minutes all to titillate the patrons' sensibilities.

"But hark, my love, before we fit like hand and glove, let us bathe before we lay...for sleep."

Lizzy did a good job of sidestepping, good girl, Stasha thought. The crowd went wild. Most of them had seen it before and knew what was coming but with that bobby-cop hanging on French the veil trick would guard the establishment's respectability. Leon ran along the stage front shuttering the lights low.

Lizzy read on as they slowly undressed each other behind the screen. She and Melba were actually nude, of course, as they climbed into the empty, high-sided copper bathtub. The gauze and the low light didn't give anything away.

"With warm waters lapping, and a heart a-fire, I could bear no more; I swooned and fell into her arms."

Stasha took Melba in her arms and they embraced but before their lips touched, an unforgivable act, they slid below the rim of the tub as lovers lying down together. The piano struck a bright cord, the brass section blew, and the curtain whizzed shut.

Stasha and Melba quickly rose. A stage hand, with eyes averted, brought them thin silk robes. All three quickly lined front stage and the curtain was drawn. They took a bow, this time careful a breast didn't flop out, and the curtain closed again.

The Dory-Rory girls were already in the wings with their corsets strung tight and accordions in hand. There was nothing like a squeeze box to make cleavage dance. The Sisters of Sappho hurried off to their dressing room.

Post late show, right after the last performance, was a dangerous time with all the stage hands and inn workers hot and agitated, a little drunk and feeling loose.

They didn't yet have enough money to fund Stasha's dream of going to New York City to escape her predicament and dance once again.

"Keep your heads," Stasha told her stage mates sharply. "French will be along, maybe with company of the sort that won't abide. Don't drop the act."

French knocked on the door. He always knocked with a prearranged rapping code. Stasha quickly made sure they were all decent before opening the door. French rushed in, shut the door and leaned his back on it.

"That was close. You did good. Keep it...artful for a while, all right?"

"What about our tips?" Lizzy asked. "The more we risk the more they put in our jar. How will we make it up? A good girl needs a decent wage, you know. I'm not resorting to whoring."

Stasha let Lizzy do the talking. She was the front girl, even if Stasha called the shots.

"We could take up Big Al's offer. He's offering twenty-five a week, each." Melba added.

French twisted his mustache like he was ringing out lice. He was a cheap son-of-a-bitch, but he wasn't stupid. Cops or not, he wasn't going to let the cash cow go find greener grass. More money and less obscenity suited Stasha fine. In New York, they'd be respected. They could say honestly they never whored, and they weren't dance hall can-can sluts, either. They were performers dancing Greek Poetry, real actresses. Better actors than French would ever know.

"Alright, alright, twenty five. I still get half the tips."

French left but he wasn't upset. Macintyre wouldn't blow the whistle. The crowd would keep coming, and the bobby-cops would stay away as long as the Sisters of Sappho walked a tight line, something they did well.

The carriage came at the usual time forty minutes after the second show, an hour past midnight. By this time, the drunks were mostly in the gutter and the cops were mostly sleeping in their beers. Still, women walking home at that hour weren't safe. The carriage man wanted sex for his service, it could have been a free ride, but Stasha had made monetary arrangements instead. Paying the taxi wasn't cheap, and it slowed their exit, but the price prevented rape.

The cab dropped them across the street from Saint Michael's Rectory. They had the entire second floor of a boarding house. The entertainment business paid well. Stasha followed the other two up the outside stairs. Melba's rear end swung before her eyes like a church bell calling and Stasha was ready for the revival. Miss Campbell, the maid, opened the door.

"Our bath ready?" Stasha asked Miss Campbell.

"Yes, Mum. Piping hot. I'll be taking me leave."

Miss Campbell was grateful for the extra income. Working at the church didn't pay much, so she provided services for the sisters late night. Campbell never lingered and never talked. Stasha stood at the window and watched the housekeeper hurry away until out of sight. She then closed the drapes.

Stasha stripped her frock as she made toward the oriental screen that surrounded the bathtub. She dropped the dress on a chair and wiggled out of her petticoat. Melba and Lizzy were already in the tub face-to-face washing each other, covered in suds.

"Should I recite Sappho for you," Stasha asked as she put up her hair, "or shall we act the poem?"

"I'm tired of acting," Lizzy cooed.

Lizzy leaned forward and kissed Melba passionately. Melba's lips parted with a little sigh, her breasts glistened in the lamplight. Stasha, satisfied with their answers, slipped into the tub. Her lovers were good actresses, the best, but home was no place for stagecraft.

**END**

# THE JESUS PROBE

We were in hot isotopes, me and Mike. I expected the announcement when it came over the intercom—,"Angels First Class Gabriel and Michel report to Control immediately,"—but I jumped anyway, not smart in low-G orbit. The last time I heard Control demand our immediate appearance, they were real unhappy. Instead of preventing a religion, we started one. But it wasn't our fault.

We wore ship-whites, all cleaned up, even our wings were groomed, white on white on white. The corridors, floors, and walls—even us—all gleamed white, company policy. We bolted from our cabins at the same time. I almost crashed into Mike. If Mike's wings weren't fluttering, I'd have run him over. He was as nervous as a sacrificial dove.

On our way to the meeting we hardly said a word to each other. With all the spy-ware onboard it wasn't smart to talk off the top of our heads. All sentry ships were the same. With so many races working together, only factual honesty was permitted. The ship's computers saw to it that everyone knew what everyone said. Just ask the computer for an accounting. No holds barred. Thankfully, our thoughts were our own. At least we had that union rule to rely on. No mind reading.

We walked in silence. The corridor walls, floors, ceilings, and every part of this ship were stark white, but I wasn't feeling too bright.

Speaking of dull bulbs, Mike voiced one thought aloud.

"You know, Gab, this isn't our fault. We can't help what a stupid probe thinks, especially the AI-7."

I answered him as anyone on this ship would. Mike knew I was giving him the pat answer. "That may be so, but, we're still responsible."

Mike's face went glum. "We shouldn't have used an AI-7. We screwed up. We trusted Control," he said. "Artificial intelligence is fine for gathering intel, but you never know for sure what they're thinking, or how they decide an action. They're not much different from Control in that way."

Mike laughed. I couldn't help it, I laughed too. It was a good joke. This was going to cost us. No need giving the computer any more ideas so I didn't share what I was thinking. But, to cover our asses and rub a little salt…"Hey, we didn't want any probes on this job, remember?" I said. "They ordered it and got what they asked for."

Mike rolled his eyes as we entered the conference room. Blind spot in the ship's eye scan system, management had to miss it. It was a small gathering, just the ship's captain, two project controllers and a rep from the Record Keepers' union. The Keepers were a throwback to the old days, but they did have value. They recorded what the computers could not, they sensed emotions. You never knew what they were feeling themselves because of their environment suits. I could ask the Keeper, union rules after all, but it's hard to hold a conversation with an eight-foot bubble and maintain a straight face.

Me and Mike were the only bipeds on this mission, actually the only beings on board that looked Earth-human at all. Take away the wings and feathers and we look exactly like them. Resonance shift cloaking changed our skin and hair, and hid the wings easy enough. Our union brothers walked with humans undetected for thousands of years. Infiltration was easy; the rest, not so much.

That's how we got these great jobs in the regional Planet Molders Union as field operatives working for the Primitive Planet Economic Development Department of this sector's Galactic Operations Detachment. In one way or the other, everyone onboard worked for the G.O.D. But God, as me and Mike liked to call them, was never happy. It wasn't our fault that God made unreasonable demands.

Our ship's contract was based on progressive results and this planet keeps going backwards. Only mature, rational beings can join the trade conglomerate. Our job was to help Earth's people evolve mentally by feeding people bits of technology, like metallurgy, and dissuading logic-killing social trends like mythologies and religions.

It wasn't going well. If things didn't turn around soon, Me and Mike would become the ship's next sacrificial lambs. Unless, of course, Control really screwed up and took the hit instead of us for a change. That would qualify as a miracle.

We took white plastic chairs at the white metal table. My wings were buzzing like hummingbirds sucking plutonium. They only had two chairs. The other crew members didn't have asses to sit on. The Control guys were both Salmelions. They looked like hairy five- hundred-pound Earth slugs with a spiny mane. The front and back looked exactly alike and were interchangeable. With the ass-chewing we were about to get, I thought, these two chairs were about to become obsolete.

The Captain, who passed for a giant four-legged tree frog, popped up his eye stalks. The Controller's spines bristled. The gestures meant both men were serious. The Recorder, well, inside his environment suit, it was impossible to say what he was thinking. Damn tinted windows.

"Mr. Mikilow, Mr. Gaberilow, so glad you could break away from your busy schedule to join us," Control One said.

I hate when Control's sarcastic.

"What is the status of the probe?" He asked.

Control Two chimed in. "We don't have to tell you two how important this project is. You know the Empire needs the resources this planet has to offer. With this recent turn of events, it may be another thousand years, if ever, before the G.O.D can invite them to join the trade conglomerate."

His spines were blue with malcontent. He needed another six hundred years before he could retire. Of course he figured it was our fault. Management always blames the peons. I think it's a job requirement.

"I hope you two can salvage this mess," Control Two said. "The contract is due for renewal in only one hundred years and that will not happen unless we show the PPED progress. What is your report?"

I swallowed hard. I felt like an asteroid without an orbit. This really wasn't our fault, I reminded myself. We only do what management tells us. Why are we always in the hot seat when their directives don't work? I wanted to ask but I had to report.

"As you know, this probe is an AI-7," I began. "It's a device well known for having bugs. I know that's no excuse for letting it get out of hand, but there were difficult circumstances."

"What kind of circumstances?" Control One asked. His bristles rippled a sign of displeasure.

Mike jumped in. "We didn't pick this probe you know. I didn't want an AI-7. We needed a twelve to override the damage Moses did. This one wasn't designed to reverse the effects of religion. You guys know that."

Control didn't like Mike's contribution. Union rule number two: cover your ass, if you have one.

"If you had extracted Moses quietly, as instructed," Control One said, "we would not have this problem."

"Sending a boat was too visible," Control Two added.

Mike was about to blow a portal seal. Job sent that boat down, not us. Junior management did that one. So I kicked Mike under the table. Management is always right, right? I need my job.

"Stick to the current facts," Control One and Two said in unison.

"Yes, Sir," I said and began my report again. "Things were going well. The subject seemed perfect for the probe. He was a Hebrew, right bloodline, and the woman was never pregnant. We couldn't have asked for a better receptor. The probe went in nice, not a hitch."

"Not a hitch," Mike repeated. "She wasn't even married yet."

I kicked Mike under the table again.

"But," I continued, "by the time the subject was thirteen-years-old, in Earth years, we started having problems. The human was tentatively accessing the probe, apparently, but the probe did not report it. The probe and the subject wanted the same things in life and—."

"I should have known something was up when the probe named itself 'the Holy Spirit,'" Mike interrupted.

I kicked Mike again. Thankfully he shut up. The Controllers were not all that well informed about Earth's social structures and how that worked within religions. We didn't need to open up a can of antimatter.

"You did not detect this anomaly?" Control One asked.

"No," I said. "When a subject and probe are on exactly the same cerebral bandwidth it's imposable to read their interactions. This was a real fluke. Who would've thunk it?"

"Go figure," Mike said with a half-smile. "I bet the probe liked it, too."

"You should have been looking out for that," Control Two said. "We had this sort of problem with the Moses probe. We had to pull the Enoch probe."

I didn't need the reminder of past failings, and Enoch was a low blow. That thing should have been scrapped eons ago. Both probes had different technical issues due to rushing the use of equipment that wasn't tuned properly for humans. It was management's bad call. Never use the wrong tools. I let them push me. I got blamed for that one. I should have called the union rep.

My wings fluttered uncontrollably. Were these guys trying to sell me down the river? I needed this job. The unemployment rate back on Heaven was ridiculous. What'd they expect from an experimental probe anyway? This AI-7 probe was tuned right, but still, it was untested. I continued.

"So, the probe and the subject melded, we're not sure when. But the last three years of the host's life showed us something weird was happening. We stayed back, tried to figure it out… but, although it was going off script, the probe was working correctly."

I took a big breath. I really didn't know if it ran right or not. I kept talking.

"The subject said all the right things to counter-act the earlier bad social consciences implants. You know stuff like, 'forget Moses, here is the new way.' People were following. Social molding was in full swing. Things looked good. But soon after…the probe clearly lost control. The subject took over the probe."

Everyone in the room knew the implications, and how unlikely that was—a new binary life force with so many complex variables just didn't spring up like that. There was either something special or something spooky about Earthlings.

"So why did you not immediacy kill the subject and extract the probe?" The Captain asked.

"We tried," Mike said. "We even sent in our S.A.T.A.N. kill-bot. The robot tried everything. No help. Satan eventually tossed the guy off the Temple roof. The subject must've learned to access the energy stream, he just floated away. Then, he turned around and killed the kill-bot!"

I interrupted again. Mike had a tendency to say too much.

"They were working together," I said. "The probe and subject were going in the same direction. Rather than use an ionizer nuke, scrap the whole project again, and really set us back, we tried direct intervention. We became part of the subject's inner circle. We steered him. We thought it was working."

Control Two sneered in green, "but things did not stay good, did they?"

My stomach was in my mouth. I almost spit up a feather ball. Never preen before a big meeting.

"No, Sir," I said. "When things got hairy, pardon the term, we tried to isolate them and nuke them, small scale, without major impact on the population. But it was too late. They just wouldn't leave the populated areas: Too many damn disciples.

We didn't want another Sodom on our hands. The salt fallout alone cost us millions to clean up. We made a perfectly good sea into a dead sea. We switched to plan B. We'd try and get the probe as the guy died."

"We got lucky on that," Mike added.

I kicked Mike again.

"The guy actually believed he was a real deity," I continued, "but a few nudges at the Sanhedrin, a few dreams planted in the governor's mind and he was a marked man."

"We set it up real nice," Mike interjected, "all we had to do was tail him and wait."

Control One and Two looked confused. Their bristles stood straight up.

"What is tail?" They said together.

I ignored the question. My gullet started grinding. We almost lost the game. As I searched for my next words, Mike jumped in.

"We couldn't predict how hard following would be. The entire city turned out for this guy. They were in the streets. We couldn't get within a hundred yards of him. The government had him, sure, execution was a done deal, but we couldn't get close enough to do a probe rescue."

Mike and I were both gritting our teeth at that memory, thongs of people pushing and crushing us. My wings are still a mess. We almost didn't save ourselves, much less the project.

"We got lucky," I said. "The guy, the probe, and the people were going nuts. The city was on fire with emotional turmoil. We were desperate. We had to get out. The raw emotions were going to wipe our holographs. We jumped over a city wall and landed in a refuse dump. We decided to hold up there and rethink it. Then we saw, the guy was hanging on a tree on the hill overlooking the dump. He wasn't even dead yet!"

"It may not have been luck," the bubble said.

Everyone made sounds of agreement. Maybe the AI had regained control.

Mike went on. "So we saw our chance, see. The guards were keeping people back. Gab and I became guards. We got in on a dice game so we got real close, we needed to extract at just the right moment. I talked to the probe in mind speak. I let it know we were ready. I told it to give me a signal, give me a sign when it was ready to evacuate."

I cut Mike off.

"After a while the probe took over. The guy was nearly dead. This human was way ahead of his time, fully integrated. When he said, 'into your hands I commend my spirit,' Mike stuck the extractor into the guy's side and sucked the probe out. Just in time. The guy dropped dead, and started to glow."

Control One was not happy. A glowing dead guy was not a good thing. I braced for the hit.

"It is good that you removed the probe," Control One said, "but a host body will not decay normally. You must remove the body. We must not leave evidence on the planet. If we break regulations, we don't get paid."

He was right, of course. But not many Earthlings saw it. Mostly Romans and nobody local believes them. Jews hate Romans.

"They're a primitive people," I said. "We all know it will be a long, long time before they become rational."

"Nonetheless," Control One said, his bristles showing annoyance. "We can't leave a host. What are you going to do about it?"

Mike beamed with that big toothy smile.

"We already took care of that," he said. "It was simple. After the riots calmed down, about three days later, we went and got the guy. He's in sick bay now. The probe programming department wants to see what makes him tick so we don't make this mistake again."

Control's bristles went pink with approval. No real damage done. So I took the opportunity and offered an idea.

"Once he gets through re-education we could use him on the team," I suggested.

"We could really use a local adviser," Mike said.

"That is good," Control One said, "I am sure he will make a fine crew member."

"Did you get away clean?" Control Two asked.

"Pretty much," I said.

"Please clarify," the Captain directed.

"No big deal," Mike said. "When we were collecting the body, a couple of women walked into the tomb. His wife and mother, I think. We weren't in holograms so they freaked and ran."

"It won't be a problem," I added. "Females have no status in this primitive society."

"Make sure, send him back, to explain," Control One said.

"Are you sure that's wise, Sir?" I asked. "I mean, remember what happened with—."

This time, Mike kicked me under the table and I shut up.

"Don't question my authority," Number One said, bristling irritation. "Had I been more involved, this would not have happened. Just do what I ask."

I was thinking to myself what an ass. He doesn't know squat about Earth. Mike and I have been on the ground for a thousand years. I was getting really ruffled, my feathers, too. I knew this was a huge mistake, but I needed this job. I had to bite my fork-tongue.

It was then I noticed Mike's sidelong smile. He'd be happy to let Control One fall flat on his face, or whatever passed for a face, which may have been his ass as well. Mike had something up his robe's sleeve.

"Yes, Sir," I said. "I will go and brief Jesus."

Number One looked perplexed. "Who is Jesus?"

"Christ, this going to be interesting," Mike said fighting to keep a straight face. "I can't wait to see how Jesus works out as a crew member."

Mike loved to mess with Control. Control didn't know sarcasm from sacred prayer. I smiled widely, hoping the bubble saw it as approval regarding Control's newest bad call of a decision, and not the way I really felt. I knew in my soul that the next ass-chewing to come down from G.O.D. wouldn't be chopping on me and Mike's asses. I'd bet my union halo on it.

**END**

# GOD'S CONTROL ROOM

"Will you look at this place," Carl said. "I can't believe the dust in here."
"What'd you expect?" Larry said. "We've not been in this control
room for ages."

"Too long," Carl said as he pushed his standard issue black-rimmed glasses
up his nose.

Larry did the same. "You'd think with all this technology they'd give us glasses that fit."

"We build and destroy planets," Carl said, "but we can't get decent glasses."

"Better check the boards," Larry said. "We're awfully late. I hope nothing's
wrong, or we'll get chewed out by the Big Guy again."

Larry rubbed his pointy chin as a revelation dawned.

"Hey, we were told to attend that luncheon in full dress, wings and all," Larry
said, "not our fault we're back late."

"Let's get this place cleaned up. I can't see the dials," Carl said.

They went to work dusting. It was no easy task wearing formal wings and
dress whites.

"What a mess!" Larry said. "Black dust everywhere. You look like the Dark
Angel."

Carl narrowed his eyes. "Don't align me with that guy, not even in jest."

Carl sat. A puff of black dust shot up around him. They stopped to laugh but
quickly resumed their task. Time was short. They busied themselves adjusting,
scanning, tracing history and pushing up their glasses. Their mood turned glum
as their assessment progressed.

"Man, we're screwed here," Carl said. "We let it run way too long without
controls."

"Yup, we got problems. They developed intelligence while we were at lunch,"
Larry said squinting at Carl's board over his glasses. "What should we do here,
boss?"

"Follow procedure," Carl said. "What else can we do? If we don't shut down and start over, chances are, they'll not achieve the higher plane."

Larry rubbed his dusty forehead, knocking his crown to the floor. "What if we let it run? I mean they got a 50/50 shot. It looks like they're pretty sophisticated. The mentor seeds had engaged. They may become spiritually aware without a reset. They did pretty well with just the basic implants, right?"

"Correct," Carl said. "They're doing fine. But I don't see how they'll make it. Almost every implant was eventually rejected. They already have nukes and enough greed to use them. If they do, then we're really screwed. We'll have to start all over from scratch anyway."

"I'd hate to start from zero again," Larry said. "But, we spent at least six billion years on this one. And look here," he said pointing at a gage. "They're evolving on their own. It's only a thin thread, but could be enough so we don't have to crash everything. We could do a quick-restart."

"I don't know," Carl said, rubbing a finger along his sagging jaw. "We've scuttled this one a bunch of times."

"What's one more time?" Larry pushed his glasses up and scratched his cheek. "I hate to lose that last fifty million years. We put a lot of work into sentient development. Can't we roll it back a bit? Say twenty thousand? We've done it before."

"No way," Carl said, "too many rollbacks already. It won't hold up. The matrix will break. We need to wipe human life and start another version. We're lucky that the ice age thing worked out without losing the threads last time."

"The Big Guy is going to scream," Larry prompted.

"Give me a minute." Carl said. "Let me think."

"Don't think too long, boss," Larry said. "One minute is a few hundred years to them."

"I got it!" Carl said. "Intervention! That's the ticket."

"We tried that. Remember Jesus? And Buddha? They came back flummoxed," Larry said.

Sending prophets wasn't a good idea, according to the manual.

Carl looked over his glasses."That's not what I am talking about, Larry. I'm thinking direct intervention, something radical. Let's show our cards. Get some humans involved. They'll be gatherers. I'll have them collect some decent samples. Once we have them on the storage ship we'll wipe out the corrupted human lines. Once the smoke clears, we'll reintroduce the better genetics and combine them with the survivors. Use better seeds to rebuild the race without trashing the whole planet. What do you think? You're the technical guy."

"It might work." Larry said. "We'll have to send On Site Observation a bigger ship but it's worth a try. Should I call the Big Guy and get the go-ahead?"

Carl rubbed his jaw and adjusted his glasses. "I saw Gabriel and Michel at the luncheon. They were on the first away team. They don't have a field assignment right now. They know the territory. They could beam over and get things going."

"Sounds like a plan," Larry said. "I'll call the Big Guy."

Larry picked up the red phone and explained the situation. After a time, he held the phone away from his face and into the air. Carl heard the tirade as well. After a while Larry put the phone back to his face.

"Yes, Sir…Yes, Sir…Will do, Sir…Right, Sir…I will tell him."

Larry hung up. "Who's this guy think he is, God or something? Everyone knows you're God on this project. He's just some dumb-ass bureaucrat. He doesn't know half of what we do."

Larry pushed his glasses back for the millionth time.

"Right," Carl said as he pushed his glasses back as well. "Let's show him who God really is, get that ship on the horn."

Larry grinned and picked up the blue phone.

"I hope them guys like a challenge as much as we do."

"If we pull this one off," Carl said, "we'll make employees of the month, and get the bonus credits, too."

Larry blew the dust off the white phone and dialed.

"It'd be nice to speak at the luncheon for a change," Carl said with a faraway look behind his slipping glasses. "We'll get to choose a gift."

"Screw the spotlight," Larry, ever the realist, said. "But, I don't mind the gift. I'm asking for new glasses."

**END**

# THE PENIS FACTORY

A man and woman waited in a typical medical facility's reception room. Sharon looked around while exhaling a depressive sigh. Long buried feelings came to the surface. Forgotten emotions tore at her wellbeing but she corked them. Man up, she told herself.

This place reminded her of the abortion clinic she had used fifteen years before. She went there to ensure her place in the business world, but her career had not improved. She came to this clinic for the same reason, career enhancement, but of a different kind. She sought a medical procedure which guaranteed her career would finally accelerate. That's what she told herself, as she sat with her eye twitching. No past regrets. But, when she checked her makeup with her favorite compact, her fearful grimace accused her. She redoubled her resolve to be happy, happy about past decisions and this one, too.

The man, being a man, watched her with interest. She thought he noticed that she was attractive. She passed for thirty although she was thirty-seven and the clock was ticking. Men always ogled, but it didn't help her. For business sake, she went so far as to wear her hair short cropped in the style of an executive and she dressed down in unfaltering serious-business pant suits. Nothing worked.

The guy made her feel even more edgy, but it wasn't his fault, not really.

How could he not help but notice no matter how hard she restrained it? Her hair was perfect, her skin clear, and her body thin. Her mundane suit could not hide her sizable yet firm breasts.

He was compelled to speak to her, of course. Distressed and pretty was hard to ignore. He spoke in a voice of concern, but it was a ploy, had to be, it always was.

"So, what brings you here?" he said. He smiled like he had a wolf inside. "I'd bet my paycheck they don't get many women here."

Sharon was thankful for the distraction, even if it was a guy hitting on her. It was better than thinking about surgery. She turned toward him.

He was a pleasant enough looking man, short and a bit pear-shaped with thinning gray hair. Typical middle-aged office worker by his clothing, but oddly, his face was soft despite his spotty beard. He had the face of a sixteen-year-old, like some kid growing his first wispy beard. Even not-a-chance nerds hit on her. It never ends.

"I'm sorry," she said and then lied. "I am not available. I have a lover."

The automated response rolled over her lips like a telemarketer's script. She said it before she could stop herself.

"Well, that's good for you then," he said, "but I'm just curious. You look sad."

A thought struck Sharon. This was the first guy she had met in ages that was able to, or cared to, notice her emotional state and she insulted him. Sensitive guys were rare.

"And frankly," he continued, "Until they install my new penis, I'm not interested. Most women would rather not date a man with a vagina, I should think."

"What?" Sharon exclaimed. "I'm sorry. I'm distracted. I spoke out of habit. I'm sorry."

He put out his hand. "I'm Bill, Bill Thomas."

She took his hand and noticed he had a very small hand, for a man.

"You must be distracted," Bill said with a friendly smile, "if you're here. You're obviously in the wrong clinic, unless, of course, you're applying for a job or waiting for your man."

That pissed Sharon off. She was more than tired of men thinking they needed to think for her and tired of their expectations that, perhaps, she isn't thinking at all. I don't need any help from you, she though, but answered nicely. She hated conflict.

"I'm here for the same reason you are."

Bill's lips contorted into a sneer. "You do realize this clinic grows penises in the laboratory and installs them?"

"Yes," Sharon snapped. "And I'm getting one."

"You're not a transsexual," Bull said. "Why would a normal woman want a penis?"

"It's for work," she blurted. She had not said it openly before. It felt good. "Respect, power, I want it. You lived in the women's world, you know. I'm totally underpaid, passed over, ignored! Why? My lack of penis."

"I don't think it's that simple," Bill said. "A penis will not control your emotions positively. It won't enhance your ability to do your job. This isn't a smart move on your part."

That tore it for Sharon.

"I've had it with men telling me what's smart or not," Sharon tried not to sound as angry as she felt. "This pre-operative transsexual woman in my office, Tiffany, got to the top in six months. I've been there fifteen years! The chick with the dick got my promotion!"

"It's a fluke," Bill said. "Read the hate crime statistics. Transsexual people are the favorite target of bigots. You're setting yourself up for bigger problems."

"We'll see. I can't believe you're protecting the male power structure," she said seething with anger.

"Have it your way," Bill said quietly and picked up a copy of *Guns and Ordinance*. The nurse came out.

"Sharon. Sharon Portrack. You're up, Ms. Portrack."

Sharon grabbed her overnight bag and marched straight past the nurse. She paused at the door, turned and glared at Bill. She had words loaded but failed to shoot.

Bill shook his head.

"What a bitch," he mouthed.

He deflated her in that instant. She never did take criticism well. He raised his *Guns and Ordinance* magazine and flipped the pages ignoring her.

*I'll show him and every man in the word once I get my cock.*

Her vacation stay as an inpatient went well. After medical discharge, she had a week before she had to return to work.

The science of growing and grafting material taken from the patient was fool-proof. Everyone carried the genes of both sexes. It was only a matter of switching on the right dormant genes and culturing the parts. Sub-molecular morphology instillation was fast and painless. Organ transplants weren't ever considered any-more. The industry of cultured organs had grown like wildfire.

Sharon's new organ performed like any penis. She tested it at home and it worked just fine. It looked like the picture in the catalog, got hard, due to weekly testosterone shots and so it behaved normally. Other drugs blocked beard growth and the deepening of her voice. It produced orgasms so intense they made her teeth hurt—that was unexpected.

They could have given her testicles and, as such, the ability to produce testos-terone and semen. But she didn't want irreversible procedures. She was a woman, not a man and she knew it. She wasn't willing to give up her vagina, just add a little job security above it. By the time she went back to work, three weeks later, she was ready for business.

Morphology was controversial. It inspired a resurgence of right wing zealotry. Human cloning was illegal but religious leaders used the clone specter to raise fears. They preached "abominations would bring the wrath of God." But, mor-phed organ recipients, burn victims, and amputees trumped political faith. Sha-ron ignored the controversies, for her, it was a passkey to the corporate penthouse not a moral issue. There was no morality in business that she ever saw.

The owners of Lawhouse Publications were right-leaning Christians, but more so, they were businessmen, not saints. Business trumps Jesus every time.

"Big swinging dicks always win," Tiffany said once. "The small head runs the man-show around here and the largest small head always wins."

Sharon knew Tiffany was right. She routinely saw the evidence. The wiener did the thinking for every man she ever knew. Men respected what each other's wiener thought. Sharon had gotten a big one. That would make her popular. She didn't know how wieners could take over one's life: that side effect wasn't listed in the brochure.

## *Six Months Later*

The two Lawhouse brothers and the firm's top two executives, stood side-by-side at the urinals of an ordinary men's bathroom. The walls were emblazoned with pink. The executive bathroom was far above so they used this one. They stood with eyes traditionally averted staring at the little multicolored specs on the wall.

"The fucking wall's pink!" The younger Lawhouse said.

"What did you expect?" The older one said. "Every since Portrack got that dick she's taken over, from quiet efficiency to a loud mouth bitch in one easy step."

"This is your fault," the younger said. "You had to have your trans-lover on staff. Tiffany started a trend. All the power hungry women in New York are getting dicks. And the women that don't, well they don't want the she-males in the women's bath room. Now we're stuck with it. We can't afford a discrimination suit."

The older man snapped an angry reprimand. "Stop using the S-word. You know it's derogatory. You're bucking to get us sued. It's hate speech. I promoted Tiffany because she's good, not because I like what's in her panties."

"Right-O," the younger said sarcastically. "Talent or not, you wanted her, you'd have given her a job regardless."

"Keep it down. I can't have this getting back to my wife," the senior partner zipped his fly. "I don't care what's in her panties, she's a great editor."

"She's outrageous with a blow job, according to the rumor mill." the junior partner said.

"I didn't find that out until much later, long after hiring her. She gives incredible head. Any girl with a dick has got to be an expert."

Junior zipped his fly.

"What about Portrack? She's made a war zone out of the administrative processing pool. I say fire her. Dick or not, she's a no talent distraction."

"No talent?" Senior said. "She was a top performer before. With her new found…attitude…She's acquired aggression, that's useable."

"Meaning?" Asked the younger Lawhouse.

"We can't fire her even if she sucks at her job. There's only one thing we can do."

"What might that be?"

"Promote her, what else? What's one more screaming middle manager?" The senior partner paused. "You may experience for yourself how a chick with a dick…er…performs."

"Not my cup of tea," the junior partner said. "I don't like she-ma…transsexual women."

"Ms. Portrack is straight," Senior said, "letting her suck you off is not remotely gay."

"Never thought of it that way, perhaps I'll give it a whirl," the younger Lawhouse said.

"At-a-boy, you do that. You'll not be disappointed. Her lips will serve you well."

The two men walked out into the hall strutting like lions. Neither man washed his hands.

Sharon did not unlearn her feminine habits easily, even though new masculine habits began to dominate her. She still sat to pee. She was on the toilet when the Lawhouse brothers came in. On instinct, she pulled up her feet at the sound of the men's room door opening.

After they had gone, she stayed there a while frozen. She heard every word. She wanted to cry and would have before testosterone, but she punched the stall's metal door instead. Strangely, she felt better. Adrenaline fueled resolve. She didn't wash her hands either. Tearing someone, anyone, a new asshole was dirty work anyway. She kicked the washroom door open.

"I'm not getting on my knees for that asshole. Fuck him, too!"

Her co-workers in the hallway parted like water plowed by a deep-V hulled boat. She steamed to her cubicle fighting tears and rage. She spent the rest of that day barking at anyone who dared look at her. The next day, Sharon was moved upstairs as the new customer relations office manager. Edward Lawhouse, the junior partner, was her new boss. Sharon saw Tiff in the hallway three days after that.

"Goddamn girl," Tiffany said. "I heard you were up here. That was fast. You only got your hot-dog, what, six months ago?"

Sharon's face showed the panic she felt, she was good at hiding her feelings before. Now, her game-face wasn't convincing anyone.

"Is everything okay, sweetie?" Tiff said.

"I don't understand," Sharon replied. "You said it would improve my work situation, not make me more a sex object. I wanted to be recognized for my work."

"I said, it would open doors," Tiffany responded, the smile gone. "I never said it would improve your skills or intelligence. You were the top girl in the pool, everyone knew it."

Sharon clenched her fists, wanted to cry but had an overpowering need to hit something. She screamed at Tiffany instead. "You lied to me! Why does it work for you and not me?"

"It did work for you. You're promoted, aren't you?" Tiffany said calmly.

"This is not what I wanted. I can't stand it, can't concentrate." Sharon cried. "Everyone I work with hates me. I'm berating people for no reason. I hate how I feel. I keep punching stuff."

Sharon offered her knotted fists for inspection. Her knuckles were scabbed and red. She went on. "All I can think about is sex. But no one comes near me; I don't even know who I would sleep with. Only the goddamn perverts want me! And now work, I can't handle it. I don't belong in management."

This time Sharon let the tears flow but she hated herself for it. Luckily she wasn't wearing makeup, but then again, she didn't bother anymore. Her face seemed too hard for it.

"I was really good at my job before. Everybody liked me downstairs. I don't know what to do."

"You better figure it out, Sharon. Every ambitious girl in New York is getting a dick. If you want to keep working here, you had better either go back to the processing floor, or get on your knees for Edward, figuratively at least, and master your job damn fast."

Sharon balled up her fists once again, she wanted to hit Tiffany but instead she swallowed her frustration like a whore swallowing an overlarge load. But, she managed to choke up a question.

"Why is it so easy for you, how do you handle it?"

"Simple," Tiffany said. "I 'm transsexual, not a genetic female. I've dealt with it my entire life. Frankly, I can't wait to get rid of it."

"How will you keep the firecracker editor job?" Sharon asked.

"You don't understand. For whatever reason, I was born with a brain not matching my body. I was forced to adapt, seek answers, be creative, and ask questions people never ask. It sharpened my mind. Dick didn't make me smarter. Figuring out how to live with it did."

Tiffany pulled a tissue out of her purse and wiped a tear from Sharon's cheek and said, "Look, honey, you're my friend. I'll help all I can. I got your back, so hang in there."

"What if I stop the testosterone?" Sharon asked glumly.

"You'll be much less aggressive, that's for sure. But, Mr. Happy won't be happy or make you happy. You'll hate dragging that thing along. You'll know exactly how I feel."

Sharon felt crushed, just like that day she had the abortion, deep in her soul, then and now, something wasn't right. Sharon turned away and stumbled straight into the open elevator and pushed the button for the ground floor.

#### 

Ed Lawhouse ran into his brother in the hall the next day.

"So," Bob asked, "how's your new office manager working out?"

"She is a firecracker," Ed replied. "I've never seen the staff work so fast or be so unhappy about it. Shit's getting done. I like it."

"Any screaming idiot will do," Bob said concurring. "What about the blow job? Any luck?"

"Nope," Ed said. "She must be a lesbian, but I don't care. She motivates people. They are scared shitless. You don't have to be good at blow jobs to yell at people all day."

Bob scratched his balls. "Where is he-she now? I'd like to see her in action."

"Called out this morning, medical problem," Ed replied. "She has sick time coming. I can't bitch."

"The hell you can't," Bob said. "She's management now. Tell her to get her ass back to work."

"No way," Ed said. "I don't need her up my ass either."

"I can relate," Bob said.

Tiffany waved at him from the other end of the hall. She wanted his attention. If Ed ever figured out Tiffany never gave it up, not even once, he'd be a laughing stock. He had no choice but to kiss her ass. He had a reputation to maintain.

####

Sharon arrived for her scheduled weekly testosterone shot. She still didn't have the balls to give herself a needle. The reception room was full of well-hung power-player genetic females. The group grew every week. Business was booming. She no longer felt pride in the fact that she was the first regular girl to have the procedure.

Normally she saw the nurse, got her shot, and then went to work. There was plenty of time before work started. Today, she had no intention of getting her T-shot or going back to the customer service floor. She had an appointment to see the doctor. She resisted the temptation to read the new *Guns and Ordinance* magazine that her company published.

Sharon asked the women sitting across from her, "Is that a fertility clinic down the hall?"

The woman was chewing gum so hard and fast it reminded Sharon of a typist getting paid by the word. Steel Jaws looked at Sharon like Sharon was crazy.

"What about it? Who the fuck wants to get knocked up? Bad for business."

"I know," Sharon said. "I know."

The woman sitting next to Sharon complained to a girl down the sofa.

"I don't understand why it's hard all the time. It's really distracting me."

Another woman answered. "Don't worry about it, you'll get used to it. It's new. You need to adjust. You'll see."

Sharon tried not to, but like the man she had met in this waiting room months before, she had to look. The girl wore tight stretch slacks. She looked like gnomes pitched a tent in that girl's panties. Her eyes wandered to the woman's ample breasts.

The girl noticed Sharon and quipped aggressively, "Hey! What are you queer? Knock it off, bitch!"

Sharon would have gotten up and slugged her last week, but today, she let it ride. More insults came but Sharon didn't listen.

"Sharon Portrack report to pre-op," the intercom blared.

"What are ya queer?" the women continued to taunt.

Sharon sprung up. "Not anymore," she said.

A small fist slammed the coffee table as she walked to the door on clouds. She was having her aggression surgically removed. For the first time in a long time, she felt right.

When Sharon left after her procedure and recovery stay, she wandered to the medical mall's fertility clinic. She wasn't sure what drew her there. She waited at the entrance. The reception area was nothing like the abortion clinic or the penis factory. There were flowers, pretty pictures happy people, and music.

Sharon crossed the threshold with reservations. The smell of baby shampoo washed over her and the regret she fought for fifteen years vanished in a flood of newborn hope. Motherhood was a bad career choice that was certain. The job was everything but now she felt a more satisfying vocational calling. She went to the reception desk and made an appointment. She couldn't wait to start.

**END**

# GOING UP THE MOUNTAIN

The Second-in-Command, and captain of this rag-tag conglomerate of nomads, picked his way across a vast desert camp. At least forty thousand people were jammed into this rift valley. They were hemmed in by two steep, unstable hillsides and a craggy mountain. Why Number One led them here was a complete mystery and an irritant for Number Two. The Commander seldom shared his reasoning.

This place made no sense from a defensive standpoint. The mountain at the farthest end of the valley was a tiring, dangerous loose slope climb that ran into a pathless puzzle of sharp spires. It provided no protection for this mass of civilian wanderers. Yet, the mountain was sacred to the tribes, local and distant, who had joined their contingent uninvited. There was no way to stop them. More came every day and more numbers meant more troubles. This holy pedestal before him meant nothing to Aaron, except it was a natural hindrance to escape if such need arose. Was was common on this primitive world. The Egyptians would slaughter them handily if they found the nomads here.

A low plateau on the mountain was Number Two's destination. He was called to a meeting there. Aaron made his way slowly though throngs of people, angrier and more frustrated with each step. Around him various groups gathered according to tribe, clan or religion.

Many celebrated with abandon in this supposedly holy place while others sat in ash wearing sackcloth muttering prayers. Most of the people feasted, wasting food that was in short supply. They worshiped tribal gods, each to his kind, under the mountain.

Captain Aaron came upon a young girl of his people eating an oversized piece of barley loaf. The girl had it dangling from her fingers and was about to drop it on the ground.

"Why are you wasting that!" He called to her. "You have enough for two! We are on rations!"

"Sir," she said with downcast eyes. "This is the gods' gift. It is bread from the stars. Surely the gods will send more. And, are we not here to celebrate the gods?"

The Captain caught himself tightening and relaxing his fist at his side. It was his way of relieving frustration.

"First of all, this food came from Heaven, not the stars," he said in a measured, gentle voice, "and Heaven is a space station, not a magical bakery in the sky. Gods have nothing to do with this. We won't get another airdrop for three weeks. This food must last."

The Captain squatted on his haunches to look into her blue eyes.

"Haven't your parents taught you anything about our people?" He continued. Now his tone grew genuine. "That's not even the right word. 'Bread' is an Egyptian word, you are not Egyptian. That's 'manna' you hold, not bread."

The girl now looked at him, wide-eyed. "Manna from the Space Station Heaven?"

"That's right," he said. He turned and walked away satisfied.

Soon, his frustration returned. Too many of his people now practiced the primitive tradition of burnt offerings. Aaron mumbled to himself as he walked. "Waste of resources. All for nothing."

He reached a circle of people gathered around a wooden effigy of a bull freshly clad in hammered gold foil. The figure had once served as a teacher's model of the constellation Taurus. They had melted gold bullion and covered a once valuable educational device transforming it into a tool of ignorance. He could stand it no longer.

"What are you doing?" he screamed. "We need this gold! It's our only trade-worthy commodity!"

An old man, potentially the group elder and cult leader, mumbled in a language Aaron didn't understand. The Captain spoke many languages, but this one was new to him.

"For the love of Earth, stop babbling will you?" Aaron exploded. "Speak a civilized language!"

But, in response, the old man babbled more.

"Curse you!" Aaron said, releasing the anger in his heart. "You Sumerians can go to Hell! Better yet, go back to where you came from, the land of Babel."

This was all a bad joke. His kind brought writing and civil language to the Tigress Valley. The humans there changed it beyond recognition and spoke it so poorly now he could not follow. He walked briskly away fuming like the wasteful fires around him. The more he walked the more he passed primitive things that he did not like and people he did not know. When he made it to the base of the slope. he cried, "I hardly recognize my own people!"

No one heard him over the din of many celebrating tongues. He made the slogging climb to Base Camp One. Aaron arrived at the flat top of the first foothill where tents of camel skins were pitched. One housed the Commander, Moses, who sat on ship made silk pillows. At four hundred years older than Aaron, the Commander's long gray hair and beard made him a very old man in the eyes of the locals who were lucky to reach thirty years. The Commander, in truth, was one thousand and twenty years old. His short time on Earth wore on him fast and it showed.

Aaron, as the second in command, entered without fanfare. He pulled over a cushion made from a goat's skin which was a gift from one of the local tribes and sat.

"When are you leaving?" Aaron asked Moses. "Has Heaven Station agreed to your retirement?"

"Yes, soon. The project is yours now. Before I go, we must decide how best to preserve the people."

"What people?" Aaron said. "I hardly recognize anyone. Our own people have gone native. Between intermarriage and interspecies breeding with the humans, we are no longer a people at all."

"We stayed in Egypt too long," Moses said. "Our people have intermarried, adapted to the primitive life. If our labor contract hadn't run out, we would be there still. The kings…"

The Commander had dressed naked pigs as best he could. Only a god could have done better. Moses earned no shame but failure still shadowed his face. Aaron felt bad for him, perceiving a defeated man.

"We needed work, we needed food and gold." Aaron said. "How else could we rebuild our society?"

Moses made no reply. For a long time, Aaron counted the rocks at his feet while he kicked at the pebbles in his mind.

"Egypt wasn't bad," Aaron continued. "We were isolated, our enclave segregated. I am more worried about the nomads. Our eight thousand colonists have grown to forty-thousand in only thirty-nine years. Our natural birth rate can't produce so many."

"Settling in Egypt was a mistake," Moses said. "It opened the door of assimilation. It is true that Egypt gave us a reprieve, one better than extinction. But now how many of our own people remember we were once their gods? I will rejoice when the transport comes. I'm done."

This hurt. Aaron did not believe he, or anyone, could fill the Commander's sandals.

"At least you will finish your days in the comfort of Space Station Heaven, but not even that, the last bastion of our great civilization, will last much longer. Nine thousand years have passed since the floods and our gene pool is corrupted, too dispersed within the primitives. I fear we have lost…without your—."

"The primitives have gotten the better of the exchange," Moses interrupted. "They grow more intelligent with every generation. Even their life span has increased while ours has decreased. Methuselah will be much interested. If only their war-like proclivities would fail."

"It's hopeless," Aaron said. "We can't even preserve our genetics. Breeding sanity into this crazy, primitive world to make it livable again defeats us."

"No, we will win by the long road," Moses said, adjusting his sheep's wool shawl. "Eventually they will mature. They'll become fully human eventually."

He paused and looked at Aaron carefully. "But, we must slow the mixing of races."

"I don't know how," Aaron remarked.

"That is why I brought us here," Moses said. "I have a plan." Moses lifted Aaron's chin with the tip of his staff. "What do we have left of our portable technology, Captain?" Moses asked.

Moses' eyes sparkled and his voice pierced, his old self shone.

"One handheld radio, a hologram, a dozen handheld laser cutters," Aaron answered. "What good are electronic tools if we can't convince our own people that it's not magic?"

The old man lifted an eyebrow, but then he laughed long and hardy. "We are not without hope. We only need foster our bloodline, increase our people, so our genetics will root. Already the mixing of races elevates the primitives. We will survive through them."

The old man was forever speaking in riddles Aaron did not understand much of what he said, but this made sense "Separate wheat from chaff," Aaron said. "How?" '

"Our kind, even mixed as they are, will continue to live long lives," Moses said. "There is time enough to spread our seeds. Start with imposing mandatory sanitary procedures and dietary restrictions."

"I can't separate mulled cultures!" Aaron said. "It can't be done."

"Religion," the Commander said calmly. "We use the same tools that dismantled our race to bring us back. Make them reproduce. Make rape and pillage a mandate of God. Start with Jericho."

"Can poison cure sickness?" Aaron said. "Impossible. Religion breeds stupidity."

"It will work," the Commander insisted. "If we call our influence the word of God, after we tailor it to our needs, they will become a separate and strong people, people that carry our genes. We'll convince them that God earmarked them as a special people."

"I don't like it," Aaron said. The immorality of it made his blood cold. "We must use reason. Religion takes us backwards."

"Look out there," Moses said pointing at the multitudes. "Religion has already captured them. That is why they gather under this mountain. Teach them religious purity, and so avoid diseases they no longer understand. Make them a people ruling the pit-trap they already accept."

"They won't believe me."

"They will believe messages from God."

"I don't see how it can be done," the Captain said. In their former society, social manipulations never worked.

"A cohesive religion," Moses said, "one that binds them. I will make a new god, one god, who will tell them how to live, to be a people above all others."

"You're out of your mind," Aaron said.

"I have the initial plan worked out," Moses said, ignoring Aaron's insubordination. "It will work. The Station's anthropologist agrees. This will preserve our race. The method is counter to our heritage, plays to their reality, not ours. Will you do it?"

"I always respect your orders."

An idea sprung to Aaron's mind. The Commander gave him the out he needed. He'd use the existing command structure to form a priesthood to preserve scientific understanding. Their traditions of fostering knowledge and technology will not be lost—a goal inside the goal.

"Good," Moses said. "Tomorrow I'll go up the mountain with the hologram and put on a light show they'll never forget. One of the fighters will rain fire from the sky. This is the perfect opportunity. When I come down from the mountain, I will tell of a new god, the one and only god and present the law. The law will bind them and oust the ones that won't bite."

"So strange, it may work." Aaron said.

"It will work. I will bring stone tablets, written by the finger of God. In reality, I'll use the handheld laser." Moses fluffed out his long beard.

"Do as you will," Aaron blurted. "Go on, go up the mountain, Moses. Leave me with all this trouble."

"Aaron, I'm leaving you with hope, not a burden."

Only one more Hebrew ship ever landed on Earth. It was the transport ship Jehovah which took Moses from the Earth much to the stunned amazement of Aaron's new believers. The day of Moses' departure solidified the people forever. Enoch himself stood on the gangway of the shuttle Jehovah with Cain and Adam. Together, they welcomed Moses aboard.

Moses' trick had worked, much to Aaron's surprise. The people would never forgot that Jehovah had gathered the patriarchs and took them to Heaven.


**END**

# THE WITCH CHILD

A lthough it was the twenty-first century, life in Hillside, Colorado, hadn't grown or changed since the village elders made a pact with Chief Still-water in 1810. The Indians, then the railroad, then mining agent pros-pectors, then big cattle ranchers and finally the real estate developers had come and gone. They had been frustrated and didn't know why. Each party had come to take Hillside and failed. The village remained free and independent of the outside world. Situated on the border of the Indian Reservation, even the govern-ment left Hillside alone. The white-man town below Hillside did its best to ignore Hillside's latest rendition, dismissed as a hippy commune or cult.

But Eva changed everything.

Hillside survived on high country farming, sheep herding, a waterwheel saw-mill, one wind generator and a water-powered gristmill. Everyone in the village took equal part in their primitive communal life. Hillside lived quietly, peace-fully, self-sustained. The valley folks felt spooked but they let the villagers be. Mutual hands-off lasted for a long, long time, but times were changing.

Eva was delivered Midsummer's Eve, 2021. In that year, the stork brought Hillside a girl child six-weeks-old. Nobody expected it except the oldest witch. Two thousand years of age had made her half-crazy so folks didn't really listen. Eva's unannounced arrival called for a Village Council meet.

Bob Crain, the lead elder and innkeeper had been busy pouring thick, strong stout from the village keg as folks filed in. On such an occasion, the village need-ed strong libations, Bob reckoned, but the apples were just brought in and the cider wasn't fermented yet. The wine was green, too, no brandy yet made. He had no choice but to open last October's brew early. It didn't seem a good omen.

Bob, seeing that all the villagers that agreed to coming had arrived, called the meeting to order with the bang of a rusty horseshoe on the Inn's Ponderosa pine bar. He quickly mopped up the rust flakes with his barkeep's apron. The room settled.

"Would the priestess please proceed," Bob said.

Alice Wood stood. Her long black dress and black crocheted shawl flowed around her like the devil's shadow on the wind. Alice raised her hands Christ-like and chanted the required prayer:

"Oh mighty Queen of Life, Mistress of Magic, Mother of Earth, grants us the wisdom to abide in your ancient ways, keep us pure of heart and guide us in this needful world. By the light of Gaia."

Everyone there, nine elders and forty villagers, said together, "Amen, Ra."

"All right," Bob said. "The Goddess delivered us this here girl-child," Bob pointed to the woman near the big window sitting in a bentwood rocker.

The woman, Millie Beers, had the swaddled babe on her breast.

"We reckoned," Bob went on, "that we'd never see another witch child again. It seemed the Goddess had withdrawn."

"The times are a-changing," ringed the room in a whisper.

Everyone knew the Goddess had fallen into sleep but nobody knew why. Bob heard people say she would wake before the next Age of Great Change. But that was all conjecture; nobody knows the mind of the Goddess.

Dan Wood stood up from his chair and pushed his mustache out of his mouth with a puff. The smell of dark stout cleared a path for his words.

"How do we know this here's a witch child?" He asked. "May be some hippies' dropped her off. Remember when them-there hippies was up here communing?"

"That was forty, no, make that fifty, years ago, Dan," Bob said. "No sir, this is no abandoned child. We got witnesses. Millie and Jack found her in their cabbage patch. It had rained the night before and there weren't no gosh-darn footprints save that of a stork. No sir, that child came by air delivery."

A murmur of agreement went around the crowd. Many eyes turned to Millie Beers. Her husband, Jack, sat near rosy-cheeked with pride. Just the fact that the Beers' cabbage patch was so mature far past planting season proved the Goddess's favor. There was loose magic afoot, that's what folks said.

"We got to report this child," someone yelled. "We ought tell the State, can't afford any bad attention. Magic's weak of late."

Cathleen Sutu, the baker's wife, raised her hand. Cat and her husband, Armo, escaped slavery in 1850. They were the last known witches to receive the Child-Gift. When they escaped, bounty hunters killed the boy. He hadn't mastered magic yet. Armo, out looking for food, got back too late. Cathleen couldn't stop them. Armo made the bounty hunters pay, turned them into snakes. Everyone remembered that tragedy. Those who didn't still recognized it; it was etched in Cathleen's eyes.

"We don't want anything to do with the State," Cathleen said. "Don't you see? We need to raise up this girl proper-like as the Goddess would have it. Colorado would make her into a mush-head like the rest of them."

With that, the debate started. The Council quickly decided that Colorado would not get the girl. They would resister the child born to the Beers since the Beers found her. However, the child was a gift to the whole village. It was the Goddesses' nature, that sort of life blessing.

In the old days when witches were hunted and killed regularly, the Goddess was generous with the Child-Gift. Witch children were as common as frogs and even given to non-witch families. The need of more witches was great and there was no better hidey hole than the enemy's own digs. But things got too hot, too modern, it wasn't safe no more. That's why the coven pushed west and higher up. In the heights, they found safety.

The Indians understood. The Red Man respected Earth magic. In the first years, the coven grew fast. Witches from all over came to survive. But with safety, there came no more Child-Gifts. The world went on without them. The need for magic vanished. Science replaced them, increasing the need to hide, and the blessings the witches seeded into the Earth faded.

Magic could still get you killed, or worse locked up in an asylum, worse still—a forced job with the government.

Folks had long understood there was nothing left to them but to live out their long days until there were no more witches. Some folks thought it was past time for magic's return to the wider world, they been saying it for over a hundred years. Some thought it was time to leave the village. Some wanted to go whole-hog into the world. Bob wasn't convinced spreading thin like that was good for old Mother Earth.

The elders were perplexed. Bob Crain, though eight hundred years alive, was still sharp as a woodmen's ax and just as careful with a swing. Bob had a way of seeing though the cracks. His words had weight.

"It may be," Bob said. "It is time we joined the world on the world's terms. It may well be that the time for magic is over or maybe not. This is hard for us, so set in our ways and not understanding things below. A child can learn fresh, right from the start, and maybe she can teach us how to get along in the valley."

No one could argue that wisdom.

So it was decided by vote that the village would bring up the child and no one would talk of or do magic. The girl would go to school in town and she would learn how to live on the outside. She'll never know that she is a witch, if the village could prevent it. That was the way to protect her, and the village, until such time as they all could leave. There was no point upending anything until they knew the will of the Goddess.

"The child hath cometh to teach us," cried the coven, and old saying from the book of witches.

"There is one more thing," Bob said. "She needs a name. I propose Dawn or Morning Star, to honor our Indian partners. She may well represent the eve of a new era of witch lore. What say ye?"

The coven chanted. Their voices blended and swayed with the Goddess's sleep time voice which forever swam high above within the four winds. They sang Earth songs until one voice cried out, "Eva!"

And so the child was named.

Bob wasn't sure how it would go. He wasn't convinced letting a witch child go among the regular folks was safe, for her or the village. As long as Eva and them bottom-landers didn't know, what harm could it do? Bob poured a tall mug, dipped his finger in it and flicked some brown suds onto the floor. As usual, he'd trust the Goddess to sort it all out. He took a deep swallow and let the foam slather his lips with Earth Mother's bounty.

### Part Two: Eva's Twelfth Birthday

Eva sat on her horse at the trailhead that went down into town. This well-worn path started near the carpenter's shop and overlooked the valley below.

It was Saturday, September 10, and Eva's birthday. She knew it wasn't her real birthday, she knew that by feeling, but that's when everyone celebrated it anyway.

She wore her backpack as if she was going to school. They didn't have internet access in the village. The weather wasn't good in town. It was raining below, but where she sat on her palomino the sun shone warmly. Her wispy blonde hair fluttered around her wire-frame body like cotton chaff floating around the gin.

She couldn't understand why the weather was always better upland. That's not how it was supposed to be, at least not according to Mrs. Thomson, her science teacher.

"What do you think, Spark?" Eva asked her horse. "Should we go to the library?"

Spark picked up his ears and brushed a foreleg across the rocky ground twice—Spark's way of saying no. Eva was torn. She really wanted to go on-line and talk with other weird kids. She had nerd friends in cyberspace but, then again, she didn't want to spend her birthday away from home either. Her Facebook friends cared about her birthday unlike the townie kids who didn't like her at all. Her parents and relatives cared too much.

"Goin' below?" Asked Uncle Buck, leaving his wood shed. As the master carpenter in town, he had made her an elaborate desk and chair for her birthday last year. Grown-ups were always so practical, and boring.

"I don't know," Eva said, "looks wet. Spark could slip and get lamed."

"I wouldn't worry none. That rain won't fall on you, and aside, a young gal needs to have fun on her naming day, I expect. And ol' Spark, why he's as surefooted as a six-legged goat."

Uncle Buck rolled back his shoulders and stuck his thumbs under his arm pits. His off-white home spun cotton shirt was stained there. Eva wondered if he had smelly thumbs.

"I guess so," said Eva, "I'll go, bring back the mail, too."

"There you have it," Uncle Buck said, "'I'll let your folks know."

"Thanks, Uncle Buck."

Eva slapped her reins against her store-bought jeans. She didn't need to nudge her horse. Spark descended the winding path without instructions. Eva felt colder the lower they went. She zipped her L.L. Bean brush coat against the cool mists, but the cold nagged her anyway.

"I'm the only one in the village with store clothes. That's not fair," Eva said.

Spark whinnied in response. Eva understood what Spark said. I was another talent of hers that she couldn't tell anyone about. Who would believe it?

"So, Spark, this is between me and you don't tell them."

Spark hesitated on a switchback and stamped his foot. He hated secrets.

"My parents and the entire town want me to be like any other girl, right? That's not happening, no way. I'm not like townies, not one bit and I don't want to be either. Everyone is such a bitch there. Okay, so I like learning a lot, that's contradictory. I hate it outside! You better not tell anyone. What am I saying? Nobody understands you...or maybe some of them can."

Eva held her tongue. There was no point in getting Spark upset, putting him in between her and everything. Maybe some of them could read horse thoughts. Many of the villagers were odd. They always seemed to be hiding something. If they knew she talked to horses they'd think she was oddest of all. The pair dropped another five hundred feet and the sun emerged. They were just outside town when a new thought came to Eva.

"Spark, are there any others like me up home? We're all related, I'm told."

Spark wasn't talking. Then something else sprang to mind.

"How can I be related to any of them, everyone looks so different? Aunt Cathleen and Uncle Armo are black. All my life everyone says we're all related but they never say how."

Spark tossed his head and shook it. He refused to answer. He didn't want to. Or, was he told not to? Maybe he couldn't. They were on the edge to town anyway. Spark's eyes got dull in town and he acted like any other dumb horse. He even smelled worse.

There was something about town that wasn't right. Or perhaps, there was something odd about her village? Eva's class had a field trip to South Park. The kids and the town there were just like here but more of it. Eva's millstone was grinding with too many new thoughts that didn't make flour. She didn't like it at all.

She felt deep inside things weren't right and nobody would say why—not even Spark. She dismounted, tied Spark to the light post near the edge of the library's parking lot and un-slung her pack. Other kids were getting dropped off by their parents, parents driving pick-up trucks or mini vans. Her folks drove a buckboard wagon.

They gave Eva everything. She was sure that when she turned sixteen they'd find a way to give her a car, too. The problem was, Eva didn't want a car. She liked living close to the Earth. It seemed that everything in the down-lands was all about taking from the planet without returning anything. At least computers and the internet didn't cause such direct harm. Some things were off up home, but down here everything was.

Eva adjusted Spark's saddle as Lisa and Cherry Sharp got out of their mom's SUV. They only live a few blocks down Main Street, for Pete's sake. The SUV left the parking lot and went back the way it had come.

Eva took an intercept course and cut off the Sharp sisters at the library entrance. It wasn't hard to do. They saw her coming, but they were both too roly-poly to do anything about it. They were way fat on fast food unlike thin-quick Eva, whom Pa says gives the wind a run for it's money.

"What's wrong with you guys that you can't walk half a mile?" Eva asked.

"That nasty car exhaust puke winds up on everything."

"Get lost freak," Lisa, the older one, said. "Go back to your crazy survivalist compound and let us normal people alone."

Eva was fixing for an argument but Lisa struck at the heart of what she was feeling and couldn't name until now. She repeated it.

"Normal people."

"That's right," Cherry, the younger sister, chirped like a scared bird. "You people up there aren't normal. Grandma says there's an Indian witch up there, warlocks and demons and everything creepy. Bunch of hippy weirdoes, if you ask me."

Cherry believed the rumors. Nobody ever said it straight up, but the townies were afraid of her and her family. But, Eva believed that 'normal people' were the real monsters. They were the one's ruining everything.

"You're destroying the planet. You crap where you sleep and that's normal?"

"What are you talking about?" Lisa exclaimed. "What a freak! Come on, Cherry."

"You're full of poop," Cherry said over her shoulder. "Poop, poop, poop."

The sisters went inside. Eva didn't follow. A power came over her. She felt it streaming, a blend of anger and sadness. She hated what they said. She hated how they lived. Her thoughts brought a storm. Emotions came upon her all at once but it seemed like slow motion.

She was warned about her period, but this wasn't like that. That was easy.

Against her will, she raised her hands and thrust them at the library. Horse and cow manure from miles around swooped in and streamed into the building. She didn't know how long she stood there, but people covered in filth flooded past her. The Sharp sisters stumbled out covered in poop and crying.

"Who's full of crap now?" Eva remarked.

They were long gone when she lowered her arms. The storm of manure motivated them to run home. Good they need exercise. Eva walked slowly to Spark. She was spent, like working in the field all day at harvest. By the time she mounted Spark and turned for home, a bunch of kids and some grownups had arrived. They scattered when she rode toward them. She patted Spark's neck as they crossed the road.

"What will I tell Mom and Dad?"

Spark usually never answered in town. "I don't think your folks will be mad, they already know," the horse said in plain English.

When she crested the trail onto the flats and into the village, a small group of neighbors waited for her. She trotted toward them. When Uncle Bob reached for her, tears filled her eyes. Spark stopped and knelt. Bob scooped her off and embraced her while the others gathered. Eva cried and cried and cried without knowing why.She did know one thing. She knew she wasn't normal. She cried until Mom came and brought her home.

####

Eva woke up and got ready for school on Monday. But she didn't go. Eva had to dial the phone for Mom to call the school. They had the only one in the village and it was fifty years old. Nobody used it. Mom never touched it. Now, she treated it like a live rattler. She held the phone far from her unhappy face.

"Eva is sick," Mom said, but Eva wasn't.

Eva's perfect attendance record was ruined. Eva didn't care and that was weird, she always cared about school before. Now, she didn't know what to care about. Not after the weekend of her folks explaining the facts of life and not the normal kind: The witch kind.

"Trouble's brewing," Mom said. "We have a meeting at the inn. This here's your first town meeting, so keep your eyes wide and listen."

Eva and her folks took the buckboard to the inn. It wasn't far, only three miles, but they rode anyway. She never thought about it before but why have an inn in a place where nobody ever comes? Uncle Bob kept the place up like he was expecting guests any minute.

She asked Dad. "Ain't for guests, it's for council, village government, a place to congregate and just in case lowlanders come up." He looked at the mountains and pointed up. "This place is our church and refuge," he added. "The congregation's got to meet somewhere."

That put Eva's mind on another path. They didn't raise her in any religion. She knew about religion. Everyone in school went to church. They didn't have a church in the village. She knew they didn't need one, but she never understood why.

Questions radiated from her like fractal geometry. Okay, so they were witches. So was she. That didn't make sense either. She wasn't like them. She had a foot in two worlds. She had too many questions about her identity and history, but she formed her own answers.

She instinctively knew far more than told. Whispers on the wind spoke real words.

They pulled up to the inn. "Remember to hold your teeth," Mom said, "no chattering."

It was eight o'clock in the morning, but Uncle Bob poured everyone strong wine from a cask. The room held about thirty people. She knew them all, but some from the outreaches she only seen in passing. Everybody was hiding from her and each other. She suddenly felt the fear they carried, it weighted on their hearts like an anvil.

Uncle Bob asked for an invocation and Alice Wood, dressed like Halloween, stood up and recited.

Eva instinctively knew the prayer even though she never heard it before. She whispered the ending with everyone else, "Amen, Ra."

Everyone dipped a finger in their red wine and flicked a droplet to the ground before guzzling the rest. Uncle Bob must have been the leader because he ran the meeting. It went on until noon, debating about her like she was an idea and not a person. Everybody had something to say and everybody got to say it but her. Eva had to chew and swallow her unsaid words. It started tasting bitter.

The village had forgotten Eva and her needs. They were more worried about surviving the incident. In the past, everyone agreed, they would have been burned at the stake. Today, exposed by her magic, they feared jail or a psychiatric hospital. Finally, Eva couldn't take it anymore. She slumped deeper into her chair and tried to tune out. But the arguments got heated.

"We ought to stay put," Uncle Buck said, slamming his fist on the bar. " If-in we go down we'll catch hell, it's dangerous."

"We should all slip away, we can hide among them if we scatter." said Aunt Cathleen.

"We can't," Dad said in his angry voice. "They have that electronic magic. They'll track us down like wounded deer and wipe us out."

"We'll make a stand here," Buck said. "Combine our magic. Make a war. They can't kill all the power of Mother Earth!"

"They can and they will," Eva said in a voice so clear and strong it rang through the place like a bell. Someone spoke from her, someone of the same mind, but not from her own mind. Eva floated from her chair. Her hair danced around her face like fire on the wind just like when Alice Wood prayed. Eva could not control herself.

Alice Wood who was the last witch child brought that lived, cried out. "The Goddess awakes!"

"I gave you this child, do what she says," the Goddess said from within Eva. "She is the peace maker."

Eva levitated to the ceiling, eleven feet high. When her head bumped the plaster, the spell broke. She floated down like a feather, swinging back and forth in slow motion until her feet touched the ground. She stood there blinking, her mouth was dry, and her lungs felt like a twister had passed by on its way to her mouth. Everyone was on their feet, waiting. She had no clue what to say.

"I'm hungry," she finally said.

"My Goddess, can't we see," her mother said, "we're so caught up in spinning troubles we forgot our child's needs…and our own."

That was true enough. Eva hadn't had breakfast. It was past noon and no vittles in site. The meeting stopped. Some people went into the kitchen. Others went to see about the horses. Others set out plates and cups. Coffee was poured. Cold chicken, fresh made bread and butter and sweet potato pie was put out. People ate and talked like it was any other day. But Eva knew everyone had an ear bent toward her.

As she chewed she thought and she had an idea that wasn't like anything the others said. She hated the idea because she didn't want things to change. She didn't want to go away, but what she wanted didn't matter. What mattered was her village.

These people could not live in the modern world, of that she was sure. Perhaps they weren't witches. Perhaps the villagers are some kind of human anomaly, special, not magic. Maybe the Goddess herself was the living mind of the Earth and the Earth is alive, aware. It was physics and not outside of nature, just rare.

"This is what I think," Eva said. "First, me and my parents should go to town, and set things right. We could cast a few small spells so the people will believe it was a twister crashing into a truck full of dung. That's what splattered the library, right?"

Murmurs of doubt sounded. Mom had told her they stopped using magic long ago out of fear. But even if they didn't know it, magic came out of them anyway so they might as well admit it. It's what protected the village and why the crops grew where they shouldn't. It was time to use it for real, but carefully and not like Uncle Buck's way of hitting everything like hammering a spike.

"What'll we do about them fearing us?" Charlie Rose, the miller said. "The suspicion is thick. They think we're queer, and queer things make folks unkind."

"That's easy," Eva said. "We face them. We have a working nineteenth century village. Let's open up for tourists. Tell them we're New Age pagans. Anything will distract them. Just don't show them real magic. Not yet."

Light appeared on the faces around her. That solution was simple. But the next part she didn't want to tell. It tore her heart in half to think of it, but it was the answer she felt in her bone marrow. She had to bring magic into the wider world, but not here and not now.

"By the time I'm old enough for university, you guys should have the tourist thing humming. I'm going to study psychics. You will let them know we're okay."

There was much crying and congratulations, and drinking in between. It was the bravest thing anyone had ever offered to do and folks were grateful. The Goddess had sent a prophet and the prophet had accepted her call.

And it came to pass that the village adopted the name of Hillside and became a tourist stop. That required people traveling through the town below and so the town folks didn't mind the income. The townies and villagers slowly became partners.

Eva became a prominent physicist and her theory of planetary consciousness set the world on fire. After her paper's weight sank into human awareness, religions fell like domino's. Planets spoke to each other while Earth and her people listened. Common people learned rudimentary magic. Offers from industry poured in for Eva. To become rich beyond reason, she needed only to say yes. Instead, she cursed the planet killers and went home.

Once home, she wasn't quiet. Eva married a non-witch townie and gave birth to Richard Sharp's witch children. She wrote the best seller, *The Practical Science of Magic*, from home. Magic and the healing of Mother Earth began in Hillside. Healing was done best at home. Homes have special magic. Home is holy.

"Mother Earth herself is our home and the seat of all things holy," Eva wrote.

With Eva's help, magic spread from home to home and Mother Earth began to heal, but this was not the end, it was a beginning and a very difficult one at that. Evil, greedy men fought the changes and the road ahead was rocky but under hard stone lay soft and loving Earth.

**END**

# A CAT'S TALE

I t's clear to me now at the end of my nine lives. As I fade, I understand. Had I known, in the beginning, I would have failed more. I'd have been less of a cat.

When I first met Edward, I was confused. I was a spirit, uncertain of my own nature, trapped inside a young black cat. I was but a kitten, compelled by feline ways.

Many years passed inside that first cat and the eight cats after that, before I had control enough over my cattishness to know myself. It was better that way, not knowing. I didn't understand that only an innocent could receive Edward's heart, or influence it.

Edward was my reason for being. I know that now.

From the start, I projected feelings into him. For what purpose, I did not know then. We were linked spirits and neither of us knew it. On his deathbed, he still didn't know.

It was 1962 when his mother found me lurking about by the front step. It was then I first realized I was sentient, and I panicked in the knowing—knowing I was a cat but not a cat.

I cried out, "Save me madam! Remove this cattishness from me." But all that came out was, "meyoll, meyoll."

She bent down and picked me up with mirth. She was a stout woman, young and strong. From her arms I surveyed the world. Her home was a little post-war shit-box as they called it. That is to say, it was a long, low ranch house and very small indeed.

I looked from her arms and saw a crude road carved out of a farmer's field. There were two other houses down the hill that men were building in this place which was little more than a ruined cow pasture.

Cows mooed from the field across that fresh gravel road and I hissed all my confusion at them. That field was never subsequently developed. Such was my power, which I did not yet understand. When I died the second time, Edward's dad buried me there among the cow bones.

"Now, now, what shall I call you?" she said, holding me up by my cattish armpits. I dangled there not knowing my own name. "Lucky thing them cows or cement trucks didn't squish you like a slug. Lots of slugs around here; mice too. You'll come in handy, lucky for me and lucky for you. That's it! I'll call you Lucky."

Then, she took me in her arms and scratched me behind my ears. It felt nice. It felt right to be cattish—for the moment. Other cattish things came to me then. I felt a pang of hunger in my stomach. I tried to tell her, but all that came out was "meyoll."

"Oh, you're hungry I see. Come inside and have a bite. Meet my son and daughter. No school for them yet."

In a panic, I struggled to be put down, but my cattish stomach would not let me run from the idea of food. What could I do? I was a spirit in a flesh body and that body needed sustenance. This much I knew, though I did not know *how* I knew it.

I was whisked into the ranch house. The aluminum screen door snapped behind us as she carried me in. The bang of the door should have frightened me, but I saw a baby playing on the floor, a little boy in a cloth diaper and little dirty t-shirt. My heart leapt and my body followed. All at once I knew he was for me and I for him, but…how did I know that? I went to him and rubbed my cattish head on his face with joy. He giggled and said, "Kitty, Kitty!"

"Ha! I'm the lucky one," Mother said. "You're just what I need to keep my two year old entertained. Lucky meet Edward."

"Meyoll," I said.

She proceeded into the kitchen, which was only a step away from the living room, and opened a can of tuna fish. The smell of it drove me into the kitchen. How disturbing! I had so little control over my own body!

Cattishness was firmly in control, so I gobbled it up before I knew it. When I came to my right mind again, I realized this family was poor. This shabby little house, although new, was cheap, the clothes they wore were rags, and the beat-to-hell furniture was probably picked from the local dump. That can of tuna was a sacrifice. Would her husband be cross when he got in from work?

I decided right then and there I would fend for myself and not cost them anymore than necessary. I decided to become a mouser that day—as soon as I was less of a kitten. I dedicated myself to be the little boy's best pal as further repayment.

I had found an awareness of my place in life, although I did not understand exactly what my role was. The cattishness in me ruled my body, usurped my mind, but one thing was clear, I was for that boy Edward and he was for me. Somehow, behind it all, I knew he was my charge. Call it instinct, not cattish instinct, mind you, but an inner knowing.

Over the years of his youth, I taught him humanity such as kindness to animals and others, to love in small ways. I would comfort him when he was spanked, or sick, or failed his test. I curled at his feet when he drew pictures or read books or watched TV. When he became complacent, I scratched him until he went outside to play. Outside, I'd follow him cattishly. Outside, I would warn him when the mean boy came around.

Edward was deathly afraid of that bully.

Once, when Edward was eleven, I spied the mean boy, Gene, hitting him under the big oak across the street. I quickly climbed the tree and fell upon Gene with raking claws. The bully eventually grabbed me and dashed me to the ground. Edward, inspired, attacked him with doggish courage and Gene withdrew. Together we defeated the enemy.

From that day onward, Gene would pitch rocks at me and later, shoot at me with his bow and arrows, but by that time I had grown so cat clever he could never get close enough to cause me harm.

Edward grew into a confident teenager. And that was good; for I became so cattish I was no longer of any help to him. We had the same problem. Edward was distracted with females, as was I. I was the biggest tomcat within half a mile, and as such, always fending off challengers. My ears were nicked, I had scars across my face, and I had ripped out a nail in a fight with a bobcat! Cats and dogs gave way wherever I roamed after that, but, in my pride, I forgot to look after Edward.

Perhaps that is why I died that first time.

I was in the house that day licking my paws and dressing my most recent wound, a gouge behind my ear where a hound dog had bitten me not long before. Edward came to me. He was seventeen and was in need of comfort.

"Lucky," he said, "This girl broke my heart!" he shoved a photograph toward me where I lay. "I don't know if I should shit or spit!"

I was in no mood. The battle was still upon me and my cattishness would not let me think straight. He reached for me, soothingly, and I lashed out. I slashed his hand with a claw.

"God dang cat!" He leapt back. "What's your problem?"

He swatted at me the way Mom did when I jumped on the kitchen table. I stood and hissed, raised the hair on my back. War was upon me again. I did not know what I was doing.

"Great, when I need you, you turn on me. Just like Kathy! Screw you!"

Edward came at me. I tried to run for the cat door but he kicked me viciously on my way out. The blow knocked me through the little flap and over the stoop's edge. I bounced off all three concrete steps on my way to the lawn.

I was badly hurt. At fifteen years old, a cat is practically ancient. My reflexes had failed me or I would have not been so bad off. Such was the blow that it knocked the cattishness right out of me. I lay there panting and thinking—and dying.

Then I remembered why I had come. I had come for Edward and I had failed him in his need. I began to cry in my cattish way. I cried for Edward's pain, I cried for Mom and Dad left to raise two children without a cat. I cried for all of them until a realization bathed me in light. I could not die here! Edward would never forgive himself! But my hip was broken! My guts were bleeding inside of me.

"Edward!" Mom called. "Go see what that fool cat is whining about."

"I'm busy Mom!"

"I'll give you busy! He's your cat."

"All right, soon as I hang up the phone."

Funny how not cat-like I was in dying. But, one last time, I summoned my cattishness. There was a vent hole thought the foundation wall near the stoop. I had long ago pushed the grate out. With my front paws I dragged myself to the hole and crawled through.

"Mom, he's gone, ran off someplace. I'm going over Kathy's."

I heard his footsteps. His car's motor started. The gravel of the driveway crackled, then the chirp of tires on pavement. He was gone. This would not do. They would smell me rotting, so I crawled in the mud until I was well away from the vent hole, and there I passed.

And so my first life ended and I returned in another cat and another. I was always black and they always named me Lucky—all nine of me. But, my luck has now run out.

Edward, seventy-eight years old, died a week ago. All during his cancer treatments I laid in his lap. I did all I could to absorb his sickness to no avail. I got sick, too. I died full of cancer at the foot of his bed just after they took his body away.

Now, I am a spirit again floating free. The light calls me but I cannot go. I will not go. What of Edward's grandson? Who will watch over him with me and Edward gone? Edward's son had been killed in war and Edward, such a good man, fought to prevent wars since. It had been his life's work and passion.

Edward had fought the good fight. Who will teach his grandson kindness in this bitter world?

As I hover over Edward's funeral service, the Light above grows stronger, pulling me. I can't resist it much longer. How can I rest in peace knowing Edward the Third is alone? I am a failure in my duty to him. I must stay!

But look, the family is leaving the parlor. The light pulls me so strongly. I am higher now. I know if I don't let go, I will cease to exist as a spirit.

But wait—there is a white cat on the stoop. It follows the little boy. Grandmother grabs him up. As I fade into blackness I hear her say, "Lucky for us you came along, little Edward's going to need a pal."

I let go and all became light.

**END**

# KEEP AN EYE ON THE PRESIDENT

It started about a year after President Bill Bush was elected; the first independent president ever, even if his grandfather was George W. People figured he was something new. Yeah right. I never paid much attention to politics, I had my own problems, but even I knew it was all a bunch of bullshit.

So anyway, I heard a knock on my door one day. In the peephole I saw the fucking Blues Brothers! Two guys, a fat one and a skinny one. They were standing there in black suits, dark sunglasses and black hats. I was thinking: Oh shit that's all I need is the god damn Jehovah Witnesses. The Witnesses were the state church's strong arm department. Since Homeland Security morphed into the thought police, I had to lay low. Any kinky, bisexual, pagan girl had too. The last thing I needed was Bible thumpers that break fingers at my door. I get enough religion shoved up my ass on TV. I didn't need any lube, thanks.

"Open up, CIA," they said.

"Fuck you," I yelled. "I am not buying it. I'm calling the cops."

"Look behind me," the fat one says.

I saw two regulars standing back a ways. So like an asshole, I opened the door. I had them come in and sit on the sofa; I pulled a kitchen chair over and sat down. Thank Goddess I keep my stash stashed good. With them inside my little efficiency was bulging like four fingers of weed in a two finger bag.

"We been watching you carefully Shelly," Fatso says, "watching a long time."

"Why," I said, "I ain't doing anything wrong."

"Don't give me that shit," he says. "We know about you; what you've been up to. If the church finds out you're fertilizer."

I was freaking out, but I clammed up. He kept talking.

"Cooperate and we'll prevent state-church from hearing about your escapades, we can protect you, give you a job."

I looked at him like he had three heads and I asked, "What the fuck?"

He says, "Because your great, great grandfather was Bill Clinton. We have a duty and a responsibility to watch and protect the families of ex-presidents including his illegitimate children's line, people like you." He didn't look any too happy about it. The skinny one just sat there with a huge bulge in his pocket.

I couldn't resist. I looked at Skinny and said, "Is that a harmonica in your pocket or are you just glad to see me?" He didn't flinch, what a tight ass. I guess he never seen the Blues Brothers movie. It's a classic.

"Ok I'm listening," I tell Fatty. So Mr. Blues lays it all out. They want me to work for Bill Bush; a receptionist job, go figure, so they can protect me. I had to bite my lip to keep from falling out. He went on about protecting the good name of the Presidency and how I got to keep shit secret. Yeah right, I was thinking. Somehow I knew there was more to it than that; never trust the government.

I don't want to tell my whole life story, but because I am distantly related to a dead President I was someone special. That was Fatty's main point. I figured jobs were hard to find. I could use the work. The economy was in the shitter. But, because I'm pretty hot for thirty, I always find work. I didn't need them. That not so 'secret' secret the CIA had on me, to convince me I should take the job, was a problem. They could've fucked with me real bad.

I didn't care what people thought of me, lots of people don't accept the church and just do what they want. But with the rightists in power, a freedom loving girl having fun could get herself killed or jailed, same shit. People killed for gas and food for Christ's sake; there was a lot of hate and desperation out there. I took the job.

I soon found out the real reason they wanted me. Not to protect the sanctity of dead Presidents or me. Turns out, the current President was crazy over kinky sex. My specialty, I was a shoe in. Ok so I sucked the President's dick for a living, a girl could do a lot worse. I think Bill especially liked it because I'm related to the Clintons. Hillary must be rolling in her grave. If she only knew about Bill's other family... anyway.

I ain't playing; this was serious shit.

So I go to work. For like six months, it's cool. My desk was just outside the Oval Office door. It was a real nice fancy red stained wooden desk, all inlays in it and junk. I had a bank of phones, some paper and the holy rolodex: he didn't trust computers. I actual had to work, I kept Bill's appointments straight, screened his calls, spent some time under the desk. It was ok; he had a nice pecker and no diseases.

One day Tom Dexter, a big honcho from the CIA, stops in and calls me over. I saw Dex all the time. He was one of the regulars. The President was out that day. I was thinking, oh great he wants a blow job too. I'm famous for it, what can I say? But no, instead he says, "Shelly I must have a talk with you. I have a new project for you."

"Project," I say, "I'm doing my job."

He says all snap-ish, "I'll tell you what your job is, get me? We brought you in because of your special ...ah...capabilities to be sure, but we have a problem."

I looked at Tom thinking how can this guy have a problem? And, what's this we shit, he's the most powerful man in the world; he controls the super secret CIA. Even the dammed Pentagon kisses his ass. If you asked me then I'd say Bill Bush wasn't shit. This guy and his cronies were the real powers here; regular puppeteers. I'm no fool. And he's got a problem? So I look him over, well if I have to blow him, at least he's good looking. Tall handsome guy in the classical way, a little round in the gut but he was over fifty.

I gave him a sexy smile and say smooth like, "So, what can I do for you Tom?"

"It's not like that," he says. "We have a national security problem and you will help us."

"How do you mean?" I say.

He snaps out of nowhere, "Asshole! Don't you watch the fucking news?"

Of course not, I'm not stupid, it's all propaganda anyway. I thought, man this guy is wound up like a pimp on crack. "No, I don't," I tell him, "But I'm listening."

So long story short, the Iran invasion is going bad. The oil is running out and everyone knows it. The terrorist from Russia have nukes and they have Kuwait hostage with a nuke they smuggled in. Meantime, the Chinese are getting ready to march a huge army toward the oil fields. Our forces are tapped out. Everyone is running for the oil, only we got no steam left. The Saudi's are scared shitless begging for the U.S. to help and our army's a joke. No money, only a smitten of troops left, but we got the nukes. The President says he's going to blow up the Russian rebels first, then lay nukes on the Chinese. There's more to it than that, but you get the drift. Things were fucked up for real.

So Tom tells me, "Look this is serious. He's getting stranger. There's a fair chance his actions or words will touch off a nuclear holocaust. Every time things start to improve, he pulls some bone head move and inflames the situation. It looks to the world's eyes and mine, that he is single-handedly instigating world war three."

"Yeah," I said, "I notice it too. He's getting really weird all right, secretive as a hermit. He hardly ever has me under the desk anymore."

So Tom says, "You have to spend more time...ah...under the desk, make an effort. I need to know what he is doing in there; who he's talking to on the phone when I can't get my phone tap working. Why don't my bugs work?" Dex looked dismayed.

I never saw him like this before. He's a cool cucumber. "This is some serious shit," I say quietly, "Ok, I'll help."

But, he just kept talking like he didn't hear me. "Things are serious, Shelly. Over the next few days we'll setup fire control, by his request, right here in the outer office." Dex waves at my foyer. " If that bastard wants a nuclear incident, he'll make sure it happens."

"Well," I tell him, "there's lots of room. This foyer's bigger than my apartment."

"Shut up!" Tom barked. He leaned in, lowered his voice. "Look...if you talk, you die, understand?" I nodded a yes. He went on. "If this gets out of hand we'll take him down. I don't mean kill him, just arrest him for treason, arrest is possible under the law. If he's insane we'll send him to hospital. Whatever happens, he must not continue this course. Oil or not, we don't want this war."

I was sort of shocked. Dex backed off of my desk. I almost shit my chair. Holy shit, I was thinking. This is some serous shit! They always want more war and this a-hole is trying to avoid one.

"Ok, I'm in."

So I cozy up to Bill real good and did extra duty. First class blow jobs. I made like I wanted to be his girl for real, not just a depository for his tensions. He warmed up to me pretty fast. The smartest men are dumb shits when it comes to a pussy. The awkwardness of the first six months faded faster than knock-off Levi's. Next thing I know, I'm in his office all the time, sitting on his lap while he talks shit with all kinds of big-wigs. I feed Dex everything. But Tom just gets more depressed. Nothing he can use. Old Bill is a pretty slick pickle.

I tell Dex, once in a while Bill makes me leave; he'd look at his watch and get fidgety, not like Bill at all. He was one cool cucumber. So Dex tells me, "Next time he asks you to leave, insist that you stay."

"How am I going to do that?" I say. "I'm a snake charmer, I don't do hypnotism."

"Find a way," Tom says, "or all of us will be out of a job…permanently."

Things got really strange near the end. In my foyer they had a whole military setup. There were guys all over the place with card tables and laptops; cables and phones everywhere. Generals were in and out buzzing like vibrators on steroids. Everyone running all over like it's the end of the world. And me, I was sitting there doing my nails and answering the phones.

Bill was ragged out like the fucking grim reaper. His eyes had black circles, his face got thin and pale like he was dying a little more every day. He had this insane look in his eyes. People would talk to him and he wouldn't answer or he'd babble about the apocalypse. Bill acted like a strung out street preacher junkie. The crap spilling out of his mouth sounded more like a milk-crate profit than a politician. Even so, he still liked getting his knob job; typical clergy.

So, I was in his office just finishing up and he says, "Shelly, get lost. I have a private call due. I need to be alone."

This was my chance; he was in a good mood, really mellow after that hummer. So I said, "No way Bill, I want to be with you. Please let me stay? All those men out there leering at me makes me feel so weird. Let me move my desk in here." I gave him the doe eyes, poured it on thick.

He reaches into his desk and pulls out a little .25 auto and puts it right up to my face and says, "Ok Shelly, I could use some company in these trying times, but if you say one word to anyone about what goes on in here, especially my wife, I will blow your brains out. You can't hide from me. I have ways of knowing what's going on, ways you'll soon understand."

I told him OK, but I was thinking: Yeah right, like he really knows what's what. He's in left field picking dandelions. He didn't even have matching socks on. What a trip.

"Not a word," he says, "get under the desk until I tell you to come out."

I could see he was getting off on this idea. We were going for a two-fer I figured.

So, there I was under his desk, but he's not letting me touch him. I was just glad he pulled the gun back. Suddenly, I heard what sounded like a choirs singing church crap, but I can't make out the words .It gets louder and louder. I sense Bill's getting stressed.

"Don't look Shelly, here they come."

All of a sudden, BOOM! A blinding light explodes into the room. Good thing I wasn't looking directly. When my eyes adjusted I saw papers flying around. I heard fucking wind, god damn wind inside the building! I was fucked up here. I started to talk but I got cut off by a booming voice, it saying, "Silence!"

"Oh shit," I whisper, it wasn't Bill's voice.

Next thing I know I see two sets of legs standing near. Looked like men in bright white suits, even the shoes were white. I bit my lip so hard I bled. I was shocked and it takes a lot to shock me.

"Oh mighty herald of God," Bill says, "How may I serve the Angels of the Lord?"

The light backed down some, the music stopped. I saw the angels weren't wearing matched socks. I was thinking: If there's a God he's a sloppy son of a bitch: his guys can't even get their socks straight. The apple does not fall far from the tree.

So the angel says. "Our work here is almost done .You have served us well. You will have the arming computer placed here on your desk, correct?"

I guess Bill motioned a yes.

"No one may prevent what you must do. When the time is right, you will insti-gate the command to launch and thus together we will begin a new world order. You will open the door to God's new world. The honor is yours."

"I understand," Bill says.

I about shit my pantyhose, for real. That guy was better at manipulating Bill than me! I watch these two sets of legs walk away from the desk over to the side wall, the one with no pictures hung on it. I peeked out from under the desk and saw two guys with wings walking into a light on the wall. It looked like the eye of a hurricane paint-ed there only it moved and shimmered. Then poof, they and the light were gone.

I was pretty freaked out but something did not sit right with me. My guts don't lie. You can't bullshit a bull-shitter. But maybe Bill was right, I thought if these guys could do that maybe they'd hear what I say to Dex. I decided right then to keep my mouth shut.

I moved my desk into the Oval Office and over the next few days the army set up the launch buttons on Bill's laptop. Dex liked my move but I clammed up on him. I lied and said nothing new was happening. This was bad news to Dex, but I got to take care of myself first, I figured.

The world was glued to the TV. Everyone was going nuts. It looked like nukes were the only way. The Chinese ran over the coalition forces and were heading for Saudi Arabia. It looked like they'd take the oil fields unless Bill launched a nuke and fast.

Bill was somber in the last days. The end was in sight. So I said to Bill, "wouldn't it be a hoot if I go down on you while you push the button? Those angels said I was your gift; you can do whatever you want with me, right? Let me be a part of history, K."

Bill smiled like the devil. He seemed like his old perverted self for a hot second. "Sure why not, may as well go out with a bang, eh Shelly?"

He laughed a long time at his own joke. I pretended to laugh, too. I didn't know what I'd do, but I had to be there. So we agreed that I would be under the desk on "D" day. But, two hours later it was time, shit I was freaking out! It was happening too fast!

The music starts playing and I get under the desk. Bill seemed like he was into it so I unzip him and go at it. His laptop was in front of him. I went to town. The light explodes and only one angel appears this time. It's good I close my eyes when I give head because I could see OK when I looked out.

So, the angel says, "It's almost time, get ready Mr. President."

I had Bill on the edge then. The timing would be classic. But, I noticed Bill lowering his hand toward me. That fucker had his .25 on me. He was going to blow me away when he pushed the Button. That really pissed me off. We're all dead anyway. So, I bit his dick really, really hard.

Everything happened all at once. He dropped the gun. I grabbed it and pulled it up. He must have sensed it because he kicked like a maniac and hit my gun arm. I squeezed and the gun goes off, sent a round right through the desk, boom! I killed his laptop.

The angel starts screaming, "You asshole, you dim wit...!"

Bill's feet go on the attack. But I'm not taking that shit, no way, so I put a cap in him. But he's still kicking me, maybe I hit a nerve. So I rolled out from under the desk, but as I do, the .25 goes off. This time I hit the angel between his shoulders; some angel. He falls over dead almost on top of me, green blood everywhere and on me, too. So I stand up and drop the gun while trying to wipe off that slimy, green goop. The light suddenly got brighter.

Dex came running in yelling, "The system crashed! We launched from Earl!"

"Who the fuck is Earl," I yell.

Bill had pushed his chair back and was bleeding buckets from his balls. Dex rushed to Bill. I step back to get the fuck out of the way and tripped over the dead guy. Last thing I saw was Tom's look of astonishment as I fell into the wall.

The blood on me activated the automated rescue system and beamed me directly to a local-space hospital ship; surprise, surprise. So here I am a guest of the Intergalactic Fission Harvester Union.

Those angel assholes set off bombs on organic inhabited planets because of some bio fission reaction shit. They seed planets with life then blow them up to collect some special atoms. I fucked up Captain Buark's renegade plans. He knows he's not supposed to blow up planets with intelligent life on them but he got greedy, the bastard. He saw what was going down on Earth and decided to help things along—illegally. He tried for a quick buck without using his own nukes; cheapskate. So he pushed Bill and got caught; thank you very much.

It turns out the one nuke that was launched got shot down and crashed into the White House with a little help from my new best friends, the Galaxy Ordinance Detection department.

I don't know how they do it. I guess the G.O.D. works in mysterious ways.

You know the rest. I don't know shit about Earth anymore. I'm a hundred thousand light years out on my way to a hero's welcome. Some environmental group on Prime Five thinks I'm the shit. I saved a nice planet they say. What a bunch of dumb asses, nice planet my ass, but they did offered me a job.

Go figure.

What the hell, I could use the work. I told them I'd take the job.

**END**

# THE NATURE OF GOD

Captain Steward scanned the officer's mess, which also doubled as his stateroom. Every inch of this spaceship and every person onboard served multiple purposes, and many crewmembers were well respected by the Captain due to their performance and attitudes. However, his senior Special Project officers, a group of eleven cleric/scientists' seated before him, filled him with disgust. They may have been excellent clerics, some were even decent scientists, but their esotericism interfered with ship's functions. Senior officer clerics were conflicted and as such undesirable crew, but he was stuck with them.

The cabin was cramped, as could be expected on any spaceship, which added to the room's tension. This was no place or time for heated arguments especially a theological debate between religious scholars whom disagreed on everything. The ship was about to drop out of null space within one hundred thousand parsecs of God. Captain Steward needed cooperation and discipline, what he had seated before him were the children of God fighting like two year olds.

His eyes strayed to his book shelf as the debate raged. Having his collection of heretical books, real paper books in plain view, never set well with this group. Every family on board was allowed a few personnel possession and he chose controversial books.

The main library was electronic holding millions of books for anyone's private enjoyment. None of the Representative Religions Crew much liked his public display. Steward visually picked through his shelf of titles. *That one will do nicely, it always gets their attention.* He pulled Nietzsche off the shelf and slammed it hard on the steel table sounding a terrible crash.

Everyone stopped bickering. Rabbi Goldberg, the ships biologist, glared at Steward with wild eyebrows raised and said. "Captain, must you be so crass. This is an important discussion."

"Important? I don't think so," Steward said. "All you people ever do is debate. You think it's your primary duty, but, your foremost responsibility is to this ship.

The debate is over. Stop theorizing for a god damn minute and think. We are about to get the hard facts. No more speculative hokum is required."

Mullah Mohamed Al Alee stood, faced the Captain and said. "How can you speak with such disrespect for Allah, we are about to face him, we must decide how to address him, we must agree on our humble approach. We must not look at him directly."

"The approach is between me and the helm," Steward snapped.

"That's right," Rev. Patterson said, ignoring the Captain, "Things must be agreed upon. We can't just run up next to God and say, hey man how's it going?"

Steward wished he could stuff a rag in Patterson's bloated mouth. How to address the anomaly had nothing to do with the real conversation. It was a tactical problem, crew safely, a flight vector issue. *If he spent less time eating and talking and more time at his navigator's post, we'd have had the approach programmed weeks ago.*

The youngest man at table stood to speak. All eyes were on him. The Catholics back on Earth elected him Pope recently. It was a coup for the Church. The Pope of Earth advocated so the Church would have their top man addressing God. Thought wave generators made communication with Earth routine. Mission Control received progress in real-time. Pope John Paul the $6^{th}$ was widely considered deserving of his title on Earth and ship-side as well. He was the best studied religious scholar aboard Spaceship Seeker. John-Paul's job as sanitation officer gave him leeway and time to study. Ejecting shit into space didn't take much duty time.

As a scholar, the Pope was respected, but not by Captain Steward. Atheist Steward and his like-minded military personnel ran the ship. Only good performance earned respect in Steward's estimation.

Steward shot John Paul and angry look. The Pope stood his place. The Captain had no tolerance for lazy crew with minimal duties. Others worked hard. *John Paul should pitch in at hydroponics, give others a break.*

"Sit down John," Steward said, distain in his voice. "There's no time for a housekeeping report. We have technical work. We need a final approach vector; not cleaner toilets."

Everyone turned to the Pope for his reaction. He was a tall, lanky man of twenty seven years, soft and pale. He spent little time at the gym, but there was power and arrogance in his interactions. His steel-gray laser-eyes burned holes in debates before he opened his mouth. He did not sit. He faced Steward with his face hard and focused.

"You may be Captain, a place no atheist deserves, but I am the spiritual leader on this mission."

Steward sat down wearily, tired of fending off this challenge but, he would not relent. He replied with a hard but quite voice. "Major, need I remind you who the Captain of this ship is. Continue insubordination and you will be watching this anomaly from the brig."

Pandemonium erupted, but not due to Steward's comment. The Pope's more grandiose ideas were not well received. Only John Paul saw himself as the ship's spiritual leader. The debate started anew but now on a different trajectory. Steward grabbed another book and slammed John Locke on the table.

"Jesus Christ," Steward screamed. "Will you people ever grow up?"

Half the room nearly fainted at his profanity, the other half gave him the evil eye; religious terms as curses were strictly taboo on this ship, even for him.

"Now that I have your attention, this is how I'm handling it. As you so called scientists can't think past religious consideration, you will do as I say or go to the brig." The Captain shook a finger at them as if castigating a naughty child. "I should have known better than to ask your opinions on this matter."

The eleven murmured disapproval; they wanted a hand in the process, of course, but they had no choice. They had to obey orders. Marine Securities and the regular Navy crewmen were loyal to the Captain—their survival depended on him. Professional spacemen accept that their preservation relies on discipline and order—this group, less so. Steward continued.

"From what astrophysics tells me the force behind the anomaly is ejecting so much matter that we cannot drop out of the hedge any closer than one hundred K parsecs. If we do, we'll get battered into oblivion. We are safe enough in null space, or in the hedge. But it seems the anomaly..."

"That's God not an anomaly." John Paul said with fire in his voice.

"The anomaly appears to be sucking up Null space ahead of it and it is causing a forceful gravity well at its bow. We can't get close behind and we can't get in front of it. Therefore, we don't dare over shoot it. Light speed is out. If we get too close to the peripheral, we'll be drawn into the black hole."

Many were visibility upset with the idea of God as a black hole but they held their tongues. It was long established that black holes eject as well as suck in matter.

"The best we can do is to drop out from the band well behind it, into real space/time, as to avoid the asteroids and plasma streams of its wake."

Ping, the Buddhist and astrophysics officer, was unaffected by the black hole comment and motioned to speak. He was the most civil cleric on board and would not engage in infighting. He was also an effective scientist. Steward respected his balance.

"Permission to speak granted," Steward said.

"Sir, as you know, I am the 5th generation of scientists to examine this phenomenon. My family has worked on this problem for two hundred and fifty years. We have modified the Unified Theory of Matter many times but we did not anticipate a gravity-well in Null space. It appears that God, for the lack of a better name, eats Null space to create matter."

Steward knew how Ping could ramble and he had heard this all before so he cut him short with a wave of his hand and said. "Ping, please, tell us your latest findings."

"As you know, the edge of Null space, known as the Hedge or Band, the place between our physical space/time and non-space/time is unaffected by God...except in front of him. Behind him, God is disinterested. To obtain good readings, we must get close. The further the distance from God the more matter normalizes. To understand creation, we must get closer than proposed."

Steward inwardly cringed at the way Ping used the God word to describe what Steward saw as an unexplained physics issue; but, at least Ping was rational about it, as any good scientist should be. Ping waited for reactions and comments but no one responded. Steward musing in his own thoughts as well suddenly had an idea and broke this rare silence.

"If we ride the Band at light speed we'll gain on it, then we'll drop into normal space at a safe distance in the less dense matter stream on the edge of the peripheral. Once in real space we'll plot a near approach and thread our way in, get as near as we can, scooping up data as we go."

"Until we enter real space," Ping agreed. "We can't plot a closer approach. It is a risk; much matter is generated. At seventy five P distance, we should avoid collisions long enough to allow the AI to do evasive navigation. Matter is expelled in great chunks and doesn't break up until after one hundred parsecs." Ping rubbed the stubble of his shaved head before going on.

"The plasma stream is wide, but it has gaps. We can drop in right behind and aside God at seventy five and have a good chance of survival. Navigating around larger bodies is less difficult than negotiating asteroid fields. We approach at one quarter sub light. I don't know if God hears prayers, we certainly hear him speak. Pray we don't drop out of the band and into a world."

"The only thing to decide is do we take that risk?" Steward said. "We could depart the hedge right into a matter stream and be incinerated. The question is; go forward, or study it at a safe distance. I don't see any advantage to maximum penetration other than speed of data gathering. We came a long way to do this. You're officers; your families are on board as are three hundred other souls. Do we risk it all to understand this anomaly a little better, a little faster; or do we take what we can get and go home?"

"God," John Paul said steadily, "It is not an anomaly; it is Him, it's our God."

For the first time Steward felt inwardly out of control and fearful, but his face did not show his doubts. Long ago it was decided that major risks would be decided by an officer's vote. Steward's guts were grinding, he knew what they would do and he did not like it. In his mind, the purpose of life was to live, not take risks that could get you killed. *What if this monster really is alive and hungry?*

The Pope stood up and called for a vote, of the twelve, only Steward voted no. It was decided. They would dare to meet God up close. Most left the stateroom quietly, pondering what they were about to do. Others were excited or elated, jabbering to each other. Steward only felt fear.

The last three years held little for him to worry about. Null space it's self was a wonderful matrix material that could be made into anything and there was nothing in Null to impede travel, no solid objects to crash into. With one hundred and eight scientists on board no unsolvable problems ever came up. They would never run out of fuel or supplies. His fear was not just about the risks of real space. *What if this thing is a sentient being and what if it doesn't like intrusions?*

Steward made for the bridge directly after the meeting. As he entered, a few crew members hailed him with, "Hello Patrick," or "what's up Cap." The Captain ran a tight ship but he did not stand on ceremony, the clerics lived for ceremony, he would not. He lived for his ship and crew.

There were only six crewmen on the bridge, a room that held twenty work stations. No need to fully man it as they were holding steady in Null space at two times plus point seven light speed, pacing the object in real space.

"Hey there boys and girls," he responded mimicking his usual easy tone unconvincingly.

"What's wrong Cap," Veronica asked?

Bill added, "You're really stressed Pat, what gives?"

"Everyone is about to find out right now. Bob, activate the ships intercom send out an attention alert... please."

Steward settled uneasily into his command chair and waited while Bob set up the 'all hear' call. He flipped on his microphone. Everyone on board could see and hear the entire bridge now. Monitors lit up all over the ship, Steward felt the hush.

"This is the Captain. Council has decided we will break Null space and attempt to get closer to the anomaly. I want the bridge fully manned, all emergency stations on line. All hands on deck. We will slip into the Hedge in one hour and then into real space/time as soon as ready. All crew take stations; rig for impact. You all know the risks. That is all."

Steward did not blank the ship's bridge monitor system. Everyone had the right to see what was happening. This was why they were all here.

"Holy shit," Bob said, "here we go."

The rest of the bridge stared at Steward with amazement. They knew he was against this.

"Get busy people," he said quietly, "its' show time."

Within twenty minutes the bridge was alive with activity. The normal battle stations crew of twenty one morphed into thirty. Many of the religious faction leaders were on the bridge. Thankfully, many were qualified to man a station. Steward was forced to push some of his favored regular bridge crew out of a chair to make room for faction representatives. Steward and his regulars were not happy about it, but this was pre arranged long ago. Each faction had the right of representation in the final moments.

Steward took the manual controls himself with Bob as back up at the sub command station; Ping manned the science and sensory arrays with Rabbi Goldberg running the bio scans. *I'm glad Ping is up front, I need a level headed man at that station.* Most of the eleven were actually doing something constructive for a change.

The Pope had no technical reason to be on the bridge so he and a few others sat in observation seats behind the activity centers. Steward thought it bitterly funny that John Paul was on deck. There was a lot of crap on the bridge and the sanitation officer may come in handy. If somebody shit himself he'd have the Pope clean it up. He smiled with strained lips at his inner joke but this was no joke; they all could die.

Transition to the Band went smoothly. Sensory data was sketchy as usual in the Hedge, but Ping, along with the Hindu, a mathematics officer, Jay Patel, made the best calculations they could and set up the jump into real space/time.

Ping gave the signal, Steward engaged the drive, and a moment later they were in real time.

Immediately, impact alarms screamed; the impractical crew members jumped with panic. The regulars held their stations. Thought-wave communications did not work in the Band or in Null space so incoming message alarms added to the confusion. A barrage of incoming Earth messages assaulted them.

"Communications shut alarms," Steward barked. "Deal with messages later; if we survive."

Rev. Patterson turned the blaring alarms off. He was probably too distracted to be offended by the Captain's authoritative demeanor now.

Steward was busy dodging huge solid masses and magnetic gas fields. They were still traveling at fifty percent of light speed. It took fearful minutes to slow enough for the AI to get acclimated. Steward did the flying. His hours at the simulator paid well. The plasma stream was nowhere near yet so he threaded the needle.

"The computers keep rebooting," Someone called. "Its trajectory plotting is overloaded."

Everyone held their breath as the Captain struggled to keep them alive, only the regulars calmly worked with him. The others sat petrified, or prayed.

"Computer control's ready Captain," Bob barked out professionally. "Engage," Steward called out. Mohamed just sat there.

"Engage you fucking asshole," Steward exploded. Mohamed pushed the button. Finally, they were safe in the electronic arms of the navigation AI.

The bridge was silent until Bob broke the reverie.

"AI's got our whole word in his hands…he's got the…" Bob sang it under his breath but everyone heard.

"Jesus, Mohamed, if you can't do the job, get the fuck off my bridge," Steward said not bothering to hide his anger. "Helm, hold speed steady. Find us a holding course at seventy five P. Science station see what this plasma is made of, full sensory array. We're not going one meter closer until we know what we're dealing with."

For the next hour, the crew busied itself with data gathering. Every few minutes the ship would make a hard maneuver to avoid some unseen obstacle. After a particularly violet shift something pelted the hull like runaway bell clappers.

"What in the hell was that?" Steward said. It was not a rhetorical question "The AI is supposed to hold a safe course."

Bill responded and moved to the AI station and checked the screens. He reported briskly.

"Sir, the computer is making emergency adjustments. Not all the objects in the stream are solids or gases. The computer is dodging energy flashes as they are detected. Matter is spontaneously forming within them."

"What's AI say about it? How's that possible?"

Ping answered. "Its light-plasma energy transmutation, it's not originating in the matter stream—never heard of anything like this."

Goldberg excitedly called out. "The bursts contain bio-chemical matrixes; they carry a full complement of life stuff. The cabbalists were right. God sheds sparks of goodness and life."

"Can the religious crap Rabbi, I need hard facts, not conjecture," Steward said. "We need to stay alive or no theory is worth a shit. We get hit with an energy bursts, we're holy toast."

"God would never…" the Pope started to say but Steward had no time for it.

"Cut the chatter!"

"We can't dance with plasma forever," Bill said, "sooner or later one of those bolts will hit us. No logic to their pattern."

The Captain noticed a congregation around the helm as he said, "We're going, getting out of here ASAP. Ping, how's the data coming?"

"We need more time Captain, can you give me more time?"

"I can't get data, no fix on God." Goldberg said. "The Torah says, we can only see his shadow, only where He has been."

Many around the room shook their heads in agreement. Steward ignored the idea and checked his positioning screen. They had closed in and were well past seventy five P out and now only forty P from the source. Getting this close seemed impossible, but Steward was encouraged—he wanted more data, but not if it killed them all.

"Helm, can we run up and get next to it? We can't stay here much longer." Steward said.

"No Captain, every time we try to maneuver outbound it turns. All we can do is stay in the stream at forty P or drop back to exit. We accelerate, the object does too. We can't do light speed plus to overtake it, the AI will shut down. No angle to read ahead of it."

"Go light speed" John Paul said from helm station, he had moved to watch navigation close up. "We can overtake God. We must see him."

"No we can't," Steward barked. "We can't slow fast enough once we get along side it. We can't avoid obstacles traveling that fast in real time. Over-shoot, we'll get caught in that gravity well. We must drop back. Helm, ready forward engines."

The ship rocked violently. Steward took the hint. "Abort aft thrusters, prepare to brake!"

"Can't stop now," John Paul said, "we must see God!"

"My ass, we're getting out," Steward said.

"Engine's ready," Helm said.

Before Steward could order braking, the collective of clerics that had gathered around the helm symbolically leaned in together along with the Pope and pushed the light drive activator joy stick.

Suddenly the ship took a hard right and accelerated. The vibration and sudden force knocked anyone standing off their feet. It took Steward a moment to collect himself as he was thrown from his chair. Once he regained his feet he screamed. "Get them out of here!"

The regulars descended on the helm's chair and bodily removed the clerics. Ping sat recording all the sensors could gather while the crew fought to regain control of the ship. The conspirators had set up a three second light speed burst. The ship was back in sub light before anyone knew what happened.

Steward had resumed control within half a minute.

"Vicky, take the helm; brake, brake, brake." Steward cried, "Bob, jump to Null; execute as soon as ready. I want a million parsecs between us and it!"

It took only split moments to get far enough back to jump. A second before the jump, someone yelled, "look at that, holy shit!"

Everyone looked up at the visual monitors. The Pope's maneuver worked. They saw the profile of a gigantic worm, light years long, with a gapping open maul wiggling through the void of Null space; its tail was in real time/space and was the source of the ejection. The trader helmsmen had plotted a hooking course. When light speed engaged, they got a glimpse.

The ship jumped from real time to Null space and safety.

Ping remarked, "Holy shit is correct, apparently what God excretes is creation."

Steward sat in his chair and laughed right out loud. His laughter was more a release of tension than for humor's sake, as they now floated in Null space and were safe. The eleven were flabbergasted. Two were crying and others appeared about too. Ping's face was as green as a jade. The regulars were too relieved and busy to think about what they had just seen. Damage reports were coming in. The ship came first.

John Paul came up to Steward and touched his shoulder. The Captain spun in his chair. John Paul was as white as the bulkhead.

"I'm sorry Captain, I had to see…to see God. I put them up to it. I take responsibility."

"You're a complete asshole, you almost killed us," Steward said, "Light speed in a plasma field is playing chicken with laser beams. It's a fucking miracle we survived."

"More than you know Captain," Ping said reading his monitor. "A plasma beam hit as we jumped. We passed through at giant planetoid in the Hedge as dispersed electrons. Truly, we ought to be dead. The beam saved us. We never encountered anything solid in the Hedge before. It, that thing, saved us."

Steward pounded a finger on at John Paul's chest and said, "Total asshole."

John Paul had withered, even the arrogant fire of his eyes no longer flickered. But he suddenly puffed himself up.

"I may be an asshole as you call it, but I am in good company." John Paul said with venom in his voice. "It seems that all of creation comes from the asshole of God, as you say, and I am near to Him."

"That explains it," Steward said. "Religious leaders are closest to God. Why? It takes an asshole to know another one. Security escort his ass-holiness to the brig."

This time Steward's rancorous laughter was for humors sake. In his mirth, Steward cried out, "Jesus tap-dancing Christ!"

For the first time since leaving Earth no one cast an evil eye at Steward's sacrilege, no one complained. With data secured, and much to study, the Spaceship Seeker made its way back to Earth with many shipboard clerics resigning their vows along the way.

**END**

# THE TRADITIONAL ENDEAVOR

Bill sat in his office overlooking the herd. As usual for this time of year, thousands of cattle were gathered two hundred feet below his office. His back was to his desk which faced the interior. He hummed a popular tune while gazing at the landscape through a floor to ceiling maxi-glass panel wall. He rested his feet upon a well worn raised horizontal pane divider and leaned toward the herd for a better look.

John Eagle, the University's Dean of Students, walked through the open door. Bill saw him reflected in the glass, but heard his footsteps first. John wasn't the stealthiest Indian.

John said to the back of Bill's gray head, "You actually admire the view, don't you?"

John Eagle, like everyone in the city, didn't care to see the world outside. It frightened them and for good reason: outside is deadly. Bill spun his chair around with a smile. John backed up half a step.

"Those mountains and grasslands are natural wonders. I never get tired of it."

John Eagle shivered and said, "I'm glad somebody's monitoring it, and glad it's not me."

John hovered by the door. John didn't want to go near the city's taboo outer shell. People within domed cities generally avoided direct-view observation rooms. John, like most citizens, was only concerned with what went on inside the city's protective sphere. After all, the natural world wasn't safe. Bill loved it anyway.

"It's a pity that more folks don't come and have a look," Bill said. "I have an excellent view here and my door is always open to tribesmen." Bill knew it was a ridicules offer. "There's nothing here to worry about." Bill spun in his chair and kicked the glass as proof. It sounded dully, like thumping a plastawall bulkhead.

"Only crazy white people go near windows." John said it with a good humored laugh. But then his voice turned serious. "Maybe it's you they fear. It is rather spooky up here, and, in fact, you do like it. That's nuts."

"Guilty," Bill said slapping his metal desk with a meaty, rough hand. "I must be crazy; I'm training your unhappy-to-be-here students. Ok, Students are naturally grumpy. Forget that one, but it's not on me."

*Indians hate herd management.*

"Naw," John said with a crooked grin, "It's not that you're crazy, that's a given. I think it's that nasty job your people do down there." John pointed at the ground floor. "However, the fact that you actually like it confirms insanity." John laughed. Then he rubbed his sparse mustache thoughtfully. His mood changed. "Crazy or not you're damn valuable down there."

Of course the Tribal Consul would much rather employ a tribe member in such a key position but no one would take on this traditional endeavor. Part of John's job was to develop someone that would. Bill liked John, they got along just fine, but the red guy was trying his best to replace the white guy.

"That's good to know." Bill said. "That explains why I've not been scalped yet. This does need to get done, right? The Tribe needs the wings and I like the money. So here I am."

"I don't know how you stuck it out so long," John said. "And, it's not just the money, come on now."

Bill felt his perpetual smile widened, he rubbed his chin to try and lesson the effect and said, "Any work is good work, that's my philosophy. And, besides, it's about my workers, your students, not the work. I like having young folks around; keeps me sharp."

"Actually," John said, his tone less serious, "The kids really like you. In spite of the fact you're a short, ugly white guy in a red man's city." Quietly John added. "You do have a way of smoothing over combative students."

John gripped the file he had in his hands a little tighter and took a step closer to the desk. Bill almost shrank back in his chair but backing off wasn't his style. *Here it comes.*

"I have a hard case coming up to see you in a few minutes. One of the Lightfeather boys; His father is a major player in the Tribe, as you know. This kid's not happy about mandatory work details, least of all this educational one." John dropped the file on Bill's desk like a dead scorpion-bug.

Bill whistled and said, "Another Lightfeather; nothing like a challenge. I'll get him on board, don't worry buddy, I'll hog tie him if I have to."

"I hope you can…ah…rope him in," John said with tight lips. "This kid's father is a major supporter of Tribal Traditions and the University's trust fund. Big chief daddy will be awfully beholding if his prodigal son learns the importance of this tradition."

"I'll see what I can do," Bill said evenly, "I'll corral him, don't worry."

"I wish I had your freedom of persuasion. He's damned spoiled; drives faculty to distraction."

"Well this ain't campus," Bill said as he cracked his knuckles. "We can't afford bull-crap. People can get hurt round here. This is a working ranch, not a playground."

"Time for Mr. Lightfeather to enhance his education," John said.

Bill detected glee in John's steps as he backed to the door and left. The law protected students on campus from harsh treatment but here inside the shell wall, Bill was the law and this was no joke. John knew it, too. Bill spun back around and looked out on the plains leaving the file were it was.

Resources gathered from the natural Earth were not needed within the city's environmentally controlled enclosure. Harvesting bovine wings was a traditional endeavor and not required for survival. Bill knew well that this industry was far more important than tradition. But, getting tribal citizens to do this kind of work was nearly impossible. Thus, the Student Work Program was mandatory for all freshmen. Outsiders like Bill were brought in as permanent staff. Citizens considered it below their status, and yet this immensely unpopular work was necessary by directive of Tribal Law, a popular law.

Bill leaned back and locked his hands behind his head, his attention now on the huge herd of winged cattle. "Beautify, just beautify, money in the bank," he said. "That's a whole lot of job security on the hoof."

Each animal had a thick, tough hide, and was covered in a tangled matt of long, thick, black hair. Each animal had two sets of wings on its' back used to fend off the relentless swarms of man-eating insects. Some paleontologist think bugs were why dinosaurs developed feathers early in their evolution. Wings were natural fly swatters and also a much loved delicacy. Wings were always in demand.

As herd manager, Bill oversaw the clipping of wings, release of unharmed harvested animals, and directed the work force of students and regular employees. Gathering wings was especially abhorrent to tribal environmentalist, philosophers and bio students. Bill was a pariah to some tribal social circles, but he enjoyed the job anyway. He lacked respect, but overflowed with anonymity.

The door chime caused Bill to jump. No one ever used it.

"Come in," Bill called out.

A young man scuffled a few feet into the room, his head bowed, and his long, thick, black hair hung down covering most of his face. He was tall and thin but his hunched posture and downward shoulders made him shorter and sad looking.

"Sit, please," Bill said pointing to the chair on the other side of his stainless steel desk. "You're from the biology program, am I right?"

The student sat down without taking his hands out of his pockets.

"Why so grim? This ain't such a bad place."

The young man looked up, pushed his hair back and said, "This is a horrible place."

Bill didn't need a heads-up to know this kid was a University student. His facial expression, uneven hair, and expensive clothing told that story. He had seen that face a thousand times in his thirty years with Herd Management. Bill puffed up his chest and pulled a folded blue plastic cover-all out of his largest desk draw. He tossed it to the student.

"Here, you'll need this, messy job, lots of blood."

The young man's grimace turned to disgust. "I'm not wearing this!"

Bill ignored him and leaned forward in his chair. The student slumped deeper into his seat and his hair flopped back over his eyes. "Look, I know you don't want to be here." Bill said. "But here we are, there's no choice. First things first, let's do the basics, go over your duties."

The student pushed back his hair and glared at Bill.

"What's your name, let's start there." Bill said calmly.

"I'm Lightfeather, Tom Lightfeather," he said his voice nuanced with pride and privilege. Lightfeather pulled himself upright in his chair.

"Ah Mr. Lightfeather," Bill said, "Call me Bill. A little about me first OK, then I will explain what we do here and why."

Lightfeather's slumped posture returned and his hair fell back into his face. "I'm not interested."

"You will be tested on everything I say," Bill said, "Best pay attention. Everything counts as course credit. Listen up and remember what I tell you." Lightfeather fidgeted and scowled. Bill looked right into Tom's dark eyes and said, "I don't play no favorites see, everyone pitches in here, everyone. You're not the first or last Lightfeather to sit in that chair."

Bill grabbed the blood-suit and tossed it into Lightfeather's lap and he let out a low but audible groan. "You ain't going to skate through the Work Program on family name. I trained your father you know."

Tom's eyes widened with revelation and he blurted out. "Hey! That's not fair!"

"I have your attention now, Good. Like I said my name is Bill, just call me Bill. Like it or not, we don't stand on formalities here. This isn't Center City and it's dangerous. I have worked for the Natural Products thirty years so I know what I'm doing, got it?"

Bill pointed to the left wall were a framed certificate hung. "I have a bio degree, too. You will find that what we do here is less about science and a lot more about what my ancestors called…ah…ranching. Our job is simple enough, but the traditional importance of it cannot be understated—."

Tom rolled his eyes condescendingly, his nose wrinkled like an academic snob. Bill thought *I'm losing him already.* So he cut his usual welcoming speech short and spoke abruptly.

"You hate it here, of course, but besides that, you're extremely unhappy. What's on your mind, Tom?"

"It's Mr. Lightfeather."

"I will call you Tom, damn the formalities. If we are going to work together in this dirty, bloody, dangerous environment, we must have mutual trust. Your life depends on it. Let's get that straight right from the start."

Tom clutched and twisted the jumpsuit as if he were ringing John Eagle's neck. "I can't stand it, it's horrible!" Tom cried, spilling emotions. "Cutting wings from live animals! They can't live without their wings, wings keep the swarms off, or they'd all die out there. Anyone outside without a bug suit would die. You're taking away their ability to protect themselves! It's barbaric!"

Tom pointed to the great outside and said, "Look, look what we did to the environment, messing with it. We ruined it for people. We should leave the natural animals out there alone. We did enough damage. Can't you see?"

Bill exhaled thought gritted teeth. "Environmentalist huh; no one's getting

damaged. We don't turn them out unprotected to die. Great Spirits! We don't impact them negatively at all. No animal is killed, ever. They don't feel a god-damn
thing, trust me. After we clip we coat the entire critter with a harmless anti-insect
gel. They roll in the dirt as happy as a jackpot winner. Then a hard crust forms.
They love it. The flies can't touch them. By the time the crust breaks up the wings
have grown back, new and stronger."

Tom pushed the hair from his eyes. He leaned forward in his chair.

*He's interested.*

"I'm not convinced. It's still not fair to them; gathering them up, forcing them
to come here; disrupting their natural lives. We have no right to do that."

"If anyone has the right," Bill said, "historically, it is your people, this city,
your people Tom."

Bill stood up and turned toward the window, he motioned Tom to come over.
Tom hedged over to the window as if he neared a cliff's edge. The brightness and
enormity of the raw outside was no doubt strange to Tom. He looked startled and
fascinated—like most young people did on their first view. But when Tom looked
down on the herd his red skin turned white. Yet, despite fear, Tom could not take
his eyes away. Bill had seen that reaction many times before.

"Aren't they beautiful," Bill said beaming.

"Lovely," Tom answered with reverence.

Thousands of creatures were huddled close together below, the weakest jock-
eying to get nearer the center for better protection. The strongest air currents
were at the center vortex. The animals pressed close to the corral's entry shoot.
A few slipped inside.

"That is odd," Tom said. His color improved. "No interference from the
stronger animals, they let the little ones in first. The herd's wings beat constantly,
en mass, like an orchestra."

"That's right. The youngest herd members are always in the middle of the
throng. They have smaller or immature wings so they are protected by the rest
that way. They collectively generate an air column which forces swarming flies
to amass above, trapped in a torrent."

"It's like…like they make a dense black dust cloud," Tom said.

"Artificial wind keeps most of the flies from descending." Bill said agreeably.
"It ain't dust, it's bugs."

Tom's eyes were wide with curiosity. He pointed a trembling finger skyward
and said, "Look, look up there."

Above the cloud, birds and winged reptiles gracefully dove and strafed feeding on the insects. They watched as one bird got too far into the cloud and was
engulfed by its former prey.

"That's one bird that will never see open air again." Bill said. "After all, it is
the natural way of things."

Tom's environmentalist face suddenly reappeared. He backed away from the
window. "But clipping wings is not so natural IS IT?"

Bill turned to Tom and said evenly, "Nature is a changing thing. It's always
in flux, you know that. There was a time when we could walk free on this Earth.

But, we failed to evolve like they did." Bill trusted a thumb at the window. "Those critters evolved wings to keep the bugs off; just as they've gotten used to the clipping. They need it now. The new wings will be stronger than the old. It ensures their survival."

Bill slapped his hand on the desk. He paused a moment and then shifted into his most sympathetic voice. He put a hand on Tom's shoulder.

"And that crust we give them, well Tom, don't you see it gives them some peace. For them, this is now natural. If we stop clipping these critters, why, they'll eventually lose their lives to the damn insect swarms. Just like all the other large mammals did. What we do here is more necessary for them than it is for us, by far."

"That's a nice speech, but I am not buying it. There's more to it." Tom stepped toward the window and pointed to one of the dozens of rusted herding robots out on the plain and said. "Look at that. Without herding bots they'd never come near this place."

"That's not true, sorry to bust your bubble." Bill said it with a half smile. Burst bubbles were as taboo a subject as it got on the reservation. "Those bots haven't moved in five hundred years. The bovines come here all on their own, and according to their timing, not mine. I have nothing to do with that. Like it or not, we are of their ecosystem now."

"That's just what I'm talking about. They are totally depended on us. I can't see how that's good." Tom said his voice desperate.

"Look now," Bill said rubbing his chin, "your people have always been a part of their ecosystem. It's always been a symbiotic and symbolic relationship. Always the same: It's just evolved, that's all. They've adapted like all survivors do, it's just evolution."

Tom looked exasperated. "That may be so Bill, but we created this situation. It's just…it's just all wrong. We're why so few mammals are around anymore and why insects rule this stupid planet. Even worse, science has found a way to wipe out all the insects. The latest is, they can selectively engineer bug DNA. Fix it so they can't reproduce at all."

"What would you have us do?" Bill said.

"I know we can't bring the world back to the way it was before. The more they do the worse it will be! I don't even know why they sent me down here. I hate all this. The terra-formers will institute the DNA manipulation, I just know it. What's the point? I don't want any part in this." Tom's eyes welled up but he fought off the tears.

"I am sympathetic, Tom, but you know we have a job to do too. And the tribe supports what we do here big time."

Tom only scowled and scuffed the concrete floor with his shoe. Bill needed to draw him in.

"I agree terra forming solutions are the wrong move. I don't think it's a good idea either, I'm with you Tom, yes sir." Bill paused for effect; an empathetic look appeared on his face as he said, "Just look at the history of biological manipulation. Our once teaming planet is now mostly bugs and grass. Remove the flies and what will the birds eat? I am with you on that Tom, let's leave well enough alone."

Tom looked at Bill with respect for the first time and said, "you really mean it?"

Bill smiled crookedly and thought *he's coming along now. Get along little doggie.*

"Of course I do. But on the other hand, look at it this way. At least the herd is protected and at peace. We can make that much right. We can keep the herd healthy and safe. After all, the relationship between them and the reservation is tens of thousands of years old. We owe them critters that much."

"We should respect them," Tom said, "and turn back time for them. Make them independent again, and then leave them alone. Make them free from us! We can do that much I bet. Don't you think we owe them their freedom?"

"It's too late for that." Bill shook his head sadly. "This ecosystem is too well fixed. It may develop further on its' own one way or another in time. But, our days of bio-manipulations are long over. The Earth is on its own now. All we can do is ensuring these bovines survive and hope for the best."

Tom thrust his hands into his pockets, scuffed his shoe and stared at the ground.

"Tom, you know messing with it now, to force things backwards, will only make all this worse. Like you've been saying, bio manipulation is a real bad idea."

"That's just an excuse, it's justification to keep things the same."

"You can believe that if you want," Bill said, "but the reality is the herd is far too valuable and precarious for us to break traditional ties now. The city will never forgo this link to its' past. And besides the rich people, you know the tribal leaders like your dad, that are supporting your education by the way, will never let the terra-formers loose or turn the herds away."

"How do you know that!? If they are paying for all this research and education, why would they not want us to use what we learn to make the outside right?" Tom's chin dropped to his scarecrow chest. "I don't get it."

"I am sure your parents can explain the facts of life better than me," Bill said picking up the blood–suit. "I'm just hired help. But the simple answer is: You know how the whales like to party, have a good time?"

"Yeah, so?"

"What would your Dad's casino be without the customer's favorite food, the delicacy they expect and pay so dearly for? Where would all these people go without hot sauce and Buffalo wings in the house? Wise up kid, without buff-lo wings, the suckers would go to Vegas, you wouldn't have a free education or a family fortune…and I'd be out of a job."

Tom looked up with a knowing light behind his eyes.

"Traditionally, economics always trumps environment." Bill said handing Tom the coveralls.

"I see your point," Tom said as he accepted the coveralls and his reality.

"At-a-boy," Bill said slapping Tom on the back, "now let's go get us some wings."

The two walked out of Bill's office side by side.

**END**

# THE VOICE OF GOD

At three AM Dr. Hillman got out of bed. He could not sleep. A solution came to his mind as he lay there praying and the prompting of all mighty God came and would not wait. He thundered into the kitchen and slapped the light switch. Dr. Weiner's home phone was still pinned to the wall. Hillman dialed.

"Weiner, its Hillman. I need your in-takes in my office nine AM, sharp. I'm interviewing them first. I've got the answer."

Dr. Weiner began his usual whining, but Hillman was too inspired to tolerate it. Hillman held the phone above his head until the siren subsided. *Weiner won't dare stand against me, I'm three hundred and fifty pounds of righteousness. Nobody can stop this herald of God.* Hillman put the phone back to his mouth when he was damn good and ready.

"Look Weiner either cooperate or I'll rifle your files. You don't want that. Give me the atheists first. That Johnson guy, the biochemical nerd, he's coming in, right? Put his chart on top."

Weiner spoke but Hillman didn't listen. Instead, his mind raced. If he could break Johnson, he'd open the faith ceiling and prove his theories once and for all. This phenomenon was no mental illness. *And it's not God, it's the devil. Has to be. Why would God talk to Johnson?*

"Have the charts ready first thing. Never mind why, just do it. Yes, yes I'll take responsibility." Hillman hung up the phone exhilarated. His career was about to hit the stratosphere.

It wasn't disease or mass hysteria, not a mote of evidence for that. There was only one answer: demonic possession. Most so called mental illnesses were, in fact, invasions of the heart. To prove it, he needed a base line. God was on his side. This study group fell into his hands like manna from heaven.

*I'm taking full credit for this discovery, too.*

Hillman had rolled all night. He didn't do well without sleep but, it was worth it. He imagined himself like Jacob wrestling with angels, or was that Job? Last night was good training for a dog-fight with the devil, he thought. His career was about to re-launch like a holy bottle rocket.

Hillman arrived early. He was tired yet energized with visions of the Christian speaking circuit dancing in his head. He lumbered down the outpatient floor's blue pastel corridor suppressing his good mood. As usual nurses and doctors scattered before him like Hebrews fleeing Goliath or was that Pharaoh? Hillman was well known at Newberry Hospital but not for his work, or girth. Hillman's religiosity cleared the halls. Nobody wanted to hear him preach. *They won't depart from me after today.*

Dr. Weiner stood at the nurses' station with the charts. Hillman pulled Weiner to him with an unfriendly traffic-cop wave. Weiner handed Hillman the files with downcast eyes.

"You read the intakes, what have you got?" Hillman asked harshly.

"Typical," Weiner said. "They claim the voice gives them salvation. But, not the Jesus story kind."

"Jesus isn't a story" Hillman said coldly.

Weiner, a small, thin and shriveled man shrank a little more. He ran a tiny hand through his thick gray hair then fingered his Star of David ring before taking a deep breath to go on.

"Well, spit it out already."

"They refused to say what they hear. All were solid citizens…until now. No prior mental health issues. No medication and for the most part, none indicated any definitive religious affiliations on the questionnaires—nothing to hang the god-voice pathology on."

"Schizophrenics always associate the voices with God," Hillman said. "Not this group, good. That's what I need."

Weiner cringed. Schizophrenic self assessments were as varied as snowflakes, was Weiner's position. "We need the APA evaluation team on this. Dozens of new cases every week—this is an epidemic. We need help."

"No, I don't need help," Hillman said. "I've got it figured out. And I know the cure—the word of God."

Weiner's jaw muscles jumped like beetles under a spandex mask. He pointed a finger at the ceiling and opened his mouth but no words came out. Weiner's forehead wrinkles deepened. He shrugged his boney shoulders, turned smartly and walked away.

Hillman stormed off toward his office and heard incoherent cries as he reached the right wing hallway adjacent to his office. Judging by the commotion, he expected a homeless man strapped to a gurney but instead he found two orderlies escorting a babbling businessman dressed in Wall Street attire into the electro-shock studio.

"Bring him to me when you're done."

Not waiting for an answer, Hillman entered his packed waiting room. He walked past the receptionist without seeing her and ordered, "Carla, five minutes. Have Johnson in."

"Yes, Doctor," Carla replied as he slammed his door.

He tossed the charts on his desk. He didn't need to read them.

Instead, he performed his usual rituals. He touched the picture of himself with Ronald Regan, straightened his Rob Johnston Theological Seminary diploma, and realigned the gold cross hung on the wall behind his desk. The cross and diploma were forever off kilter unlike his medical degrees which were more solidly affixed.

"God damn it," he said as he adjusted his wall hangings.

Sitting, he pulled a leather bound Bible from a drawer and placed it next to his "Jesus Saves" pen set. *If the Word of God doesn't cure him, Johnson can't be helped.*

Doctor Johnson knocked. Hillman grunted, "come" and without looking, waved Johnson to sit. Hillman grabbed the patient's chart and flipped to the last page. Disdain filled him as he read "Atheist" on the religious affiliation line. He expected it. He slapped the chart down and assessed his quarry. Johnson's irritation looked back.

Johnson was unremarkable: short, slight, balding; thick framed glasses colored like his mouse-brown handlebar mustache—typical academic liar. Johnson removed his glasses and squinted at Hillman. Hillman saw him as that smart assed kid he beat up in High School. Hillman cracked his knuckles. The patient didn't flinch.

"So then, Mr. Johnson, I need your background, a few questions first."

"What's the matter, can't you read a chart Doctor? Or I should say Mr. Ah yes…Mr. Hillman. I see by your wall hangers you're a theologian."

Uncharacteristic sarcasm, Hillman thought as he turned and looked at his divinity school placard. It was askew again. "That's Doctor Hillman to you, I'm a psychiatrist as well."

"Well, then, that's Doctor Johnson to you, Bucko," Johnson said twisting his mustache revealing a toothy smile. "I don't recognize divinity degrees. You have a real doctorate?"

Hillman felt his face flush. Remembering his professionalism, he took a deep breath and resolved to ignore Johnson's remarks. Typical lost cause. *Don't let that atheist nut-bag get to you. The devil is tricky.* He needed more information. Hillman proceeded.

"Fine…Doctor…I have questions. Before prescribing, I need input," He lied.

"I am a biochemical medical researcher," Johnson said, putting his glasses on. "I probably designed whatever crap you're prescribing. I make better stuff in my kitchen. I don't need medication. My brain's chemistry is just fine."

Anger took Hillman. Felt his eyes pop wide. His lower lip quivered. He exploded up from his chair and slammed his fist on the desk. Bully tactics came naturally and always worked.

"Now see here, I will not tolerate this disrespect, not from the likes of you…you…you…Heathen!"

Hillman leaned forward on knuckled fists; his shadow covered the wide mahogany desk. He expected Johnson to cower, but, he did not. His eyes twinkled with amusement. Hillman thrust his face closer to Johnson's toothy grin.

"Oh, so that's the rub," Johnson said flicking the cross in on Hillman's necktie with a finger, "You believe that junk. Sorry, Doctor. Jesus won't save you. But, I know who will."

"I'll crush you, you weasel," Hillman said. "How dare you mock my God?"

Spit ran down Hillmans chin and splashed on the desk blotter. Johnson didn't back away. Instead, he adjusted his glasses and met Hillman eye-to-eye.

"Why are you here?" Hillman said. "If you're so god damn smart switch chairs."

"No thanks. You ruined the padding," Johnson said. "But, I'll answer. I'm here to set you straight. Leave those people in the lobby alone. You need help, not them. Hear me out and you'll save yourself."

"I'm saved," Hillman said regaining his chair, "I don't need your help. Those people do."

Hillman's skin prickled. He felt a sudden fear, the buttons of his soft leather chair felt like Christ's thorny crown. *The Devil is here!* He pointed at the exit. "Get out, in the name of Jesus, Satan get behind me!"

Hillman felt like he was back in control. *That little man can't best me, this is my turf, demon possessed or not.* He began to stand, but Johnson waved him to sit. Hillman complied against his own will. Despite his resolve, Hillman's body would not go where he wanted it to.

"That's better," said Johnson pushing his glasses onto his forehead. He looked at his watch. "I'm here to share what the voices tell people. It's important. You need to pay attention."

"What imagined voices say is inconsequential," Hillman hissed between clenched teeth. "This isn't psychotic neurosis, not imagination; it's the Devil's work."

"I beg to differ," Johnson said. "The voice tells everyone exactly the same thing, most unlike neurosis, and it speaks to many more than reported. Last I checked Beelzebub doesn't help anyone. Sure you don't want to hear the message?"

"Not from Satan," Hillman said struggling to move but he could not. "You're him."

"Me Satan, that's rich. No, actually, you 're more like him, and everyone like you is, too," Johnson said. "Of course Beelzebub isn't real. That's part of the message. If you'll shut up, I'll tell you what God says." Johnson laughed like a chicken cackling but he stopped suddenly and continued. "For lack of a better word, God will do."

Johnson clucked for a few seconds more wiping tears from his eyes while checking his watch. Hillman's agitation increased with every cluck. His immobility and fury deepened until he could not talk at all.

"You look like a snapshot of Jerry Farwell on Hell's roller coaster. Finally, a captive audience," Johnson said. "I wish my students were as accommodating. Anyway, here's the dope. Everything you know about religion, forget it. It's crap. It's not like that. But, this is true. Peaceful minds hear the voice. However, it's an alien recording, not god. Nothing personnel: It's just instructions on how to escape before the comet hits. Wherever two or three of us chosen get together, at the appointed time, it opens a quantum escape tunnel."

Johnson put both feet on Hillman's desk. Hillman felt his eyes bulging in testimony of his rage.

"It's only for, you know, 'They that have ears to hear.' It's pointless to tell people like you. Sheepherders aren't welcome. But, as a decent human being, thought I'd try anyway. I see you don't believe. That's too bad. Belief in human love and coexistence, not made-up gods, is the key thing."

Johnson swung his feet to the floor, stood, and buttoned his blazer. "Follow-up on your patients, you'll find they've mostly…you'll see."

Johnson looked at his watch. "Stop medicating people. They need clear minds." Johnson leaned over the desk and flicked Hillman's ear. "It's not too late, hear me?"

Hillman growled from his guts.

"Bullies always get it wrong. Oh, they say nice things, 'the meek shall inherit the earth,' 'for the people by the people,' nice words good for manipulating the people who live by those words. Here's a new saying: The meek shall escape the comet."

Johnson paced a few times twisting his mustache until his alarm watch sounded. "Hypocrisy is damning."

Johnson turned and walked toward the door. Hillman felt his eyes going wilder, his lower lip quivered again. He regained his mobility and stood. All at once Hillman spastically grabbed up his Bible intending to hurl it at Johnson but his arm disobeyed. The book hit the desk.

"You're wrong, you bastard! You're not going to Heaven. You're going straight to hell!"

Johnson halted Hillman with a raised hand, and said. "Well, no Doctor, hell is coming here. But unless you…what's the word? Ah…Repent…you'll see it firsthand." Johnson took the door handle and spoke over his shoulder. "Spread the word Doctor Hillman, redeem yourself."

As Johnson crossed the threshold, Hillman's full mobility returned. He sprung for the door like a rocket–propelled serpent but the door closed in his face.

"God damn it!" Hillman screamed punching the door. "Nobody does that to me!"

Violently jerking the door open, Hillman called, "Carla, stop that man!" But she was not there. No one was there. Earl Johnson, Carla, and all the patients were gone. Hillman stormed Carla's reception desk. She always left a note when she left the office. Hillman snapped up the paper and read.

I've gone to the rapture. Goodbye, Dr. Hillman and good luck, Carla.


**END**

# THE REAL STAR WARS

As the last American President, I George G. Brush the 4th was asked to explain the events of the later days. Mr. Lee told me to skip the bullshit and focus on the facts. With all due respect for Mr. Lee, I'll explain it the way I see it. Details matter. What's history if it's not a plaster cast of bullshit? Conservatives still think everything I do is crap anyway. The war's over, they need to get over it.

Let me back up and start at the beginning.

First, I never wanted to be the President. The Independent Party thrust it on me. This wasn't my fault. My great grandfather and name sake was George Wilbert Brush. I couldn't imagine in my wildest nightmares I'd get his job one day. Not after what Old George did. He created the trends that made America a third world nation. Grandpa, I call him Grandpa, set up and accelerated the circumstances that ensured China would become the last world power—if you can call it that.

The harder the Conservatives of both parties worked at financial hegemony, the more it slipped away. Short sighted greed was not a good policy. China was all about the long view. Who knew? Reagan's fantasy failed, but Old George got unbelievably richer by pushing fake economics, he had to know.

I guess it worked out for him, me—not so much.

I'm of the Brush family but, Grandpa shot his money in the foot. His wealth bled off into multinationals and that means China. Worse, his Middle East policy persisted long after he died. He did more than shoot himself in the foot; he chopped off America's financial legs.

And, I wouldn't shut up about it. I became a famous Internet detractor bashing Conservatives generally and Grandpa continuously.

People liked my rants. I got a lot of hits.

That's how the Freedom Party conned me into it. America was pissed and so was I. It didn't take much to convince me. All Gramps gave me were his debts, left me and America holding the bag; a bag of shit that was on fire. Contrary to popular belief, shit isn't good fertilizer.

The end started with the election, or really my Independent Party gig before that. They spun me into the new Abby Hoffman. Ok, I have the gift of gab. I got people excited, not hard to do. I needed work so I hired on as a talking head. People needed change, not Oboner change which was just an extension of Grandpa's policies. The Party promised to be the hinge of change and I was their squeaky hinge pin.

Back then half the country was blacked out. Oil fired, and most coal energy plants, were shut down; permanently. Nuke plants were old and mostly off line. What oil we had the military took for defense. Even coal was glommed up for the war machine. Government horded and people suffered. Shit was fucked up.

By 2060 the Yukon was Swiss cheese. No help there. Some mass communication was still in place. Satellites don't use oil. Wind mills, solar panels and water wheels sprang up like fungus in cow shit. Everybody distilled ethanol. American ingenuity took over. Nobody trusted the Feds. The Government refit a handful of nuclear power plants but it was too little too late. America was sinking into an unindustrialized mud hole and I wallowed in it like everyone else.

I'm sure our new agricultural society will work out better.

And me, I was on the air. Most communities still had power enough for public TV a few hours a day. People gathered to hear the news. I told them to prepare for the dark ages. The public trusted me.

Of course, the Feds told them the opposite. The Feds shit out war-talk and spouted lies about new public programs—all smoke and mirrors, lies, distractions. I called them out.

The rats were jumping ship or more so, the rats with private sailing vessels or secret fuel reserves left by sea while the rest of us floundered. When the riots started, there weren't any bankers left to hang.

Whoever had the means bugged out, but not all of the big men split. That's how I got the Star-Wars system. True believers stayed behind for the immediate Rapture that never came. Repubnut leaders believed their own lies, naturally, but so did the liberals.

We Independents started the exodus backlash in 2061, a hard, wide swing to the left of reality. The write-in movement took on a life of its own. I was elected four years ago and I wasn't on the ballot. Everyone on the ticket was either a Republican or a Democrat which amounted to the same thing. Everyone in politics was bought and paid for, as usual, everyone except me.

People were tired of it. They didn't buy the end-of-the-world bullshit; the second coming was all media talked about. Given the choice, bullshit or reality, they stuck with me. See what telling the truth gets you? Beat people in the head with the Bible long enough and they'll run like hell.

I was a shoe-in.

Smoke screens stopped working when the oil ran out. It took a lot of money to buy oil smoke. And mirrors only reflect what is. I was a mirror. So they elected me knowing I didn't know shit about running a country. I told them that too, I wasn't a bullshitter. That's why the voters hired me.

Not long after the 2062 election my girlfriend and I moved in. We took the underground shelter under the White House's backyard. I made Erma my VP. OK, she was really just my stenographer. I didn't use the Oval Office much. It wasn't smart, easy target.

One afternoon, when things were calm, Erma and I, her idea really, decided to fuck in the Oval Office. We had nothing better to do. That's how the ageing Brush family lawyer, James West, got to me. He wouldn't have found me otherwise. I had fired the White House staff so Erma, a few civilians, and the local militiamen—who guarded me half assed—were it.

Anyone could get in.

I would have stopped James had I known he was on the grounds, but the guys were drunk and nobody called me. James would have found me anyway. All access took was a bottle of eighty proofed bribe. I guess the meeting was unavoidable.

Erma and I were about to go at it. I had one hand up her skirt, the other cupping a tit when James shuffled in. He must have stood there a while getting an eye full. When I looked up he gave me an approving smile. Something I wouldn't have expected from a zealot.

"Mr. President," he said with a look of concern on his wrinkled brow, "I have an urgent matter to discuss with you."

"You're going to tell me what a family embarrassment I am again, right James? And don't call me Mr. President, George will do just fine. I hate that."

Erma pulled away and fixed her clothes. "Ya want I should go then George?"

"Sure, but don't go far." I said, "This won't take long."

I gave James a sidelong glance, as I patted Erma's ass. He shot back a condescending look. I had not seen him in years, not since college. It wasn't a happy meeting then. I wasn't happy to see him that day either. The last time we talked he told me I was disowned. With gritted teeth we sat at my desk eyeing each other suspiciously, same as back then.

"So, what brings you here," I pulled up a bottle of bourbon. "Still drink bourbon?"

I didn't wait for an answer and poured two glasses. He gulped his down with one pull. I poured him another, and I took a sip. I wasn't much of a drinker, yet.

"Well Mr. Pres...er...Mr. Brush..." he began with pained voice. I cut him off.

"George, everyone calls me George."

"George...yes George then. So, I am here to deliver to you something important. It was left by your great, great grandfather."

"I'm out of the will, Gramps hated my guts. Why bother? Money has no value."

"It's not about money," he said.

This took me aback; everything was about money in the Brush family. "Go on," I said.

He pulled out a large envelop stuffed with papers and also a handful of computer data cards. He placed them on my desk and slid the pile across to me. He took a deep pull from his drink.

"This pains me greatly...err...George. I have tremendous respect for this office. To find you here…well…that was the last thing I expected. Your forbearer left instructions that, should a Brush find his way into the White House again, this information would be passed on."

He poured another and slammed it.

"It's access to a weapon of mass destruction. I was not going to bother, it seems to me things are hopeless. Only a war president can stop the Chinese and you are not that, more some kind of a hippie than a president, but I am honor bound."

"What honor," I said after I stopped laughing, "You and my family drove this Nation into the ground. Where's the honor in that." I used the harshest voice I could muster. Not my usual way of communicating. I wasn't convincing. "War economy mentality got us into this mess." I said. Damn if I didn't act presidential that day. "Grandpa's wars bankrupted us, gutted our resources. Even if I had an army, using it would only make things worse. Your business-as-usual bullshit killed us."

His face wasn't red from alcohol. He could suck down an entire bottle without blinking. In the words of my alcoholic dead father, George the third; 'Neo-cons sure can drink.' James was pissed. Good.

"Be that as it may, I have brought you a resource, a weapon that may well defeat China. It will remove their will for war, detour them from their impending Middle East conquest. Are you interested or not? Do you have the Brush family's balls? Will you do what's right; what's good for our Country?"

This guy didn't have a clue what was right or wrong. Fighting over the last few drops of oil wasn't going to do shit. Rather than waste my time trying to convert this sorry-ass lawyer to common sense, I let it go. I thought it better to hear him out, get the thing and bury it.

"What is this weapon?"

"Star Wars," he said, "the real Star Wars; it's an orbital weapons platform. It's been in place since before you were born, thanks to Reagan's foresight. Many satellites are not what they appear to be. Communications was a cover. We have orbital weapons that require no army."

"Are you out of your fucking mind?" I cried, "If you think I'll launch ICBMs from space you're nuts. Blowing up China won't save anyone, the radiation alone—."

He slammed his fist on my desktop. "Just shut up George, will you listen for one God damn minute? It's not that you dumb fuck."

James was always an aggressive guy, a real hard-ass in the Republican sort of way, but I never heard him scream before. It wasn't his style. He was too pious. He never cursed.

"Ok, ok," I said.

"It's an energy ray weapon. It doesn't shoot down or launch missiles," A gleeful sneer appeared on James. I'd seen it before, he walked in with it. "It doesn't kill; it changes human hearts."

I gulped my drink. "How so," I crocked the question through burning bourbon.

He smiled that same smile he had on the day he disowned me at school. "This energy ray makes solders into pansies, faggots, and better yet, in reverse polarity, it makes straight people more aggressive, it makes children into solders and women into slaves."

"Shit," I said.

He got up from the chair as my jaw hit the desk's blotter. He reached over and patted the folder he had placed on my desk. "It's all in there, how to activate and use the system, its capabilities, key codes, everything they need. I won't explain the implications; I have a schooner to catch. Hit China with this and they will stand down." He laughed bitterly before adding. "Maybe they'll fight over a bar of soap in the showers, but that's about all."

He reminded me of a deranged prison warden. He took the last slug from his drink and slammed the glass down. "If I were you…err…Mr. President," he said with a mix of hopelessness and disdain in his voice. "I would call a meeting of the Joint Chiefs of Staff and pronto."

He spun and walked out before I could say another word. I hated the military guys, avoided them like the Black Death. With my guts screaming at me not to do it, I picked up my jaw and the phone, and dialed the Pentagon.

That was my first and greatest big Presidential mistake.

####

"Mr. President," four-star general, Bob Bradley said, "You have a responsibility to the people. You must act. Without control of the oil reserves how will you feed the people? Farming depends on machines. Our very survival is at stake."

I'd been hearing this kind of bullshit rationale all morning and I was sick of it. "You mean your jobs are at stake," I said dryly. It was my last statement of resistance. No one was listening. Generals make good hunters but poor gatherers.

The other eleven men in the room were solidly behind the General. They had worn me down. They had endless positives for deployment and no negatives. After two hours of debate, them Vs me, I doubted myself in earnest.

I relented against my gut feeling. I didn't want to use Gramps' method of governing by gut. I feared repeating the Brush legacy. The warriors made it sound logical. I wanted to be logical. I forgot they were professional bullshitters. I got sucked into their spin. I should have listened to my insides. I should have known better but I fucked up. I trusted them.

"Ok," I said, feeling very presidential. "Have a plan on my desk first thing in the morning. That's it people, get lost."

I was feeling my oats. Never trust oats.

After they left, I waved Erma over. I needed some grounding. My head was swimming in power bullshit. Erma, bless her, saw I was full of myself and needed to kick down a notch. I was dripping with military testosterone. We fucked right on top of the General's staff table. Not even Clintock could make that claim.

However, to be honest, it was Erma's idea. I used to be known for my honesty, before the ray was deployed. I won't lie about Erma. She deserves her place in history. She acted dumb but was always a step ahead of me.

Erma and I talked as we got dressed. She was there for the meeting; after all, she was the official White House stenographer and VP.

"George, you're not buying that crap, are you? I mean they only care about saving their own assess, ya know." She fought with her bra a few seconds then added. "I especially don't like the idea of removing our gays. America needs them, gosh. I mean, without them what would entertainment be? It would be crap. Like it or not George, gays exist for a reason. I don't think reprogramming people's brains is going to solve anything."

In my heart I agreed with her. Things were adjusting; people were getting around the oil problem. Radical moves weren't necessary. Backyard motor-heads had cars running on corn alcohol or bio-diesel; chemistry geeks were making fuel out of everything and anything. Life was different but life went on. If anything, poor people had it better. They had work that mattered. We had farming communities. Farm co-ops sprang up like spring dandelions. Everyone had a garden, every town a blacksmith. Obesity became rare.

The wealthy had tough times, however; they didn't know how to work and they had no commodities for trade, nothing you could eat. Equality was shaping long term survival. We the people didn't need another oil war.

I didn't say what I thought. Erma would've held me to it. Instead, I said to her, "Look these guys know what they're doing; they're experts. I think we should go with it. Those guys have been doing this shit a long time."

"I don't know. I don't like it George, the foxes have run the henhouse way too long."

I responded with fake confidence, to impress her. Make her think I was handling those guys. "I got no choice really; I'm going to have to go with the pros."

I should have listened to Erma.

That was my second big Presidential mistake.

####

The PMM, Personnel Modification Modulator, or as I liked to call it the Gay Ray was deployed later that week. The effects were not immediate, but it didn't take long.

The system dosed continuously and hit ninety percent of the world's population. It rotated in three hour cycles. The Gay Ray was timed so that China got the Gay beam and America got the beam that made gay's straight and straights into monsters.

The evangelicals loved it. Wife beating was back on the table.

What was the down side? Americans fell into extreme social-gender dichotomy. It came on slowly. We didn't fully experience the effects until months later: Frogs in a slow boiling pot. Men liked it too much. Violent crime shot up, rape and pillage became an American pastime. The farm co-ops fell apart. Food wars raged. Farmers were too busy killing each other to farm and female slaves were inadequate. Beaten up, pregnant women did not produce shit.

Three and a half years after deployment, the world was a different place. Everyone was different. I was different and I didn't like it. There wasn't much time before my term ran out and I didn't give a shit.

I had relocated to Groom Lake, AKA Area 51 in New Mexico because I was as paranoid as fuck. The Gay Ray's control system was there. I had to be near it. I had override authority, not that it mattered. Erma and I lived there, underground. The conference room attached to our apartment was my office. It was really a war room. No matter what room I was in, I was at war.

The day I regained my sanity happened like this.

I was watching the news, it was good news, but I didn't feel good about it. Bob Jones was on. As an ex-gay he was able to present the news without screaming and cursing. He was calm and logical like the way I used to be. The old news team was straight, so the program turned into an annoying fist fight. I got them arrested and made the Networks hire ex-gays.

I had my feet up on the desk, drinking direct from a full bottle of scotch—I used to hate scotch. Glasses were for pussies as every American man knew. I screamed at Erma to turn up the volume.

She ran in wearing the French maid outfit that I had decreed standard female staff attire. I enjoyed watching her bend over. I had her stand next to me so I could feel her up as I watched the news. She didn't mind, or at least she wasn't supposed to mind. What did I know? So she made a tinfoil maid's hat.

The commentary started. *Our correspondent, Christy Lee is in China and reports that the last of China's troops have just crossed China's border. What's the latest?*

A Chinese/American woman came onto the screen. China had been pulling back for weeks.

*Thanks Bob. Spokesmen for China's Science Ministry announced that the new alternative energy source, that its top scientists had developed, is ready for general use and will virtually render oil obsolete. China's Minister of International Energy, Mow Lee, stated today that China would willingly share this technology with any gay-normalized Nation that asks for aid. A top source inside Beijing said, 'This is just the beginning. Due to our new creative energy, the people have achieved more scientifically in the last three years than in all of China's history.' Back to You Bob.*

I flipped out. I heaved the bottle at the TV and missed. That pissed me off even more.

Erma cowered and started shaking all over. I felt her inner recoil. She was fear personified and I felt it. It was strange to recognize her feelings again. Before the ray, I always knew how she felt, but now I had no receptivity at all. We were close before. 'We we're two peas in a pod,' Erma used to say. We were strangers now. That pissed me off even more.

I stood and back handed her sending her to the ground. I was about to kick her, then I recalled that the last time I did that, I broke three of her ribs. I didn't care. I hated myself for not caring.

While my thoughts and emotions see-sawed she cried and begged. Something a new world woman wasn't supposed to do. After the Gay Ray, all women became docile, happy slaves unless they were gay or bisexual, then they became straight but average. Maybe it was her bisexual side, or maybe it was her memories of the good old days but it was the tinfoil hat. She ventured to speak knowing it could get her killed.

"Look at you, she cried, you...you...you used to love me, you used to love. Now all you do is destroy. You're ruining us and everyone!" She fell into deep sobbing.

Somehow, her profound distress got to me. The Gay Ray did not wipe out all my sentiments. I must have had a sliver of gay inside me. I didn't kick her. I just stood there looking at her on the floor, her lip bleeding; the sight of blood got me hard. I hated myself a bit more.

Just then the phone rang. It was General Butler, the new chief of staff. He was an ex-gay thus able to act like a human being. He told me that the nuclear strike we were getting ready to launch was a go. Most of our ICBMs were raided for fuel years ago. We had been working on refueling a handful. It took a year. If I couldn't have the oil, no one was having it. Staff thought it was a great idea.

"Sir, China will share its oil, they don't need it," he said. "There's no reason to launch. They promised to give us whatever's we need and their new energy technologies for free as well. Sir, peace is offered. What do you want me to do?"

"Launch the God damn things," I screamed at the phone. Then I bashed the receiver into the holder. What Erma had said just a few minutes before came pounding back into my skull. I voiced it. "All you do is destroying."

I had that sick feeling again, something was wrong. The launch was scheduled and it didn't feel right. Even out of control with rage, a common state of mind post Gay Ray, in that moment I knew I had to ignore my rage and follow deeper guts, not the George Two kind.

I reached down for Erma. "Take my hand," I said, "we got work to do."

I had to clear my head. We went to the science lab and picked up shield hats. They were simple tinfoil lined hard hats and they deflected the Ray. Satellites re-coated every three hours to maintain the effects. We missed the next Ray shot and the next. As my mind progressively cleared my guts spoke more. I came back to myself. What I had to do next was critical, but very much out of charter with my old self.

Erma and I went to the pistol range and checked out two 45s. We then went to the launch control station and, at gun point; I had the operators shut down the Gay Ray. I stood over them with a loaded gun as they programmed the stop sequence. They were not happy.

Military men lived and breathed war. I was cutting off the junkies' supply. I had to get it done and call Butler fast. The missiles were due to launce. I only had a few minutes. Once my command code was entered and in motion, I relaxed and holstered the gun.

They didn't know the code I gave them was a self destruct order. I said so after it was too late to stop it.

That was my third big Presidential mistake.

Both techs jumped up out of their chairs like manic coil springs and attacked me. Of course the female techs just stood by. Even if I brought my gun up in time, I wouldn't have used it. I was normal again. The realization that my life was lost flashed across my mind's eye as I fell over a chair in a tangle of punching fists and kicking feet. I didn't stand a chance they would have beat me to death.

There was a defining bang, bang, and bang. I thought myself shot. But the wet I felt wasn't my blood. I had pissed my pants. Proof positive I was my old pussy self again.

I would have laughed but there was blood, lots of blood, only this time it didn't make my dick hard. I retched instead. When I regained composure Erma was standing there with her gun. She was a crack shot before all this happened and she didn't lose that skill.

She looked at me and said, "I better get a pardon for this George, you are the President you know."

Good old Erma was back, bless her. Piss isn't sticky. I looked, saw splattered blood on me and I fainted.

After I woke up I remembered I had given General Butler orders to launch. No longer under the influence of the PMM, I freaked out. I tried to bolt. Erma held me down gently. I was in a hospital bed.

"You dumb ass, you hit your head when you fainted." She said. "What am I going to do with you?"

She gave me that loving eyelash batting look which I hadn't seen in years. My head was pounding, but that look always made me feel better. I tried to speak but she hushed me and said quietly. "You have a nasty bump George, a concussion. You must keep still."

I stammered a question, I had to ask, blazing head ache or not, "what about the missiles, did Butler fire?"

"Well of course he did George; he's a loyal man, after all. But don't worry, nothing came of it, they got their own Star Wars, ya know. They took your rockets out. Who'd have thunk it?" She chuckled and then turned serious. "They made a way they'd stay gayer. All that creativity was good for them ya know."

She rolled her eyes. My heart jumped. She was so thin. Had I starved her?

"I could have told them that." She said. "It doesn't take a big brain, ya know. A little gayness is good for everyone, gosh. I just don't say that because I'm AC/DC either."

I tried to sit up, I had to get going, so much to do, to learn, but she pushed me back into my pillow.

"Now you get some sleep George. The free energy agency President, Mr. Lee, is on his way from China. You'll need to write a report so we can get some of that free energy. But, not now, when you feel up to it, OK dear?"

For the first time in too long, I took Erma's advice. I shut my eyes and went back to sleep. It was the first time in years that I had sweet, soft dreams. That night I dreamt in rainbow colors. The next morning everything was brighter.

**END**

# MY LAST DAY AT THE LAB

Walter never came to work early, but there he sat in front of the printer waiting for that printout as if divining truth from the sacred fires of laser jet. Walter is usually pasty-white, but his face was flushed; sweat pooled in the dimples on top of his bald head. I was sweating, too, and the room wasn't even hot.

This isn't good. Walter's ugly, but when he's scared he's a regular abomination.

I was scared for different reasons. I'm the kind that always does the right thing, but not every time. Ok I'm a crook. I robbed the Farberts. I stole the finger bone. I took pictures of the pictures of century's old secret texts the Farberts had. Some old-time abbot had written about the alien. I got pictures of its grave goods and samples for evidence. But, I needed more. I had to get the final report showing our research, especially how we cracked the alien's symbolic language. All I had to do was download the files into my laptop and email them to my online storage and well out of Barry Farberts long reach, and go home.

But, Walter came in early. Shit!

Walter liked working at the Barry Farberts Christian Research Institute. He took the institute's mission 'to protect the faith' seriously even though Walter must know all we really do is mostly protect Farberts' reputation and money. We research anything that disagrees with Farberts' view so Farberts can keep fleecing his flock. His mega church and billion dollar broadcasting set up wasn't cheap.

I have morals, but decent jobs are harder to find than the lost tribe of Benjamin. I bit my tongue so often around here; my tongue looked like mutton burger. I just wanted to do the right thing. I care about people and the Farberts' brand of religion wasn't helping anyone. That's how I justified stealing, but I still felt like shit. I was raised Catholic. We're good at guilt.

As I stared at Walter trying to think of a way around him sweat ran into my left eye.

"We got to destroy this data, Sam."

"Not so fast," I said as I set my new laptop down on a white Formica desk and booted. "Let's at least see the printout." We both had a good idea of what it would say.

Once I had a copy of the Origins File, I'd do the right thing—tell the world what the Vatican knows, and what Farberts was about to learn from his Swiss Guard spies and our research: Namely, The Holy Grail is real and it was an alien strongbox made of stone, like and ossuary or arc but bigger. It was buried filled with advanced technologies and a body. The Knights Templar dug it out of the Second Temple ruins in the thirtieth century.

The ancient Semite nomads thought it was God in a box. Maybe the computer still worked. The later Jews stashed it. The early Church hid it, too. They all knew it would ruin the scam. God doesn't need tools or mini angels. You just can't show up one Sunday with the Ark of the Covenant. What Farberts didn't know is its' DNA doesn't match anything from Earth. He thinks it's a midget like the Church Fathers did. They thought of it as some kind of holy dwarf. The Hebrews weren't far off, 'god' did come down from the Heavens, but not in a cloud, it was a spaceship.

As the tests came in and evidence mounted over the last week, I knew I had to do something. I sat down at my desk, knees knocking, and started the upload. I tried to look relaxed, but my hands shook. I couldn't make my stomach quit grumbling. I needed time to upload, compress, and email. It was a big file.

"Say, what are you doing there, Sammy boy?" Walter asked squinting at my PC.

"New laptop," I said, "Just trying it out." So I didn't lie.

I had to stall, not easy to do, he didn't like me, always suspicious. The only thing we had in common was marriage into the Farberts family. Mom married Bob Farberts, the family outcast and sacrilegious editor at the World Times newspaper. Barry hired me anyway, probably just to say, 'fuck you' to his atheist brother. God bless nepotistic family values.

Bob and I got along and that really irked Walter. Walter's likeminded evangelical brother-in-law, Barry, treated Walt like shit. But, what really pissed Walter off was me reading Bob's North East liberal newspaper religiously, in the lab— that gave me an idea.

"Publication!" I blurted out. "Look Walter, we need to publish this, ourselves. Think of the money. Forget Farberts. Screw him. You know Farberts is a crook. He'll holy roll right over us. He'll take all the credit and all the money."

Walter glared at me, his amber cheeks returning to pasty face as shock ran the blood out.

"Now, see here, Barry Farberts may not be a saint, but he's got a flock to feed. We've got a good job here too, you know, see, he's a good boss, a decent man, he pays well. He does a lot of good you know! He's blessed by God. Look at his money—God's good to him. Have some gratitude, man. If the media finds out he's spied on the Vatican he's finished. Have some respect."

Respect, I had to laugh. As the token liberal around here, respect for me was in short supply.

Once I stopped laughing, Walter went dramatic on me. He stood up and pointed his chubby finger at my lab coat's breast pocket and said, "What does that emblem say, right there?"

I couldn't remember, so I read it off his coat.

"Christian Research Institute of Science and Technology Inc, CRIST," I said.

Walter lowered his voice as if in church and said, "What's the first word there?"

"Christian," I said.

"That's right," he said, "Our first responsibility is Christianity. We must protect the faith for the good of the people. We took an oath, see. But you're right, Farberts will exploit this somehow. We got to delete the files. If anyone finds out about this Barry Farberts and our jobs are done and over. Barry's faithful will be traumatized. It'll hurt the faithful. Let's do the right thing and wipe it out."

Walter's right I did take the oath. I swore on a stack of bibles, but I didn't sign a confidentiality agreement. Farberts shouldn't have had faith in my faith. I had my out. But I didn't feel any better, I was still a thief.

"Guess, you're right," I said feigning reconciliation. "Give me a minute, I need to think."

I put on my best sympathetic face. But, I thought, why protect Barry? His empire was built on dispensational lies. Is warm and fuzzy fiction better than this cold reality? I battled within. This was huge, it really could kill Christianity. What would people think? The church hid an alien body just to keep the sheep grazing? Jesus! I had thousands of years of hidden religious history pouring into my laptop. This was way bigger than Barry.

But, I wasn't yet convinced dropping napalm was a good idea. Religion had merits, or maybe not. What about the abortion clinic bombing? The cops arrested a Farberts' parishioner. *Do the right thing* hammered in the back of my skull. I had to keep stalling Walter.

"Farberts' followers, they'd bail." I said sheepishly.

Walter shook his head with a grimace.

"Ok," I said as I keyed my laptop to compress the data. I had another idea. If Walter thought it was going to Farberts, fine. I needed more time and an excuse to go on-line.

"Maybe we should trust Farberts; He'll do the right thing and quash it. You're right Walter. We have to do our Christian duty here. And, you know what that is, don't you Walter? Why yes, it is to uphold the commandments! God said that if you're faithful in a few small things then He'll reward you with better stuff, right?"

I didn't wait for an answer; I took a deep breath and just kept talking. You can't live in the South without some entertainment-preacher skills rubbing off on you. I watched my PC with one eye as I spoke. Walter became mesmerized. He loved a good preaching at. Before long, I had my download ready and Walter off balance. He'd never heard me preach before; neither did I.

When my laptop chimed I finished up with, "So then, Walter, we want to do what's right, what would Jesus do! Tell the truth, right? We got to do what's right here, the book says, 'give to Caesar what is Caesar's.' So then, we work for the Farberts, right? I wrote the preliminary report last night, it's ready to go, all I have to do is hit send and it'll be on Farberts desk in the twinkling of an eye. It's the right thing to do."

I thought my impromptu plan worked. Walter was as doe-eyed as a ram caught in god's landing lights. He didn't know where the file was going. But blood suddenly shot into his face, his jaw dropped, his eyes bugged out and Walther screamed, "NO!" He shot over my desk like Cleopatra's cobra off a hot plate.

My computer flew and crashed onto the floor dead. Walter grabbed my lab coat's lapels and screamed, "It didn't go, tell me you didn't send it! I need this job, see. If he sees this, Barry won't need me anymore. I'm fifty two, where the hell am I going to go! Tell me you didn't send it!"

"No, of course not, how the hell could I!" I screamed with real anger. Now, I had no way to send the data. I wasn't sure if I hit send or not. I couldn't risk going though security with hard copy. They check everything.

"You broke my PC, darn it Walter. I just got this one. I don't even know how it works yet, Jesus!"

Lack of job security makes people do some strange things and that was way strange for such a meek and mild sheep such as Walter. He took a hanky out of his lab coat pocket and mopped his forehead.

"I'm so sorry, really I'm so sorry Sam; I'll make it up to you."

Walter had to be stunned by his own aggression. He crumpled like a whipped puppy and fell back into his chair paler than ever. I felt bad for him. Walter never gets physical. Ok, explosive in a theological debate, but he's basically a docile dude. He never moved that fast, not even for free donuts. I was afraid the adrenaline would kill him.

Just then the printer started spitting out paper. Walter grabbed the first few sheets, read them and moaned, "God Damn Catholics," and put his head between his knees.

I noticed my laptop's indicator light was still green. The hard drive was still running. Walter didn't see anything but his shoes, so I snapped up my laptop and cased it. Another idea popped into my head—plug into another monitor. I could send it from the computer lab.

"I'm going to the PC shop and see what they can do. Dang it all Walter, my new laptop! You busted my new laptop."

I baptized Walter with a good dose of Catholic guilt, poured it on like barbeque sauce. I wanted him stuck to that chair. Walter watched with narrowing eyes as I stuffed my laptop bag, but, his face suddenly flashed red and I thought he had me.

"Promise you won't talk about this, no publishing." He said suddenly frantic. "If people find out there's …my God Sam, Christianity will crash. Not a word, promise me, not a word."

He looked around wild eyed. Farberts was known to use hidden cameras to watch his employees. That's how the FBI found out one of Farberts' employees bombed the clinic.

"Farberts! You're right; we owe it to them, but no one else. Only the Farberts gets this data, see. The family will know what to do. We'll tell them."

Walter didn't want to face Barry, but Barry wasn't the only Farberts on staff, he was just the front man. This was a family operation and, 'anyone but Barry' was Walter's motto. He opened that door, not me. Bob the newspaper man outcast was family, too.

"Ok, when I get back," I said, "Only a Farberts, only family gets this data, I promise." It felt good, not to lie.

I took a step toward the door but Walter grabbed my arm.

"I promised already." I said. "Let me go. Jesus knows the only one deserving of this are the Farberts. When I get back we'll talk about publishing."

"Publishing is out of the question," Walter shot back.

We agreed at least five more times that we'd only tell the Farberts family. Walter finally looked relieved. I never mentioned that Bob Farberts was the only Farberts I had in mind and so what Bob's in publishing, I can't help that. Walter didn't ask. I wasn't going back on my word. I've got morals.

By the time I left the lab my nerves were shot. I could hardly walk with the weight of the Barry Farberts' empire hanging in my shoulder bag. Thank god the way was clear.

But, just when I thought I was home free, I ran into Barry near the PC Shop. I almost puked on his thousand dollar shoes. I told him, between chattering teeth, that I'd dropped my PC. He hardly glanced at me. Barry made a point of avoiding liberals, especially family liberals.

With a wave of his hand he said, "Carry on, I'm going to Walter's for the Origins Report."

We parted. Barry rolled his bulk around the corner and disappeared from view. I thought, once Farberts sees that report he'll initiate security lockdown. I thought I was screwed until a revelation hit me—the PC shop fire-door is nearest employee parking. I entered, ran past Phil the PC guy, and smashed into the emergency door panic-bar setting off the alarm. Outside, I ran like hell.

The file was intact but far from safe. I sat in my car for a minute catching air so I could drive. What to do next? I'd go to the internet café in town and plug in. I couldn't trust my home system. Farberts had it bugged. I had to email this file fast. I started the motor still unsure what to do next.

Walter burst out of the fire door like an evangelical commando. Farberts was close behind screaming, "You trader, you liberal bastard!"

Farberts and Walter puffed toward me like hell bound steam locomotives. Walter crashed into my closed car window just as I pulled away. Arms flailing he grabbed for the car's door handle but missed and fell to his knees. He cried out like a schoolyard kid, "Don't break your promise, you promised!"

I stepped on the gas.

I wasn't about to break my promise. Just because religions lie didn't mean I'd give myself that license. I just didn't tell Walter that Bob was the only Farberts I trusted. Bob Farberts my stepfather. As I drove I debated the wisdom of sending that file to Bob.

Did I really want to shoot the Farberts cash cow? There was a lot of money at stake here. Farberts, his kind, and their money would crucify me given the chance. I could get arrested or worse. And yet, Farberts stole this stuff from the Catholics, who stole if from the Knights Templar, who stole it from Arabs, who stole it from the Romans, who stole if from the Jews, who stole it from the Hittites. Is it wrong to steal stolen property? What exactly is the right thing?

I pulled into a motel with a 'Free Internet' sign on the marquee, parked my car around back and checked in, paid cash and borrowed a cable so I could use the TV as a monitor.

Three days later I emerged from the Cavern Hotel and went downtown for a paper. The copy of the Times I had delivered to the lab was inaccessible and the hotel didn't get the paper. I was surprised to see Janet, my section's secretary at the coffee shop in town. Janet never took a day off.

"Hey Sammy," she said in a cheerful voice, "what's happened to you, everyone at work is talking about how you just up and ran out."

"Everyone," I asked.

"Well no," she said, "the one guy I'd expect to blab is as tight lipped as a smart bass in a fishing hole full of baited hooks. Walter hasn't said two words to anyone in days. Reverend Farberts has been pretty quiet too, until this morning."

"No kidding, what happened?"

"This morning, oh my Lord did Reverend Farberts pitch a fit. Ten minutes after I dropped off your paper, Barry started busting up the lab. I couldn't believe it. He and Walter locked horns yelling something about Bobby. Next thing you know, Barry fired Walter and gave everyone the day off."

"I wonder if the Times had anything to do with Barry's melt down," I said. "Maybe he thought it was Walter's paper."

"Naw," she said, "you know Walter and Barry. They'd never read a liberal paper, not even a free copy."

"I'm not so sure about that. Guess I had better cancel that subscription, thanks for reminding me. I wouldn't want to upset things at the lab."

"That's very thoughtful of you Sammy. I don't know why Reverend Farberts never liked you."

"God only knows," I said.

Janet said goodbye and headed into the coffee shop. I looked at my copy of the Times. The front page headline said, "God is an alien!" The bi-line was Robert Farberts and Samuel Lee. I guess I'm in the other family business now. God bless nepotism.

**END**

# ACKNOWLEDGMENTS

Many thanks the people that helped me put this collection together besides Vonnegut (whom I never met). In random order: thank you Angel Ackerman my former news editor and mentor who edited this book, Lisa Cross my main proof reader and story critic, the Greater Lehigh Valley Writers Group and its network of supporters and critique partners, Kathy Roscoe for proof reading, and Gayle F. Hendricks my book formatting guru. Finally, thanks to that college professor who told me, regarding a story I wrote for class back in 1979, "hey that's pretty good." I look at that first story now and think, 'Boy is that trash.' And so goes the proof that Kilgore Trout is alive and well within me and countless other writers as well.

# ABOUT THE AUTHOR

Rachel C. Thompson, writing as R.C. Thom, began her writing career after surviving a devastating motorcycle accident in 2003. She has since published non-fiction pieces in newspapers and magazines, cartoons and a handful of short stories. *Soul Harvest* is her third novel and first released. The sequel, *Aggie in Orbit*, will follow in the fall. *Dragon Fire* is out now and her novel *Book of Answers* will be out late in 2018.

Lightning Source UK Ltd.
Milton Keynes UK
UKHW02f1822230718
326165UK00008B/183/P

9 781732 145948